FOREVER PEOPLE

ALISON LYKE

Black Rose Writing | Texas

ISBN: 978-1-68433-240-3
PUBLISHED BY BLACK ROSE WRITING
www.blackrosewriting.com

Printed in the United States of America
Suggested Retail Price (SRP) $18.95

Forever People is printed in Traditional Arabic

For Frederick Smith, my brother with wings.

FOREVER PEOPLE

PART I: ONE-SHOT DEAL

1
CAMILLE

Camille had three kinds of clients: those who were trying to extract funds or rare items from someone else before they died, those looking to find a loved one before they died, and regulars with a myriad of shady reasons for needing repeated, illegal services.

Wren Barrett was Camille's favorite type of the three. He was a balding account manager, from the Delta Zone, who'd come to Zeta City to find his son. Like most others arriving in Zeta for the first time, he was ill-equipped, soft, and confused. He washed up in Camille's office like a beached manatee: gasping for air and bleached by the sun.

Her office walls were stark white, as was her desk and other furniture, and even the floor, giving the woman herself the appearance of a smudge on a piece of blank paper. Camille wore a grey tank top, black shorts, and she was unadorned aside from her wrist mounted reality augmentation device. The device's long touch-sensitive screen and pad ran down her forearm; her RAP was an impressive piece of technology that marked her as wealthy and well connected. She also had a mop of frizzy, black hair that hung raggedly around her ears. While Wren Barrett spoke, Camille sipped on an orange juice box straw and watched him closely.

Mr. Barrett's son was dying. Sashi Barrett was born dying, even more so than the rest of us. Sashi had a heart condition that made life a painful struggle. So, Sashi did what many people from all over the world do when they want to die; he came to Zeta City.

Zeta City was the capital of the Zeta Net, so-called because the entire area was covered by a wireless network designed to upload people's consciousness at the time of death and store it in the Node's massive computer system. Zeta was not the only Net, there were dozens of others, but many people chose Zeta because Zeta was the first netted city in the world. Generations of people made pilgrimages to Zeta before the other Nets were built, and now some people superstitiously clung to it as the place to go to die. Maybe it was because Zeta gave the world the first promise of a tangible afterlife. "Going to die in Zeta" was the new "going to church on Sunday."

"You can find Sashi?" Mr. Barrett asked sadly, "you can keep him alive?"

"I can find him and keep him alive, more or less, until you're ready to let him go into the Node. I accept cash and other forms of payment. You know what I mean," Camille said.

"Of course. I'll transfer two-thousand Node Points to you, as a thank you for your service, along with four hundred in cash. Does that work?"

"No rush. We'll sort it once it's over, Wren." When Camille stood up to shake Mr. Barrett's hands, he was surprised to see that she that she was a thick woman with large breasts and the hint of a belly. He was expecting a fit, muscled mercenary. Then he realized, there was no reason for her to be fit, most of her bounties couldn't run away.

●   ●   ●   ●   ●

Camille found Sashi, who was a boy – twenty at the most – in an alley two blocks from the Water Street Gate, in an area known for drug abuse and homelessness. He was a heap of bones and in dirty, Central Charity-issued clothes. His method of suicide, a drawn-out opiate overdose, was not doing him any favors. Camille double-checked the hologram on her wrist RAP to verify his identity, and then crouched next to him.

"You wanna tell me why you're trying to die?" Camille asked him softly.

He took a moment to answer. It was clear that he hadn't carried on a conversation for quite some time. "Death in the Node has got to be better than life here." He struggled. Her suicidal bounties always gave some form of that same statement as their reason for killing themselves.

"You got enough Node Points, kiddo? Don't want to die without enough of those NPs." Camille always asked her dying bounties some form of that question.

It turned out that Sashi had more than enough Node Points to have a comfortable afterlife. The wealth that afforded his addiction would also support him in death. It wasn't supposed to work that way, that wasn't how the Founders set it up, but the Founders were long gone down the Node's rabbit hole.

"Do you want to see your dad before you go? He's the one who sent me," Camille asked.

Sashi's dull eyes lit up, and faded just as fast. "I won't make it through the hour," he mumbled.

"It's okay. I have a Confiner." Camille tapped her wrist RAP.

She called Mr. Barrett and then hovered over Sashi in the alley for the rest of the afternoon. The device within her wrist RAP stabilized the electronic version of Sashi's mind inside his body, and it would last as long as she was close to him. Once she turned off the Confiner or moved away from the deceased, his consciousness would release into the Net and, eventually, be uploaded into the Node. The technology wasn't above the table, but it was also quite rare.

Camille would have preferred moving Sashi to her place, which functioned as an office, apartment, and an occasional hospice, but he did not want to move and she was compelled to accommodate the dying. Sashi did die before his father came, forcing Camille to use the Confiner.

Camille often chased after debtors and thieves who were trying to die before they could be seized. She would hold them, in their dead, damaged bodies until they resolved their issues with their victims or creditors.

But some days, like that day with Sashi, were just sad and slow. On these days, Camille felt like an angel, guiding the broken home. She stood about fifteen feet away from Mr. Barrett and his dead son (the farthest that the Confiner could reach and still hold the dead in place) as they spoke softly and tearfully. The boy's mother, who had been estranged from both of them, showed up.

Afterward, Camille went home to her apartment, which was on the other side of a door in the back of her office. She left the clinical, white room for the for the chaos and color of her own apartment. She checked her wrist RAP to make sure that Mr. Barrett had transferred the promised Points. Satisfied, she unhooked the device from her wrist and set it on her coffee table. She sat down on her sofa and cried for several minutes before tearfully ordering wild mushroom soup and crusty bread from her favorite diner.

The next morning, Camille received a call from her least favorite kind of client, a regular named Cody. He wanted Camille to extract a young woman, named Toy, from an old cabin on the edge of Zeta's bayou and bring her to Camille's office, if possible. Otherwise, Camille was to confine Toy in place until Cody arrived.

2
TOY

"Society has become ill, and I will heal it. I am the agent of change. I am the catalyst. Nature has been defied; I will bring justice to the natural law …" Toy practiced her speech in even, steady, strong tones. "No," she said, her voice a little lower. She started again, "Nature has been *defiled*, I will bring *dignity* back to the natural order … ugh, no …"

With her beautiful full, pink lips, and round, blue eyes, this earnest young woman should have been shopping at a mall or hanging around in her pajamas and waiting for her boyfriend to call. Instead, she was prepared to die in the bedroom of this hot, rickety, wooden cabin. The bed smelled musty, and the cracked plaster walls looked ancient. When her co-conspirators had wheeled in the nanite distribution machines, Toy worried that the hulking equipment would buckle the wooden floor.

A tall, husky technician named Bernard stood next to her, fussing with a tray full of medical instruments. He broke a plastic safety seal and extracted a syringe to be filled with a fluid-suspended nano-virus. The tubes of the nanite machines snaked over each other, up the side of the bed, and across the pillow next to Toy. Bernard had taken care to place every cord they would need for the download near her, ready for the moment when millions of tiny, computer virus-infected nanites would be pumped directly into Toy's dying brain.

Toy held her straight, blond hair back from her face so Bernard could mark out a target on the temple and get a clean stab. "I like the first speech better," the tech said while cleaning the chosen spot on her right temple with a smear of orange iodine, "justice and law matches."

"You're right. I should have practiced more," she sighed. "I've never given an official statement before."

Toy looked over as Bernard filled the needle with ionic fluid, which would deliver the disruptive virus to her brain, binding with her neurons and becoming part of her consciousness, before killing her.

She said, "I don't know why you're bothering cleaning the surgical site, I'm going to die anyway."

Friends and followers lined the edged of the room and spilled out into the cabin's remaining rooms. Among the following were doubters; there were down-right cynics, and there was a smattering of true believers. Toy breathed the essence of the true believers, but the rest of them did not matter to her. It was no wonder she had such fervent followers. Her face glowed, and her blue eyes begged you to join her.

Not that her followers needed too much persuasion. Resentment turns to anger, indoctrination, and then to violent action when the poor are kept poor for too long, and the poor in Zeta were destitute for eternity. Toy was not opportunistic, she was one of them, and she was skilled, organized, driven, and, soon to be, dead.

Bernard the tech was a true believer; he was a Nirvana disciple down to the bone. Toy would have no one else plunge the thick needle into her temple. Others might hesitate, and that needle had to go in hard enough to puncture her skull. This was a one-shot deal.

"Get the cameras ready," Toy gave steely directions from her cord-draped perch.

This was the cue for a group of semi-believers, armed with cheap American cameras ready to capture Nirvana's dissent, to jump into place in front of Toy. The moment of her death would be recorded and broadcast to the entire country an hour after she died, thanks to incredibly expensive airtime on Zetacast, the network that Nirvana had purchased just days ago.

Bernard, an ever-fervent disciple of Nirvana, reached his arm towards Toy's head.

"Now," Toy said through a jaw set in steel.

As Bernard shoved the needle mercilessly into Toy's skull, she noticed, somewhat hysterically, that he was wearing pink hygienic gloves. *So, I won't get an infection. As if it mattered,* she thought darkly. Toy gave a barely audible chuckle. Her "Now" was the signal to the camera crew to begin filming, and so the first seconds of film would show Toy receiving her brutal injection of viral nanites, and then laughing at the absurdity of pink gloves.

It was strange; Toy's pain barely registered. She couldn't feel the atom-sized bots as they contaminated her brain. She wasn't sure what she was expecting, but the lack of pain seemed anti-climactic.

She looked into the camera, and began to speak:

"Good afternoon Zeta City. I'm Toy Bowen, and I am your salvation. A few hundred years ago, the group of great thinkers and engineers, known as the Founders, destroyed our culture as they created the new world. They were not happy simply engineering the gift of clean water, and then walking away after the End of Days Wars. These Founders had to burden us with the Node Point System. We earned and deserved our immortality. Thousands of years of innovation culminated in our ability to preserve our minds in a digital utopia; but instead of utopia, we got the Node Point System. Our so-called 'Founders' faded into the Node, leaving us with software algorithms that force us to pay for our eternal status."

Toy took a deep, shaky breath. "By the time you view this, I will have died. This -" she raised her hand to indicate the needle that Bernard held steady in her temple "- is pumping thousands of nanites designed to use my own neural transmitters as a virus, which will take down the Node Point system from the inside. When I pass into the Node, the Node Points belonging to everyone in this country will be wiped out; your accounts will run down to zero, as will the accounts of everyone already existing in the Node. You the people, the Founders, and the system, will have no other choice but freedom. There will be no other choice but to accept the afterlife that we *deserve*. Society has become ill, and I will heal it. I am the agent -"

Toy was cut off by a ruckus from the cabin's front room. Bernard pulled the needle out of her temple with a quick, steady, pink-gloved hand. Toy reached up instinctively to the wound and pressed her other hand up against her mouth to stifle the scream of pain that had come to her at last. Blood trickled from her temple and down her cheek, between her fingers.

"The Funds are here!" someone called into the cabin. Toy could not tell if the voice belonged to a Nirvana member or one of the Publicly Funded Police.

"Is it done?" she gasped.

"Good enough," Bernard said through gritted teeth as he frantically unhooked cords and scooped instruments into a black knapsack. Toy grabbed his arm as he tried to hurry past her.

"Do it now!" she pleaded, "Please kill me now." But Bernard shook his head. Toy looked around for someone who would help her die. The camera crew had abandoned their filming and were trying to distract the Funds, oblivious to an unsupported camera that had fallen to the floor.

"It wouldn't do any good; the virus isn't in your neural circuitry yet." Bernard tapped has computer monitor. "You gotta sit with the nanites in there for like an hour – forty-five minutes at least."

Bernard kicked aside a tattered rug and pulled open a trap door that led to the cabin's false basement storage space.

"Get down there," he directed Toy, "Stay still and don't make a sound for at *least* 45 minutes."

Realizing she was getting woozy, Toy tried to follow his direction, but she could not.

"You come with me," she gripped Bernard's arm and attempted to pull him into the cellar with her.

"No!" he hissed. "I gotta make sure they don't find you." He put his hand on the crown of her head and gently pushed Toy toward the cellar as the sounds of a scuffle grew louder; somewhere in the cabin, a woman screamed.

"Please!" she begged Bernard again.

He ignored Toy, shoving her the rest of the way down the hole and into the cellar.

"If this goes bad you run," he grunted. "Get as close to the gate as you can before you die. You don't want some Fund or mercenary to hold you back."

Toy nodded, but he couldn't see her response in the murky dark of the cellar.

"Goodbye, Miss Bowen. I'll find you in the Node – a *free* Node." Bernard saluted as he shut the trap door.

Bernard dragged the rug back over the trapdoor and placed the camera and tripod on its side over the area to look like it had been knocked over, but he left the camera recording. He turned to the back door of the room and paused for a heartbeat with his hand hovering over the knob.

A red-haired, tan-clad officer pushed through the front of the room a few seconds later. "Publicly Funded POLICE!" the officer shouted. When he saw Bernard flee from the back porch and into the swamp beyond, he yelled "Stop!" and chased after him, followed by the rest of the Funds. In the false cellar beneath the cabin, Toy began to moan softly as the nanites started to do their work.

3
CAMILLE

By the time Camille entered the cabin, it had an air of botched government job to it. In the living room cameras and audio equipment had been abandoned and trashed. She followed a trail of plastic debris and tubing into the bedroom and saw more broken equipment lying about, but this junk looked more clinical, machines with blinking lights, sterile needles, and pink rubber gloves. The Fundies had stomped around and contaminated everything without any actual accomplishment. She sniffed and caught the sweet smell of burned rubber. Camille knew this to be the smell of discharged pulse rifle meant to stun, but they were often too weak to do anything besides make you tingle unless they were set to kill. Camille sucked air in angrily.

"Dipshit Funds," she muttered to herself.

She punched in a few buttons on her wrist RAP.

"Cody, you minge," she said to her wrist, "why am I in the middle of a bad Fund bust?"

"Camille," a high-pitched male voice came back through the communicator, "Just do your job."

"I'll give you five more minutes. If I don't smell money or Node Points, I'm leaving." She turned off her screen.

Camille sighed and sat down on a naked mattress that protested her weight. She punched a few more buttons on her wrist RAP, and a transparent holographic image appeared, rotating in the air above it. Camille studied the woman depicted in the hologram. She was delicate and pretty, with shoulder-length blond hair and big eyes. Camille thought she looked a bit thin, but it was hard to tell from just the neck up.

"Toy Bowen … Toy Bowen …Toy Bowen …" Camille's communicator spoke her mark's name in a pleasant, robotic tone as the hologram rotated like a gyroscope.

Camille jumped up from the creaky bed, startled as the tray of medical equipment in front of her rolled away, catching on the edge of a threadbare, tribal patterned rug, and the toppling over and crashing. Camille watched in alarm as the rug itself moved, an unseen force below it lifting and folding it until it slid away revealing a slowly opening trap door. The human version of Camille's wrist hologram struggled from the beneath the floor. Toy and her hologram were identical, aside from the head wound and the dried blood down the side of human Toy's face.

"Toy Bowen!" Camille said at the same time as her wrist repeated Toy's name. Camille laughed, and pointed at the face on the wrist RAP, "what are the odds?"

Toy gaped at Camille, injured and confused.

"I mean, you *are* my bounty, so that raises the odds a little."

Tired of waiting for Toy to respond, Camille went on, "they don't have many basements around here, because of the swamp. I would have looked. I just don't want you to think that I'm inept."

Toy froze for a fraction of a second, and ran, not bothering to take in any more of Camille.

"Wait, wait, wait!" Camille rocketed away from the mattress and barreled after her, "I'm all alone! No backup! Just hear me out!"

Toy reached the spot at the edge of the yard where someone had hastily concealed a motorbike under a tarp and some brush. Camille took the moment while Toy cleared the brush to advance on her.

"I'm leveling with you!" she pleaded. "I don't work for nobody and I don't have any weapons except for a Confiner in this thing." Camille waved her wrist RAP. "It won't do anything as long as you're alive."

Toy paused when she heard the word "Confiner." Camille could almost see Toy's heart beat terror into her eyes as she sped up clearing the motorbike.

Camille, exasperated, blurted "Alright! I won't even use the Confiner if you die; I don't like it either. I just want you to tell me what's going on with you."

Toy freed the bike and started it up before mounting it and steering it away from Camille.

"Tell me why I shouldn't bring you to my boss and maybe we can figure it out. You'll get to die in peace and I'll get my Node Points and we can both –"

but she was cut short as Toy laughed and kicked the motorbike into gear.

"Fine, bitch," Camille grumbled as Toy peeled away. She stomped off to her own bike, parked around the front of the cabin.

"Cody." Her wrist RAP beeped to acknowledge that he was listening. "I lost her. She had a bike stashed."

"She'll be trying to get as close to a gate as possible." His clipped voice strained against the sound of Camille's own motorbike chugging to a start.

"I figured, I'm headed to the nearest one."

"So, why are you contacting me?"

"To complain. This job is awful. You sent me in after the Funds, I hate that garbage. And this little skank was in a basement. Who has a basement in Zeta? Cody?"

Camille received no response; Cody had terminated the transmission as soon as he heard her say "complain." Camille regretted getting out of bed to take a job from Cody. Jobs from Cody always seemed to suck.

This job, with the Toy woman who had a hole in her head, didn't feel like one of her preferred, guiding angel jobs. With the Funds and the basement, it didn't feel like a retrieval job either. Dread crept over Camille as she steered her bike into to the heart of Zeta City.

4
TOY

Toy was not a native to Zeta, and before she moved there she had witnessed only one death – that of her grandmother, which had affected her profoundly. Toy had grown up with her extended family on the Epsilon Net islands, a poor but dreamy tropical location on the other side of the world, both physically and metaphysically. The islands were one of the last places in the world to be connected to the Net system, aside from the no-mans-land detached areas. The people of Epsilon were rich in money, but poor in Node Points, having lost out on the fifty years that the families of older zones had to earn so-called Goodwill and stockpiled their Node Points.

The Net on Epsilon was spotty and ill kept. As a result, the poorer island folk lived close to the areas where the Net sometimes cut out. Toy's grandmother lived in a beach bungalow close to the border where the Net ended, and the coverage was scant. To keep people far away from the official edge of the Net, and mostly away from the unreliable areas, safety officers had bisected the beach with a bright red fence. This border extended to red poles in the water, posted at regular intervals all the way out to where the water would overcome a swimmer's physical limits.

Tourists and natives alike frolicked on this beach, but, never near, and especially not past, the border. If they drowned or had an aneurysm beyond that fence they were dead, but inside of it, they were immortal.

Toy's Gran, with her long face framed by short white hair, died just barely inside the red fence. Toy didn't know if her grandmother hung her laundry out to dry on a line because she liked the smell and texture of linens dried in tropical warmth, or if she hung them because she was poor and could not afford an electric dryer. Toy suspected the latter because Gran's laundry was often too heavy and wet for her to lift on her own.

Little Toy often helped her Gran, but that day she wanted to build sandcastles, so Gran had to lift the clothes by herself. While struggling to hang a sheet, Gran stopped, turned wan and she clutched her blue blouse, just below her throat. She collapsed like the clothes in the basket next to her, ragged breathing, eyes empty and senseless.

"Thank the stars she died inside the Net," Toy's mother, Ruby, said after men came and took the body away.

"She only had 50,000 Points," said Toy's father, Walter, with quiet concern. Gran was his mother.

"That doesn't seem like enough."

"On the mainland, they die with millions of Points."

That was Toy's first inkling of what the "Points" that the government issued her each birthday actually were. Before that, she knew she got them for every day that she was alive, plus more for volunteering with her parents in programs that made meals for the hospital-bound and bedridden. Toy knew that when she grew up, she'd have a job that would give her both money and more points. Her grandmother's passing was the first time she associated the Points with death.

Toy saw more death when she moved to Zeta City. She saw violent, sword-to-the-gut deaths and the end of slow, sad, opiate overdoses. Toy learned to avoid the areas around Zeta's three Node gates because they were surrounded by misery and suicide.

The day of her own, planned, death, Toy ditched her motorbike on the edge of the city. Bikes were allowed in Zeta, but most everyone walked or rode the rail, and she didn't need to stick out more than she already did with her gaping head hole and bleeding temple. She walked toward the Nouveau Avenue Gate, which was the smallest, and newest, Gate. She assumed the Funds, and the black-haired woman with the wrist RAP, would search for her at the larger gates first.

There was a casino on the corner of Nouveau Avenue and Tempete Street. It used to be flashy, but now it was just faded and inappropriate, like a middle-aged woman, well past her prime, dressed in a miniskirt and fishnet stockings. A few blocks away, a white painted line across the road and sidewalk marked the approximate location of the Nouveau Avenue Gate. The actual gate was invisible and intangible to the living. Only Founders, Node engineers, and the deceased who walked through it knew where the gate really was.

People tried to die as close to the gates as possible because of what happens after, when your mind is alive in the Net, but not yet in the Node. Some people's digitized minds – who knows how many – remained stuck in the mortal coil. Due to this glitch, hospitals were often built right next to gate lines.

Her headache worsened, and Toy realized that the nanites Bernard had injected into her brain were killing her, but not fast enough. As she traversed the city she saw giant billboard screens dotting the landscape and playing nonstop advertisements. Toy's ad spot was coming up soon. Nirvana had paid for it to be played in a loop for half an hour that afternoon, and since she was supposed to be dead hours before the ad played, being seen as a living martyr would ruin the effect. The hot sun was high above Zeta City, burning her neck and reminding Toy that she was very much alive.

She made a beeline for the casino's front doors, hoping she could find something inside that she could use to off herself. She grimly thought about smashing a bathroom mirror and slashing her wrist, but she dismissed that idea and shuddered, hoping there was a gift shop in the casino that sold guns or knives. She wanted a quick ending.

As she reached for the door, a muscular, feminine arm barred her way. It was that big girl with black hair who had greeted her when she rose from the Nirvana basement. Strands of her curls hung, sweaty and disheveled, into her dark, glittering eyes that danced when she Toy met her gaze.

"Girl," the woman sighed with exasperation, "why am I chasing you? I'm not a Fund, I'm not even a militia, I'm a one-hundred-percent private hire, and I don't give a rat's ass – "

Toy ducked under the woman's heavy arm and tore through the casino. This woman, with the crazy curls and glitter eyes, gained on her wicked fast. Toy realized that she wasn't going to lose the woman inside the casino, so she barreled through the nearest exit into an alleyway that had train tracks on the other side. The tracks were deep – four rails thick – and fronted by a ten-foot tall fence. An advertising screen loomed over the other side of the tracks, positioned to market to passengers on slow trains, and patrons to the strip mall that took over the neighboring streets. Toy saw her own face on the display screen as her words scrolled beneath.

She stopped, despite her attempted getaway, and watched Bernard's pink-glove hand plunge the nanotech needle into her head. She heard a woman on the train platform gasp and put her hand over her mouth as she watched the video. Toy was proud. The people of Zeta were tough, used to daily death, and dirt, and blood and still, Toy's creation was making an impact.

Glitter Eyes flew through the casino door. "I know your name is Toy, mine is Camille," she said through heaving breath.

"Stop!" Toy shouted at the charging Camille. "Why are to you trying to talk to me? Just kill me!" Toy raised her arms up over her head in surrender, hoping that Camille would give her the gift of death.

"I can't kill you," Camille drew up, panting, and patted herself down, "I don't even have anything on me that *could* kill you." As Camille looked up, she followed the arc of Toy's arm and noticed the video screen looming over Zeta, and looked from the advertising board back to Toy's face.

Toy glanced back at the screen in time to see the words *I am the agent* scroll across the bottom of the screen as Bernard pulled the needle from her head. She saw her own, fearful, response to the sound of the Fund infiltrating the cabin. A moment later, the video would go black and begin again in an half-hour-long loop of Nirvana-sponsored terror.

"At least I know what you did to your noggin." Camille sighed and tapped the side of her head, "But I can't kill you, I'm here to do the opposite." Camille lifted her wrist and Toy recalled that the woman had mentioned that she, impossibly, owned a Confiner.

"Please," Toy begged and then she turned and ran – away from Camille's Confiner and the casino – toward one of the busiest streets in Zeta, keeping close to the train track's fence. Camille was bigger and slower than Toy, but not by much.

Toy heard the noise that she had been waiting for: an oncoming train. When she heard it, she swung up on to the fence and climbed with all her might. If she could get to the top before the train, and jump far enough into its path, it would kill her well out of reach of Camille's Confiner.

Below her, Camille reached for Toy's foot on the chain link and narrowly missed.

"Come on, man!" Camille groaned and readied herself to climb up after Toy.

Toy straddled the fence while she waited for the moment the train would be in the right spot. As she took a quick survey of the scene below her, she could see a few people ogling up at her, some recognizing her from her terrorizing advertisements. Most people ignored the scene, though, because horror and death come cheap in Zeta. Closer, but still well below her, was Camille, fighting a losing battle with gravity in her attempts to climb up the fence to Toy.

She swung over the top of the fence and dropped, biting her tongue hard as she landed. It hurt like hell, but it gave her the adrenaline she needed for her final act. Clinging to the edge of the of the rail, Toy had just long enough to think *this had better kill me.*

Toy died with the taste of blood in her mouth and the last thought – *kill me, kill me, kill me* – echoing in her mind.

5
CAMILLE

The Funds were widely known to be the worst police in a city full of a myriad of police forces. They were also the only ones paid for by the government. Most police officers spent a few years as a Fund and then moved on to private police jobs that paid far better and garnered more respect. Camille was not surprised the Fund had mismanaged their extraction of Toy, but she was uncertain about why they were chasing her in the first place. She missed all but a snippet of the broadcast because she had been climbing up the fence after Toy at the time it was being shown. So why Toy? Dying criminals were not government territory; they belonged to the people who had been hired by their victims. They belonged to Bounty Hunters, mercenaries, and private police.

The bulk of her income came from one-time clients because most people had the need for her macabre services once in a lifetime, but Camille did have a number of regular clients, and none of them were as infuriating or as elusive as Cody. His jobs were always strange in one way or another, tending to include trips to unseemly areas and characters involved in multiple, illegal activities. Camille assumed that Cody took jobs from the Funds, but paid her from his own store of Node Points since payment in Node was supposed to be illegal. To Camille, this made Cody the worst kind of criminal, full of self-righteousness and unable to admit, or possibly even accept, his own criminality. Still, Camille had developed a fondness for him, something akin to the feelings one might have for a house spider that no one has got around to killing - yet.

The first time she met him, she had almost squashed him like a cockroach. Cody stood in the way of Camille and her bounty, a bookie named Iesus Rolland who had slimed and swindled his way through Zeta's upper, and then lower, classes. A kingpin heard Rolland was planning on escaping into the Node and had sent Camille to Rolland's grimy, public housing flat.

Camille knocked on Rolland's door, but instead of being greeted by the bookie, Cody poked his out of the narrow opening between the door and the door frame.

"Uh, I'm here to see Iesus Rolland," Camille said, realizing that Cody looked nothing like her target's scruffy hologram.

"Mr. Rolland is dying." Cody spoke in sharp tones.

"Good." Camille muscled her way into the apartment while Cody tried to hem and fuss her back out.

"Who are you?" Camille asked once she was firmly planted in Rolland's living room.

"I represent a business with an interest in Mr. Rolland. We were hoping to … extract assets before he …" Cody squirmed, not meeting Camille's eyes, and flicking a nonexistent piece of dust from his suit cuff.

He was very tall, and painfully thin, with olive skin and jet black hair. When he met her gaze, with his wide, brown stare, Camille sensed a multitude of interconnected fears swimming in his mind's dark waters.

"Yeah, well I'm 'extracting assets' too. Us and half of Lower Zeta, huh? Where is he?" Camille asked.

"In the bedroom, he's very close to death, I think it's an overdose. He says he's out of money and he refuses to pay in NPs," Cody fretted.

"Alright, I'm going to do something that will help both of us," she leaned into Cody and lowered her voice. "Can I trust you?"

"I – I don't think so." Cody took a large step back.

"What?" Camille looked at Cody with a mix of rage and confusion. "What do mean you 'don't think so'? Even people I can't trust say that I can trust them."

"Well, then, why did you ask?" Cody retorted.

Camille gave Cody her most menacing glare. "Are we good? I'm not going to ask again."

Cody sighed, "Okay, you can trust me."

"Okay." Camille eyeballed him with suspicion before continuing, "My wrist RAP has a Confiner built in. If we hurry, I can hold Iesus here and force him to cough up some NPs before I let him go."

"Those things," Cody pointed at the wrist RAP, "are extremely illegal." Cody emphasized *extremely* and *illegal*. "Where did you get that?"

"I made it," Camille lied. "What does it matter? I thought you said we need to hurry."

Cody nodded curtly, and they rushed into the bedroom where Rolland lay dying. The carpet, which was thirty years out of date, showed a pattern of wear and stain that betrayed Rolland's habit of shuffling to the kitchen to get food and then carelessly eating it in bed. The room smelled of medicine and poor dental hygiene, with the stench itself clinging to the shriveled figure on the bed, piled among grey pillows and a worn duvet.

"Are you going to do it?" Cody looked at her wrist as if it might explode.

"I already am." Camille stood over Rolland. He was much older than he had seemed on her hologram, or perhaps his looming death had aged him. He was mostly bald with a yellowing, chinstrap beard. His bloodshot eyes flew open when Camille approached him.

"I'm so sorry, honey," Camille said as she slipped her hand underneath the cover to take his.

Cody took a step backward, stunned and confused. He wasn't quite sure what to expect from this rugged young woman, but kind platitudes weren't on his list.

Camille ignored Cody and focused on Rolland, "I know that this is very hard and that you're close to passing, but I can't let you move on into the Node until you pay some people what you owe."

Rolland rolled his eyes toward the ceiling and grimaced.

"This isn't working," Cody said.

"Give me a minute, man." Camille shot him a sharp look, but she continued to speak gently to Rolland, "I did a little research on you, Iesus, your mom is in the Node, and she passed into there with enough Points to spare. You do have enough Points to pay off a few debts for me and for this well-dressed gentleman over here."

Rolland didn't answer, and Cody made an impatient noise.

Camille said, "We were hired to collect from you, honey. With this device," she tapped the RAP, "I can hold you in this body for a very long time. But, I don't want to. I just want to do my job, collect and go home. Now, Mr. Rolland put yourself in my shoes. What would you do?"

Twenty minutes later, Cody and Camille left the rank apartment with their debts fully paid.

"I underestimated you," Cody said.

"No. You would have had to estimate me in the first place," Camille laughed, "When are you going to pay me my portion of your bounty on the debt I helped you recover?" She was half joking, but Cody very seriously asked her for her account number.

After the Iesus incident, Cody called Camille from time to time with strange jobs that had large payouts. Camille assumed he wasn't telling his employers his amazing results were attributed to a sloppy mercenary and her contraband technology.

But, with this Toy hacker job, it seemed that Cody, who had, in his defense, once explicitly told her that he could not be trusted, had set her up with something beyond the normal scope of her job. She hoped that the Fund's involvement wouldn't cost her Confiner, or anything more valuable. Camille was not happy.

So, at four minutes after eleven that Tuesday morning, Toy the hacker heaved herself over a guardrail and jumped in front of the 11:15 train, exploding into a gory tangle of goop and bones. Her blood splattered across Camille's face and arms at the moment of impact. Camille, in recoil, pushed back and jumped down to the pedestrian sidewalk that ran alongside the tracks.

Bellowing steam, the train howled and halted, but the engine was the only scream. A few onlookers stopped to gawk, but most ducked against the wind and carried on, save one elderly gentleman who shook his head sadly.

"Grim," the man commented, "how everybody comes to die."

Camille backed away from the groaning train and tapped a few buttons on her wrist RAP.

"Cody Priolo," she said, and her wrist began to chime.

A few moments later, Cody's stern face appeared on the RAP's screen. He was sitting at his desk, with his hands folded.

"Do you have her?" Cody glowered into the screen. Seeing the blood splattered on Camille's face, he asked, "Are you alright?"

Camille took a breath and walked away from Toy's remains while still talking into the RAP.

"It's not my blood. Toy Bowen is dead, Cody. She jumped onto the Nouveau Avenue train tracks and went squish. No way I could confine her."

Camille walked faster away from Nouveau Avenue, distancing herself from the sound of sirens as Fund motorcycles pulled up along the tracks. The area's roads and sidewalks were cracked and uneven, making walking and video talking difficult. The screen on her wrist bounced as she spoke to Cody.

"I told you how important she was." Cody tone was deep and grave.

"Yeah, but you never told me why. A dozen more hackers will kill themselves in Zeta's Net this week. Should I play savior to all of them?"

"I'll meet you in your office in half an hour." Cody was not about to play ball, at least not on an open communication line that could be tapped. "You'll need to fix this."

"Fix what? That kid is dead, Cody." Camille growled into her wrist RAP, "She belongs to the Node now," but Camille was talking to a blank screen. Cody had hung up on her, again.

6
TOY

Toy regretted jumping in front of the train for about a second. It was a long second, though, packed with memories of her simple childhood and her younger-self, an island girl who had loved life and who never would have dreamed of causing her own death, but the Points had darkened that girl into an angry woman, an angry woman with one second left to live.

Toy spent her so much of her life rejecting the idea of Node Points, she had close to none of them saved up. The few she had earned were acquired because of her age, and she had spent those on political favors and sourcing nefarious technology. If her virus didn't succeed in maiming the NP system, she would spend forever in the Node's version of a debtor's prison. Granted, no one actually knew what it was like to be dead without Node Points, but everyone assumed it was unpleasant.

After that last pang, there was nothing for Toy to regret, nothing to feel, nothing to be. That nothing embraced her for a what seemed like an eternity of soft, warm, nothing. She loved it and never wanted to leave. *This is the heaven void of pain and desire*, she thought; but Toy came back fast and confused.

It seemed, for a moment, that the train passed through her, but Toy saw her own ruined body. She had succeeded in destroying herself so badly that Camille would have no place to confine her.

"I died! Good!" Toy spun around to shout at the black-haired bounty hunter who had chased her to the rails. She reached up to touch the hole in her temple. It was still there. *How is it there*, she thought, *I died. I dead good.*

I dead good- that's not how you say it. She realized something was wrong one second before her mind broke into a million pieces that cracked and fragmented as the Net attempted to upload her consciousness. Thoughts were no longer possible as Toy felt herself become bits of knowledge, bits that were frantically trying to piece themselves together. These snippets of memory took many forms – what the color blue looked like, how to add numbers, the shape of her father's face, the taste of potatoes and butter, how lips move to make words, her name – *Toy* – and what she had looked like in the mirror that morning. The mirror was dusty, and she had looked sad.

The train and her broken body were gone and then came back again as a new kind of vision, one that didn't use sight or need physical eyes. Pieces of experience formed together into a few whole memories that Toy had guarded and nurtured. In one memory, she was sitting on a curb with her legs stretched out, crossed at her ankles in front of her. Her father and brother were across the street buying sandwiches from a cart. In another memory, her grandmother hung heavy laundry by the beach. In yet another memory, a woman in a white dress played flute at a recital. In another, she was reading from her tablet while gray rain splattered on her window. Finally, she felt a thick, wired needle being lowered to her temple.

As her fragmented memories re-formed, the vision that was not true eyesight revealed a new world to Toy. Living people faded and a shadow world pulsed into form around her. The shadows became stronger on beats, like the quickening of a heart. They looked like people, but as time went on, they looked more corporeal than the living. When they stopped pulsing, these "ghosts" were much more substantial. While ethereal, they were still tangible; but the living people, and the world they inhabited, faded into the mere whisper of a double exposure photograph.

Standing around her were thousands of these ghosts. They were pale representations of their former selves. Strong, opaque faces faded and blended down into pastel, translucent torsos and most of them disappeared just around the knee, making them appear to float. Not all were serene: some of the phantoms were bloody and wailing, while some hovered in lazy circles, their sunken eyes staring hopelessly. A few of the specters moved with intelligent purpose.

Toy found she could move and turned away from the train tracks to face a parallel street, which was known as Eglise Boulevard to the living. Eglise Boulevard ended at an open square, where a cathedral stood with its huge statue of Jesus looming over the square. The ghosts were attracted to this area, many of them floated around the church, and even more meandered toward it. There were so many of these shades gathering there that the area around the statue looked as if it was covered in a fog.

The last word Toy had said before she died spiked through her fragmented mind: *Good.*

She tried to say it. "G–G," she sputtered.

One of the more coherent-looking spirits speed toward her and almost passed her, but halted when he heard her attempt to form a word.

"What was that?" the fat ghost said.

Toy stopped faltering and stared at the phantom man. He was short, thin, and old. Wisps of white hair tumbled out from under his flat, tweed cap. He looked Toy up and down, and then past her into the double exposure remnant of the reality that was left behind: the bloodied tracks, and the living, Funded Police with their motorcycles and perimeter tape.

"That you, eh?" The phantom man nodded to the train splatter and looked back at Toy sympathetically. He focused on the bleeding hole in Toy's temple, "What a mess." He shook his head sadly.

"G–G–G" Toy said loudly, suddenly.

The old man turned toward the church and the Jesus statue, where Toy seemed to be looking, "God?" he guessed. "No God here. But, they seem to like it, you know, moths to a flame," he said almost apologetically.

When Toy didn't respond, the man went on, "Well, my name's Alan Freed. I like to make the rounds and take those who want to go to the gates to the gates. Just doin' my duty until Nelly passes on, then me and her can go in together. I know they say not to do that, that it's easy to find people once you're in the Node, but after seeing all this," he gestured to the church and the horde of spirits again, "I don't trust it. I don't trust any of it."

Toy tried frantically to piece together what the man was saying. He was speaking at a normal rate, but it was still much too fast for her broken brain to identify. She knew some things that he said were very important, and some weren't, but it was impossible to rationalize. Bits of what the old ghost said tumbled around her thoughts. *Alan, gates, Nelly, together, trust, Node.*

"Look, I'll bring you to the next gate if you want to go, but I'm not pushing anybody into the other side. I know you died rough, and that's got to be making it hard for you to operate yourself there. If you could just say 'gate,' I'll go on and bring you to it."

"G–G" Toy tried to say "good" again.

"Close enough," Alan said.

7
CAMILLE

Toy's death on the tracks held up the trains for several blocks; Camille suspected that the whole city may be on hold. She didn't want to stand and watch them attempt to piece together the hacker's body, so she walked the mile and a half to the next station, near where she had left the bike. She thought about calling back that prick Cody, but she had reached a part of Zeta where even walking could be hazardous, let alone walking while staring at a wrist communicator screen.

The ground in Zeta was hot, and the cement was warped from the constant rain. Zeta was an ancient city built precariously, and unwisely, on top of a swamp in an ocean gulf. Vines crept from around every corner, and the streets cracked, then crumbled, from the moisture.

It was a world away from Camille's home in Prioria, which was northeast of Zeta, under the vast Sigma Net that covered several cities. It wasn't so packed, and there were fewer suicides and even fewer ghosts. Camille's Sigma home was warm – pleasantly so – and there were real trees and animals with soft fur. The only animals in Zeta were lizards that ranged in size from a pinky finger to twice the size of a person. The big lizards, like crocodiles, ate pets and children. The little ones overran the streets. A little lizard scuttled across Camille's path, pausing to look up at her as if to remind her of how far away from Prioria she had settled.

She gathered her bike from the bike rental locks at the Oasiau station. As she had predicted, the trains there were stopped too. A man in a cowboy hat asked her what happened further up the track. She ignored him and climbed on her bike, eager to get out of there.

After a bumpy ride home, Camille made the weary walk up several flights of stairs to her small office and apartment. She paused for a moment to admire her white front office. Camille has chosen all white as part of a con, to make it look pristine and pure, like she kept a tight ship.

Cody had once asked to see her records and Camille had laughed, opening the filing cabinet to reveal a soda cup lid and a half-eaten candy bar still inside its wrapper. When Cody protested her lack of actual files, Camille stood up from her desk, grabbed the rest of the candy bar from the filing cabinet, and locked herself inside her apartment. Cody knocked for about five minutes, then gave up and went home. He never asked about her records again.

Beyond the empty office, there was a full apartment with two bedrooms. It had a little kitchen with an island, which opened to a long, narrow living room. Worn sofas and chairs were adorned with loose items from Camille's wardrobe. It was messy, but well decorated, tending toward kitsch. A door at the end of the living room led to her small bedroom. The colors in her apartment were the same as the colors in the rest of Zeta, old and drab as if every bit of pigment had been bleached by the sun, with the exception of one wall that was painted black.

Camille settled onto her sofa and pointed her wrist RAP at the black wall in front of her, activating a holographic television screen. She clicked over to a news channel and saw an enlarged image of Toy Bowen's face staring at her from behind a news anchor.

"… claimed to have created a virus to destroy the Node Point system," the anchorwoman spoke in her best Breaking News voice, "Bowen died by apparent suicide, jumping onto the Nouveau Street train tracks late this morning."

Good. Camille thought, *no one realizes I was following her.*

"Now our Node expert, Doctor Ian Rames, will discuss the possible ramifications of an NP breach."

Camille paused the news, and did what a billion other people did at that exact moment; she checked the balance of her Node Point account. She was relieved to see all her 1,975,004 NPs displayed on her wrist screen. Whatever the hacker did, it hadn't affected the system; at least, not yet.

Next, she searched for the full video the hacker had played over Zeta City's ad screens. She watched the video projected onto her wall. Not as large as a street ad screen, but still all-encompassing.

"I'm Toy Bowen, and I am your salvation …" The blonde said while she bobbed her head the wire feeding the needle swayed.

Camille silently cursed Cody for getting her involved in this mess while the video played out. She was just about to press *play* on the news to see what the Node expert, Dr. Ian Rames, had to say, when her wrist vibrated, alerting her to a call from Cody.

"I thought you were coming to my office," Camille grumbled without bothering to say hello.

"There have been some issues. I'll be delayed." Cody's face looked haggard and his expression a bit confused.

"I'm never taking another government job from you, Cody. Or, any other kind of job from you. We're done," Camille said as she plodded over to her refrigerator and rummaged through it with her free hand.

"Be that as it may," Cody was breathing hard, as if he were walking briskly, "You have to see this one through, you've been paid – a lot."

"I can't help you. I find suicidal kids, lost lovers, and skeevy debtors. This hacker shit is for the security companies." Camille grabbed a small box of orange juice from the fridge and stuck a straw through the top.

"You're one person. A security company is hundreds or thousands of people. We need as few eyes as possible on this job."

"As few eyes as possible? This is all over the news."

"And you – one person, not a security company – found her and almost had her before she jumped."

"It doesn't matter anyway. She's dead. Job over." Camille moved her hand to hang up on Cody.

"No. Job not over. Not if we can find her ghost."

Camille didn't answer him, she just narrowed her eyes, sipped orange juice through the straw, and glared at Cody through the holo-screen. Cody tried to match her silence, but he broke.

"I'll be at your office in less than an hour. Stay there," Cody commanded. Camille's wrist screen went black when he hung up.

She found half a chicken sandwich in her fridge, leftover from lunch at a diner a few days before. She set a kettle of water to boil on the stovetop so she could have tea when her meal was finished. As she sat down to eat she pulled her black hair up into a clip to keep her long bangs out of her face.

Seemingly, on its own volition, the kettle whizzed off the stove top and slammed onto the floor. Camille was momentarily startled, but she bent down and picked up the kettle.

"No. No twat ghosts today. Do you hear me?" Louder she asked, "Can you hear me?"

She straightened up and placed the kettle in the sink, preparing to wash and refill it. Right before she turned on the water, she called out again, "If you can hear me, I want you to know that you're dead. You died."

Camille looked around, waiting for a sound, or a picture rattling on the wall – some acknowledgment that what she said had been heard.

After filling and replacing the kettle, Camille spun around to face her empty apartment. The hair on her arms and neck rose as her skin chilled.

"The nearest gate is the Zeta main gate. You can get into the Node from there. Go out the front door of this building, turn right, and then left onto Carnival Street. The gate is in the middle of the road."

Her kettle rattled again and her office door, which had been ajar, closed softly.

"I'm sorry you died," Camille called to the closed door.

8
NORA

Holographic screens lined the cafeteria, each of them projecting a different version of the story of Toy Bowen, the Nirvana rebel who died with a nano-poisoned mind. Nora dreamily ate her vegetable-stuffed pita and listened in on the conversation happening one table over.

"There have been thousands of attempts to hack the Node system over the last hundred years since the system became fully functional. Most hackers come from one of two groups." The man speaking was Cosmo Kadmos, Nora's classmate and a Node Studies major. This business with the hacker was his time to shine. He didn't wait for someone to ask the nature of the two groups of Node hackers; he just plunged right in.

"One group are the people who want to falsely supply themselves with more NPs," Cosmo continued to his captive audience of student diners, "this group had various degrees of success, but Node research seems to indicate that the false points would not translate in the afterlife. I mean, the Founders, all deceased, promised to guard the system from the inside out. The living population took stock in these guardians and believed that they had made sure the Node was fair and untainted."

"That's not this lady though." Nora's friend Mini had joined the group. She had walked right past Nora, which made her feel a little slighted.

"I'm getting there." Cosmo both resented and reveled in the interruption. It meant that someone was truly listening. "The second group of hackers focused on speaking to the dead. They figured, considering the dead lived in cyberspace, that they should be able to chat with, or at least text message, their dead loved ones. These attempts were never successful, leading to the creeping suspicion that there was no Node."

"Yeah, but the ghosts –" Nora let her interest drag her into the conversation.

She slid her tray over and joined the group's far side, "– don't the reverbs prove that there is a Node?"

"I'm just playing devil's advocate. Of course, I believe there's a Node," Cosmo said, "But some people believe there are only ghosts and that the Node was a trick to pacify the population and that our reverbs fade into oblivion instead of passing into the Node to redeem their eternal rewards."

"That's awful," Nora said.

At the same time, Mini said, "Toy Bowen isn't in either of those groups."

"I know. That is precisely what makes her so fascinating. This hacker's goal is a new one. We have never seen an attempt to render the points useless."

"One that was publicized," said another man in the group. He was stout, with long, curly brown hair. Nora didn't recognize him.

"Why aren't people freaking out more?" Nora asked Cosmo.

"They are, and they aren't." Cosmo nodded toward one of the many holo–screens recreating Toy's speech, "but, to most, the Node seems impenetrable and these attempts insignificant."

"I guess it was a waste for her to do it then. A little naïve at best, destructive at worst." Nora displayed her newly formed opinion.

"Are you kidding me," the student with the curly hair spoke again, "this lady is absolutely a hero. You're the naïve one."

"And you are?" Cosmo asked him, nervous that his carefully curated conversation was derailing.

"Alexis," he said, standing up and picking up his lunch tray.

"Why do you think Toy's a hero?" Cosmo asked, thinking that perhaps there was a research paper hidden in Alexis's response.

"How many Node Points do you have?" Alexis asked. He turned to Nora, "how many do you have?"

Cosmo, knowing where Alexis was headed, was too smart to answer; but Nora fell right into his trap.

"I don't know." Nora shrugged.

"Of course you don't." Alexis slammed his tray down, drawing attention from other groups in the dining hall, "Your parents take care of it for you. Just like their parents take care of it for them. Not everyone was born into Points. I know how many are in my account, down to the last one. And my parents know every point in their accounts too, but they're not saving up for me. They are saving up for their parents to make sure that they don't die without any. We are in a race against death, while people like you just stretch out. Your hours and your days belonging to no one but yourselves."

"My mother died," Nora said suddenly, irrationally. "You said my 'parents,' but it's only my dad."

"Is that supposed to make it okay that you and your family rob us? How old were you when she died?"

"You're being cruel," Cosmo stepped in.

"Am I? I didn't hear you volunteer your Node Point amount."

Cosmo opened his mouth to answer.

Alexis interrupted, "Spare me. The fact that you're getting a useless degree tells me. Either you don't know, or the number is so high that it's embarrassing."

"Four," Nora said, and the two men calmed, "I was four when my mother died."

"I'm sorry but, you barely knew her," Alexis said, "you lost something that you never knew. I will spend eternity working for something that I can never have." He walked away, not allowing for a retort.

"No one ever said that the Node Point system was fair," Cosmo called after him.

9
CAMILLE

Camille, like almost everyone else, assumed Toy had failed. But Cody must have thought otherwise because he persisted in spreading his peculiar brand of gloom onto Camille's personal space.

Cody sat across from Camille at her white desk. His hands were folded into a pyramid, pointed in toward his chest, his elbows wide on her empty desk. The dusky man brought much darkness to her simple, clean office. Cody had clipped, black hair, dark olive skin, and watery black eyes. He wore an impeccably tailored black suit and shiny, silver tie. A badge on a string around his neck identified him as a National Bounty Officer.

Camille had known that Cody was a member of the NBO, but he rarely wore his badge. Some members of NBO were just bounty hunters, but the organization also held members who policed and oversaw the city's various bounty hunter organizations. Cody could have arrested Camille a dozen times by now for her infractions, not the least of which included the Confiner. But he hadn't. The only reason he would wear the NBO badge was if he planning to arrest her or attempt to use the threat of arrest to force her to do something. She knew he wasn't going to arrest her, so she concluded that his motivation was force. Camille had an inkling of what he might press her to do. Dreading what may come next, Camille faked being busy.

Camille made a long production out of using some of her extra tea water to make Cody an instant coffee. His mug sat in front of him, cooling and untouched. He fidgeted, trying to come with the best way to scratch whatever subject itched his mind.

"Camille, we're friends, right?" He began by looking into Camille's eyes.

"Not as far as I can tell." Camille broke his gaze and glanced to the side, pretending to look out the window. "Friends don't coerce each other into unwillingly working for the government."

Flustered, and genuinely surprised, Cody broke his haughty tone. He sounded sad and a little pathetic, "Really, I mean – we see each other all the time. We're at least friendly."

Camille sighed, "Cody, you're a goddamn high school Hall Monitor. You're tolerated as an annoying necessity who occasionally pays me."

Cody resumed his professional tone, "That was uncalled for, and I will chalk it up to lack of discretion following your failure on the Toy Bowen case. Especially unfortunate because it was your first ever government case."

"I didn't ask for my 'first ever' government case. And you hung up on me. Twice." Camille pointed out.

"My apologies," Cody said, "We were both in a rush and I only had time to relay and receive vital information,"

Camille rolled her eyes and sipped her tea.

"I don't know if I can trust you with this intelligence," Cody began again.

"You can't," Camille interrupted with a grin, recalling their first meeting. She softened her tone a bit when Cody didn't smile back. "I don't want to play games. I'm sorry the hacker died, and you don't have to pay me." Camille leaned back and started typing into her wrist RAP. "I'll pay you back right now."

Cody waved a hand. "Not necessary. But here is what you can't talk to anyone about," Cody paused dramatically, "Toy wasn't just a regular hacker. We have reason to believe that she carried a virus that did some real damage to the NP system."

"Nirvana is weak and lame." Camille laughed, "I just checked my NPs, they're fine. If she did any real damage, there would be panic in the streets. I don't hear any panic, do you?" She exaggerated cupping her hand to her ear.

"Nirvana isn't as weak as—" he broke off at the sound of a loud crash from the apartment's kitchen. "What the devil was that?"

"A ghost." Camille waved her hand dismissively. "It's been here all day. I think it's an old lady. It likes my red tea kettle."

Camille got up, turned around and opened her office door. "You died. You can't have any coffee. Go away!" She spoke firmly into the emptiness of the kitchen.

Cody chuckled and relaxed a little. Camille wasn't going to bite him. "I used to tell the reverbs where the nearest Node entry point was."

"I did that a few minutes before you came in. It obviously didn't help."

"No, perhaps not. I don't think they can hear us."

Camille shook her head, "I didn't grow up here, and I'll never get used to them. There are hardly any ghosts under the Sigma Net."

"I know. I'm from a different Net too." Cody tensed up again, "We have to get back on subject here – this hacker job."

Camille crumpled. "I know what you're going to ask." She held up her wrist and tapped her RAP, "This Confiner is as illegal as it gets. I could go to state-funded prison. You could be fired."

"I gave you the job because we needed the best and you're the best. Or, at least I thought you were the best, until this morning." He folded his arms across his chest.

The ghost continued to bang around in the apartment behind her.

"Toy was carrying something called the Bliss virus," Cody continued, despite the noise. "A very real, very dangerous bit of code capable of infecting and wiping out banks of Node Points from inside the Node outward. Your NP account might not show the damage for weeks or it may never show that it has been tampered with until you die, get to the Node, and find yourself destitute."

"The Founders – " Camille began.

"The Founders might not be able to do anything about it without contact from the living," Cody interjected. "There's just no way."

"So, she could have just broken the Afterlife," Camille said blankly.

"Well, I wouldn't put it like that, but yes." Cody was glad that Camille finally seemed to understand the severity of the situation.

10
TOY

As the old man with the flat hat walked and talked, Toy began to comprehend what he was saying instead of simply hearing but failing to process. She also began to understand what she was seeing. She was inside of the Net, seeing the "real" world through a digital veil. It was like being underwater and staring at the murky ocean floor. The only things that were clear were the other sea creatures – the ghosts stuck in the Zeta Net – with her.

She supposed the Founders could have made it so she could see the world clearly, but since all the dead needed to do was navigate to a Node Gate, there wasn't any reason to waste the processing power.

She felt a sudden, deep loss. *Processing power.* She was dead. All that was left of Toy was bits of data waiting to be processed.

Am I breathing? She raised her hand up to her mouth and felt no warm air. *No, data doesn't breathe, but it can listen.* She floated along, gently guided by the rambling old man. She stopped trying to feel herself breathe and focused on the old man's words.

"—in no rush to die, Nelly will have Node Points enough for both of us. She was a nurse, they get double for every day of nursing."

"Node Points," Toy parroted.

"That's right, good for you," he said, surprised that she had said anything aside from her repeated "G" sounds, "What's your name?"

"Node Points," Toy repeated.

Alan was a little crestfallen, "Well, we tried, didn't we. You know, I've been doing this for about a year, as far as I can tell, and I know that some people come through broken, but I've never seen anybody come through as broken as you are."

Toy looked into the old man's eyes, she was sad and pleading, but so was he. She was sure the Bliss virus was the cause of her degeneration, but she couldn't communicate the problem, and wouldn't if she could. She needed him to bring her to the gate without finding out she was wired to destroy the system he seemed to so deeply believe in. Toy broke her gaze and followed him as best she could in her broken condition.

11
CAMILLE

"What are you doing?" Cody raised an eyebrow at Camille as she fussed with her wrist RAP.

"Checking to see if my NPs are still there," she said as she finished typing. "They are," she sighed in relief.

Cody nodded, "Again? Well, we would have heard from a news feed if they were gone. You wouldn't be the first one to notice."

Camille had ushered Cody through her stark white office and into her apartment where they could sit in more comfort. They were watching the news on the projector screen, waiting for any sign that Toy's sabotage was successful and Camille was already regretting her hospitality. Cody was squirming around in his seat, he clearly still had something unpleasant to talk about, and she was tired of waiting for the shoe to drop.

"Of course," Cody broke the silence and then paused for a long time, studied his fingernails, and gave a sly upwards glance at Camille. "She could still be a reverb," he said in a fake, offhand way.

"Yeah, maybe," Camille said as she shrugged.

"It's too bad we can't find reverbs." He made a show of raising his eyebrow. "Or maybe we can … " Cody continued his cloying, sly act.

Gears turned in Camille's mind, and her eyes lit with brief rage.

"You didn't hire me for this job because you thought I was the 'best.' Dammit, Cody, you brought me on this case because you knew that she would kill herself no matter what I did. You can forget it. I don't know how to find ghosts. Anything you've heard about me finding reverbs is a rumor."

Cody rolled his eyes. "Spare me." He tapped his NBO badge. "I know everything."

There was a long silence. Camille sat with her arms folded as Cody attempted to stare her down.

"Ted Walton," Cody said venomously. "And think carefully what you say next."

Considering his warning, Camille neglected to respond.

Cody went on, "Two years ago you took a job for Ted, I know about this job because Ted works in the department next to mine. Your mark died before you could confine her, but you still managed to get Ted's message to her. How?"

"Suddenly, this feels like an interrogation," Camille said, "are you officially asking with your NBO badge, or are you asking nicely because we're friendly? Which is it?"

Cody flustered, "I'm trying to be nice. I know that you brought Ted to her reverb in a warehouse in Lower Zeta. He told me you helped him speak with the ghost of his dead sister. You have equipment that lets you talk to the dead, at least, before they enter the Node." Cody leaned in hard. "You, and your partner."

Camille leaned as far away from him as she could get, she gestured to the emptiness of the room, "But I don't have a partner, Cody. Do you see a partner? Do you see equipment?"

"I've known Ted for fifteen years; he's not going to lie to me. I'm not sure you're grasping the weight of this situation. Yes, you're okay at finding and confining people, but you're right, that's not why I hired you for this job."

Camille continued to stare at him with frank rage. "I took that Walton job right before the Iesus job; when we met. You were there on purpose. You've been hosing me for two years, waiting for a chance to get at the good stuff."

"That's not important now." Cody looked a little guilty. "How many Node Points do you have?"

"Why do you want to know?" Camille lunged for him and tugged at his NBO badge, trying to rip it off its chain. "Shouldn't you know anyway? You know everything else."

Cody pried her hand off his badge, narrowly saving his lanyard. Camille rose from her sofa and hovered menacingly over Cody, who stood and matched Camille's combative stance. Camille's brute muscle was a close match for Cody's wiry height. Things seemed like they might come to blows, but Camille relaxed and Cody followed suit.

"I have millions of points." Camille sighed and deflated, sitting back down.

"Wow." Cody was genuinely shocked.

"Some people will trade anything for my services."

Cody paused in silent disgust of Camille's exploitation.

"Well, you wouldn't want to lose all those NPs, or have them rendered meaningless?" he asked at last. Cody smoothed his suit, and raised his hands in exasperation, "What about the people who have died? You must have some loved ones in the Node. What about them?"

Camille turned away from the window, "Yeah, of course, I do, but I can't find ghosts by myself. I did use to work with a partner, sometimes."

•   •   •   •   •

Noon was wicked hot in Zeta City, and most people stayed indoors until the sun was lower in the sky. Cody, in his three-piece suit, had copious amounts of sweat running from his forehead to his collar, so he stood apart from the few, cooler-blooded folks who had ventured out. Camille wore gray shorts and a pink tank top, with her short black hair clipped up off her neck. For Camille, the walk was much more comfortable.

Zeta streets were always full of puddles, even when it hadn't rained for days. Zeta was meant to be a tropical swamp, but instead, someone had gone and built a city there, hundreds of years ago. Early inhabitants spent decades fighting on two fronts, trying to raise the city above the swamp while beating back the ocean. Thy system of levees had morphed into a seawall, but Zeta had lost the battle to rise, so the world's first "Netted city" was crumbling to mud.

Cody stepped into a warm puddle, accidentally dousing his shoe and pant leg.

"Where does your partner live?" he grumbled, "Can't we just take the train."

"Ex-partner," she scolded him, "and I'm not in the mood for the train today." Camille said flatly, "I just watched a person use one to commit suicide."

"Right, sorry," Cody said, trudging on.

They walked for about another ten minutes, and Cody stopped in his tracks, "You're stalling," he accused.

"No."

"We've doubled back one street over." He pointed up the road to the left.

There were two buildings with a garden in front. The balcony on one of the buildings had a hanging garden of vines covered with red and blue flowers. He had seen it from a different block before.

"How long have we been working together?" Camille glanced up at Cody.

"Two years." Cody was confounded by the out of place question, "We were just talking about the Iesus job."

"I'll work with you for about five or six years. That's my pattern, I spend five or six years in the same situation with the same people."

"That's good to know," Cody noted.

"During those five years, I got to know the people I work with very well. I shared my life with them, and they share their lives with me. I get drunk at their weddings, and I get bored at their baby showers. Together we survive long business trips, strange situations, and deep moments; but they are just the people I work with – they are not my forever people. They are a large part of my life for a finite amount of time, and then they are memories that I wave to from a distance when I see them in the market. I haven't seen my old partner in a year and a half. He's a relic with more deep moments and strange situations than most."

"Can we please explore your hidden depths later?" Cody asked as he shook his head in disbelief. "We are too short on time to get philosophical. Now, where does your old partner live?"

Camille paused a moment and looked Cody up and down, "I was trying to be real with you Cody. How is this for not philosophical? You have social problems, and you're sweating through your suit."

"Be that as it may ... *where* does he live?" Cody replied, gritting his teeth slightly.

Camille led Cody down the street where the building with the flower garden stood, and about halfway past the door with the hanging garden. She stopped in front of an eggshell blue townhouse. Someone had just put in new, wooden front steps, but they were yet to be painted and there was no railing. The glass on the windows had all been painted black.

"This is the last place he lived. I'm pretty sure he's still here."

"What's this man's name?"

She hesitated.

"It's too late now Camille." Cody shook his head at her. "We're standing in front of his door."

"Remington Nakamoto – but it's 'Remy'." Camille stood still at the base of the unpainted steps.

"Are you going to knock?" Cody asked, gesturing for her to walk up the steps.

Camille shook her head. "This is your deal, man."

Cody rapped on the door and waited a solid minute. He was just about to turn away when the door swung open. A short, muscular guy with long, black hair answered, wearing a long black trench coat, black gloves, and black sunglasses with shields that wrapped around past his temples. An elderly Siamese cat wove around his ankles, its brown-tipped tail lifted in greeting. The man looked Cody up and down. "Whatever it is, say it fast."

"Remington Nakamoto?" Cody asked as he extended his hand.

Remy did not return the gesture. "I get my security from the City Forces, my electricity from Zeta E, and whatever you're selling, not from you." He started to close the door.

"I'm not selling anything," Cody said stiffly, thrusting his foot in to keep the door from closing.

"Well then, what are you?" Remy sniffed, still refusing Cody's still outstretched hand.

"Cody Priolo, I'm an overseer from Hawk United National Bounty Hunters – "

"Nope." Remy shook his head, "Get out of here. No bounties." He stepped toward Cody, forcing him to remove his foot.

"I'm here with your former colleague," Cody called to the closing door. He stepped to the side so that Remy could see Camille at the foot of the steps. "And, ah, she seems to bring into question your whole 'no bounties' ethic."

Remy screwed up his face in disgust. "Aw, Camille. What the hell?"

12
TOY

"Come on," Alan said as he led Toy around the corner. They faced the southern end of Carnival Street. "There's a gate here on Carnival, but I want you to stay near me, don't go toward it yet, okay?" he warned.

Toy nodded.

The gate into the Node straddled the avenue. It was a flat, opaque, white arch with nothing visible around it or beyond it. She knew there was a Node Gate on Carnival Street, but it was invisible to the living. She thought about how many times she had walked past it, or through it, without realizing the awful thing stood there, just below her threshold of perception. If she squinted, she could see the puddles of water on the real street, and ghost forms of the living walking around and through the gate as oblivious as she once was.

Blue streaks of electricity arced around the edges of the gate. Toy whimpered and looked away as the old man shielded his eyes.

"Sorry, it is a bit like staring into the sun," he said, turning his gaze from the gate as well.

Toy struggled to understand the situation that surrounded her. Her thoughts came much slower than when she was alive. In front of her was the path into the Node. She understood she was carrying the virus, but she was unsure if she should bring it into the Node. It turns out, moral dilemmas are much harder to work through after a violent death has diminished one's faculties.

"Are you going in, my dear?"

Toy turned to Alan and put her hands to her temples. She pushed and felt for the hole the needle had made. The wide needle had allowed the viral fluid direct access to her brain and her brain was the one thing that was left of her.

"Needle," she said pressing her temple harder.

"Indeed," Alan thoughtlessly agreed with what he thought was ghost gibberish.

A well-dressed, middle-aged woman rounded the corner on the opposite side of Carnival Street. She was wearing a flower-patterned blouse, and she appeared solid down to the hem of her A-line skirt where her legs faded into nothing. She floated toward the gate at an even speed with no stop, no hesitation.

"Now, there's a lady who's ready to go in. You'll want to watch her so you'll know what to do," Alan recommended.

As the phantom-legged woman approached the gate, the blue arcs became tendrils that reached out of the white expanse, stretching toward her. Soon, the tendrils became a stream of blue, enveloping her ghostly body and pulling her toward the gate. Finally, she merged with the gate as a human-shaped ball of blue light. The gate made a brief, static noise as it blinked out for a moment before returning to its original state.

Alan turned to Toy, "That's about it. Are you going to go in? Are you ready?"

Real, whole, coherent thoughts formed in Toy's mind. She remembered why she carried the virus. She was Toy Bowen, the woman who died to save the world from the Node Point system.

But she had not been meant to die so brutally. She was supposed to drift off in a drug-induced termination because they knew that Node scientists had often speculated that violent, sudden deaths caused people's minds to upload incompletely when transferred into the Net. Toy had the additional burden of carrying a toxic, cerebral virus when she flung herself in front of that train. The combination of all these factors had severely damaged her virtual ghost.

Toy knew that the Net had digital corrective properties, but the Node had better ones. Her signal may have been broken, but it wouldn't be forever. All she had to do was get through the gate. The Node should correct her, while simultaneously downloading the Node Point virus.

Toy answered Alan, "You ready?"

Alan looked on proudly as Toy glided toward the gate. She was about forty feet from the gate, at the same point that the woman was when the blue tendrils of electricity had reached out for her, but none of the tendrils reached out for Toy. Toy did not think that this was too strange, and she continued to drift into the gate.

Sudden fear shook Alan. "Wait!" he called to Toy.

Alan had been dead for almost a year; he had witnessed at least fifty reverbs go through the gate, and he had never seen one who was not enveloped by the blue electricity.

When she was about fifteen feet from the gate, a single, weak, blue arc reached out for Toy. Instead of lovingly enveloping her when it touched her, the blue stream turned white and jumped from her, recoiling back into the gate. Toy shook it off and continued toward the entrance, the tendrils of electricity arching and recoiling. In the end, Toy had to push her way through, with the gate sputtering in and out, screaming and leaking shocks of blue and white arcs.

Alan watched on in horror, vowing to never help another soul through the gate again.

13
CAMILLE

It took a few minutes for Camille and Cody's eyes to adjust to the relative darkness in Remy Nakamoto's townhouse. Every potential source of sunlight had been blocked out by thick, black paint on the window glass. A few, low light lamp fixtures were attached to the walls. The interior looked like a mix between an antique store and a mechanic's workshop. The floor was concrete, the carpet long since ripped up to spare it from stains. There were shelves of oddities, clocks, taxidermy animals, and old street signs. There was an important-looking work table in the center of the room that held a gutted computer, with its parts strewn around and its wires hanging out. This project was lit by a single semi-bright light source, a desk lamp that had seen better days.

The Siamese cat, aging but still agile, picked its way past several cases of broken electronics and settled himself on top of a closed crate.

"Looks like quite an operation you've got going here," Cody said with earnest interest.

"No." Remy held up his palm up to Cody's face. "I'm talking to Camille and Camille alone."

Remy turned to face Camille and maneuvered himself so that his back was to Cody, who shook his head and rolled his eyes.

"What's going on?" Remy demanded.

"Hi Boss," Camille said brightly, reaching down to pet the cat. "He's getting to be an old man, huh?"

"Leave Boss alone," Remy snapped, "he doesn't like it when you bring NBOs," Remy looked at Cody pointedly, "or at least people pretending to be NBOs, into our house."

"He's on hire from the City Patrol." Camille sighed and continued to pet Boss, "He put me on the hacker job that was on the news this morning. I didn't know what I was doing, but here I am."

"What hacker job?" Remy's brow crinkled.

"Oh, I forgot you don't watch simulcasts." Camille laughed and typed into her wrist RAP.

"They have subliminal messages," Remy said. Cody scoffed.

"How's this for a subliminal message?" Camille's wrist played a six-inch hologram of Toy's advertisement. The three of them watched in silence as Toy's hologram pronounced the world as sick before the pink-gloved hands of an unseen assistant plunged a needle into her temple. They simultaneously cringed.

"Wow." When the hologram was over, Remy chewed the inside of his cheek. "Did the hack work?" He addressed Cody for the first time that day.

"That's classified information." Cody peered over Remy's cold shoulder to speak directly to Camille, "Don't tell him anything."

"Nobody knows if it worked, but they're thinking it might have. Cody here is looking for her reverb." Camille ignored Cody, "she took a dive off the tracks by the casino. Right in front of me. I got her blood on me."

Camille brushed her curly black bangs out of her eyes so that Remy could get her full expression, and gain some non-verbal insight. Remy ignored her raised eyebrows, focused on scrutinizing Cody's heat-ruined, would be immaculateness and unyielding poker face.

When Remy finished sizing up the situation, he said, "No. I don't care, and I don't want any part of it. Get out." Remy turned back to his work table and picked up a small soldering iron. He didn't use it, he just pretended, in hopes of looking busy enough to make them leave. To him, Camille had always been an absurd amount of trouble, intriguing, attractive trouble, but trouble none the less.

Cody surveyed the room. He fixated on a half-completed, four-inch circuit board. "I guess I have proof of where Camille got her Confiner."

"You can't blackmail me; I have contracts with most of the city's security forces."

Cody stooped down so that he was eye level with Remy.

"What you doing there?" He nodded toward the iron that Remy was uselessly waving over a circuit board. Remy ignored him continuing to pantomime work.

"It must be hard to work in such low light," Cody said.

"I'm sensitive to the light," Remy brushed him off.

"But that's not the only reason you keep everything off in here. It looks like you have a quite a workshop going here. You must go through energy like crazy. I bet you use up most of the allowance in the first six months of the year. Four months, maybe?"

Remy ignored him but kept his ears perked.

"I can pay you in energy," Cody said slyly, "Years' worth. Decades worth."

He paused and looked up at Cody, clearly interested. Remy still didn't speak, but he waited for Cody to go on.

"How are you going to pay me in energy, man?" Remy put down his soldering iron.

"Camille told you, this is a government job. When it gets done, I tell them who needs to get paid and how. In one week, you'll wake up with ten years' worth of electricity for this place. Or we could put it in another location for you if you have any other shops."

Remy looked at Camille, "Is this for real?"

"He's paid me over 200,000 NPs, and a bunch of cash or I wouldn't work for his shady ass."

Remy calculated in his mind for a few seconds, and then nodded as if he couldn't bring himself to say 'yes.'

"Okay, good. How do we do this?" Cody beamed and rubbed his hands together.

"This," Remy looked at him with distaste, "is infringing on the territory of the dead. Please take it seriously."

Cody tried his best to seem solemn, and he stopped rubbing his hands. "Oh, I take it very seriously."

"I have cobbled together equipment, I call it a "ReV – remote electromagnetic viewer," Remy said. "Don't let the acronym fool you. It doesn't look good, and it doesn't work well," he started wandering around, loading up a crate with various odd objects, "so, how we do this is carefully."

Camille snickered but stifled it quickly.

•   •   •   •   •

There were three ways to get where you needed to go in Zeta City, you could walk, motorbike, or take one of the trains. The trains were rickety, lumbering, steam-powered monstrosities. With the frequent stops, Zeta citizens often said that walking is faster than taking the trains, and they were usually correct.

Cody was neither a resident nor a frequent visitor of Zeta, he usually contacted Camille from his home base in a climate-controlled city. When Remy suggested they start looking for Toy's ghost downtown, at the spot where she died, heat wilted Cody insisted they take the train. So, what would have been a half an hour walk turned into an hour-long train ride.

Camille and Remy sat side by side, and Cody sat across from them, with his hands folded in his lap. Remy was dressed in head to toe in black, he wore black sunglasses, gloves and a large, wide-brimmed black fedora with strips of fabric hanging down the sides. Remy had brought several instruments from his laboratory with him. A pair of glass and tin goggles were perched on top of his hat, ready to be pulled over his eyes when needed. The goggles had tiny, brass gears embedded in the frames. Remy also held a shiny steel block on his lap. The block had two antennae on the front and a mass of wires coming out of the back. Some of the wires ran down into a large, circuit board in a crate that sat by Remy's feet.

Between Cody's suit and Remy's ReV contraption. The trio was getting some startled looks from other train passengers.

"Isn't there any way to keep your equipment concealed?" Cody hissed at Remy.

"There is," Remy said with disdain, "but I'm not going to."

After a long silence, Remy asked, "What are you going to do to the hacker's ghost when we find her?"

"Pinpoint her location. Then, I'll call it in to my client, she's watching the Net. She'll extract the virus from the woman's reverb," Cody explained.

"What's that going to do to her ghost?" Remy looked at Cody with suspicion.

"We have no idea," Cody shrugged. "We've never done a virus extraction from a reverb before."

"So, you don't even know if it will work," Camille said while Remy said,

"We could kill her," his eyes narrowed, "Really kill her."

"She killed herself when she jumped onto to those train tracks, carrying a virus," Cody said. On cue, the train's electronic voice announced their stop and the three exited to Nouveau Avenue. They left the train and headed to the spot where the hacker died.

Toy's blood still marked the pavement near where she had tossed herself onto the train tracks. Camille morosely studied the splatter pattern while Remy switched out his black sunglasses in favor of his intricate, tin goggles. Cody watched with interest as Remy used wires to attach the goggles to the handheld device, which was still attached the hulking hard drive in the box. The hard drive was a chunky fusion of motherboards, wires, and switches.

Remy gestured to the open box, "Make sure nobody steps on this," he said to Cody.

Remy turned a dial on the handheld part of his machine.

Cody watched him. "What are you doing?"

"Tuning into the digital frequency for the Net in this area."

Remy stopped turning the dial and looked around. "Ah, there we are. Hey Camille, what did Toy look like?"

Camille looked up from the blood stains. "Short, real thin, with shoulder-length, blonde hair."

Remy shook his head. "That's not going to do it."

Camille pulled up the "Toy Bowen" hologram on her wrist RAP. She thought about when Cody had first sent the hologram, early that morning. It seemed like decades ago.

"That's only her head so I can't tell." Remy gingerly removed the goggles from his head and moved toward Camille. "You're going to have to put these on and tell me if you see her."

Camille had worked with Remy on and off over several years, but she had never worn his equipment. She had not once seen a ghost. Remy hadn't offered her the equipment, and she had never asked for it. She never had any interest in seeing the disembodied minds of the dead.

Camille reluctantly slipped the glasses over her head but kept her eyes closed for a moment. She could hear the whirring of the machine's fans and felt the hum in her brain. Remy stood close to her, still holding the handheld monitor and its connected briefcase.

Taking a deep breath, Camille opened her eyes and looked around. The streets of Zeta were full of ghosts. There were dozens of them. They were white and translucent, still holding human form up until their shins, then their legs trailed off into mists, and then nothing. Most of them were stationary, just standing, staring into space, but a few of the ghosts moved with varying degrees of dexterity.

"There's so many!" Camille gasped.

"A lot of people die in Zeta, not everyone makes it to the Node," Remy replied grimly.

"Do you see her? Do you see Toy?" Cody asked eagerly.

Camille watched as a living passenger walked toward the train, she stepped right through the ghost of a middle-aged man. Camille shuddered and wondered how many ghosts she had walked through herself.

"I don't see her," Camille said. "She might head toward the nearest Node entry."

"That's a few blocks down, on Carnival, near the library," Cody said.

The walk to the library was strange for all involved. Camille meandered at a measured pace, wearing the goggles still hooked up to the box Remy carried. She looked side to side every few steps, keeping an eye out for Toy's reverb. Cody walked beside the two in the same stride. Onlookers gawked at their awkward parade.

As they approached it, Camille could see the Node entry. It was a long, bright slit in space. Tendrils of light seeped out of the edges of it. Several ghosts floated near the entry.

"I see it. I see the Node entry-" Camille began, but then she saw Toy's ghost, a few yards from the entry. Her thin form was moving toward the edges of the gate's tendrils.

"Toy's here, but she's almost in the Node," Camille called.

"Okay, I'm going to see if I can get a lock on this area." Cody pulled out his tablet and began to type furiously.

Camille watched Toy move into the Node. Toy's ghost grew brighter, and the Node seemed to swallow her, pulling her in with one final flash.

"It's too late, Cody. She's gone in."

Camille took off the glasses and handed them back to Remy. Cody's hands shook as he stopped typing and lowered his tablet. "A few seconds late," he muttered.

They stood, apart and strange, covered with their odd bits of technology, staring at wonders that no one else could see.

"What do we do now?" Camille wondered aloud.

"Well," Cody paused, "I'm going back to figure things out with my superior. You two can go do whatever you like," he thought for a moment, "But you stay in Zeta, Camille. I'm going to need you to help me see this through."

"I'm not going anywhere," Camille said. "I never go anywhere."

Cody turned sharply and walked away from Camille and Remy, headed toward the train station.

Remy asked to Camille when Cody was out of earshot, "So, is he your new partner, now?"

"No, he just gives me jobs and pays well. Worried you've been replaced?"

Remy shook his head. "He seems a bit stiff for you."

"I said he's not my partner," Camille scoffed.

Remy gently extracted Camille's head from the equipment. "Do you wanna get some coffee or something? I have some questions for you about Cody. Something's off."

"You always think that something is off," Camille said with a grin. "But, yeah, you can come see my new place."

14
TOY

Once through the Node gate, Toy stood on a large, soapstone pavilion. She turned to look for the gate she had just passed through, but there was only a natural stone wall behind her with no sign of the gate. *A one-way trip,* she thought. The colors around here were a million times brighter than anything she had seen while alive. The air itself seemed to vibrate with a musical hum just below the threshold of total perception.

On the pavilion in front of her about a dozen people milled around and talked in hushed voices. "People" was a loose term, some of them were regular and human-like, others had wings, or glittery faces, or other exotic appearances. She focused on one of them, a human-cat hybrid. She was a woman who stood on two legs but had a light, thin fur that was stripped like a black and white tiger with a feline countenance.

The stories Toy often disbelieved her whole life swarmed in vibrant reality around her. She had been told that the Node was a place where you could be anything and have anything if you had the Node Points to pay for it. Toy was one of the many who sometimes secretly suspected that nothing happened when you died, that the Node was a trick to keep people in line.

At this moment in their journey into the glorious, digital afterlife, most people felt awe and hope. Toy felt nervous rage. The only hope she had was that the Bliss virus worked. As she had guessed, it seemed the gate's processors cleaned her program and the physical effects of the virus ended the moment that Toy stepped into the Node. She had been a confused ghost, but she was rendered coherent as soon as she stepped through the gate. She vaguely recalled the Node gate's attempts to keep her out and took it as a sign the Bliss virus had done its job.

She scrutinized the Node residents on the platform. Everyone around her seemed to be going about his or her or its business without any hint of a cataclysm. For the first time, she noticed the pavilion was dizzyingly high. The platform was on a plateau directly across from the top of a sand-colored mountain. From this high vantage point, she could see the sprawling city that lay between the platform and the mountain. To the left and right, the city stretched to the horizon.

Ahead of her, the woman in the flower dress, who had gone through the Gate before her, was being seen by one normal man and a woman, who floated next to her, propelled by massive, purple, fairy wings.

The pavilion was lined on one side with food-laden banquet tables with elaborately carved stone archways on either end. The other side of the pavilion held several multicolored, decorated kiosks. The kiosks had banners, reading: "Orientation," "Heaven," "Elysium," "Maybury," "Summerlands," "Wild West," "Valhalla," "Nirvana," "Wonderland" "Antiquity" and "Assorted Paradises." There was also a dodgy looking booth that simply read in cracked mustard-yellow gothic lettering, "Other."

Toy headed for the kiosk marked "Orientation," but a man dressed like a medieval noble and the cat woman she had seen earlier, intercepted her.

"Welcome to the Node," the cat woman clapped and purred, though her clapping was somewhat muted due to the furriness of her palms. "My name's Lyndsy and this is Lord Solomon Bryon Radclyffe."

The Nobleman did a curt bow and extended a gloved hand. "Bryon."

Toy shook his hand while she studied the cat woman. She was nude, except for her fur, which protected her modesty by covering every inch of her body in white slashed black stripes. She had human hair- all black- that flowed around her head like a mane.

"What are you?" Toy asked, forgetting herself.

Lyndsy gave a short, condescending laugh, "I'm an ailuranthrope – by choice, of course. We're common in Elysium and the Summerlands. Once you're through Orientation you can be whatever you want, wherever you want to be."

Toy's purpose in death, though never far from her mind, came rushing back in full force. For a moment, she wondered how many Node Points it cost to become an ailuranthrope. She glanced around again to see if anyone had noticed the proliferation of the Bliss virus. Nothing seemed amiss. The woman ahead of her left the Orientation tent and wandered over to the Maybury kiosk.

Toy pointed to the city below the pavilion. "What's that city?"

"Actually, it doesn't have a name. Some people call it New Zeta City. It's for people who are confused or who can't accept being dead. Some of them were waiting for loved ones to come through, and then just forgot who they were, or where they are." Lyndsy explained, "It's a weird place. I wouldn't go there. As I said, you can go anywhere."

Toy gave the cat woman a sideways glance. "I don't have many NPs, so my choices here may be limited."

"That's okay, for now. Hey, do have anyone in the Node you'd like us to contact for you?" Lyndsy asked.

"My grandmother," Toy said, breathless and hopeful, "her name was – is - Marian Blair."

"Do you have her date of birth or middle name?" Bryon asked. "Just a name doesn't go very far around here."

"Fleming was her maiden name," Toy said.

Bryron said, "Screen" and a screen appeared in his hand. "Marion Byron nee Fleming, please," he said into the screen. After a few seconds he said, "Hm, communication is down."

"Down?" Lynsdy look startled. "Try the System."

Byron went over to one of the two vaulted archways that stood on a pedestal on the corner of the pavilion. He fiddled with a control panel attached to the side of the arch.

"I can see where she is, but I can't reach her with communications," he said. "I'll have to go fetch her myself."

"Where is she?" Lyndsy asked.

She must be in Paradise. Toy figured as she recalled the hot sand and azure waters of her childhood visits. She was surprised when Byron announced, "She is in the Wild West," and chuckled.

"Oh my. Bring your hip holster." Lyndsy clapped happily.

"Can I come?" Toy asked, rebounding from her shock in the idea that her grandmother wasn't spending eternity relaxing on a beach. Perhaps, the Wild West is where they put people who haven't earned enough Node Points. "She is my grandmother after all."

"Well, it's irregular, but I don't see a problem, being that communications went down when you came through," Byron said, and Lyndsy nodded her furry face encouragingly.

"Come on then, I'll show you how our Travel System works."

15
CAMILLE

The sun was low in the sky, and it made heat shimmers across the river inlet Remy and Camille walked along as they took the long way back to Camille's apartment. They stopped at a café for espresso and pastries and then stopped again to watch the sunset along the water.

"Remember that awful job we did? What was the mark's name … Small Bob?"

"Lil' Larry," Camille smiled, "he thought he could get away with faking a death."

"Not in Zeta."

"Not with us." Camille took a bite of the extra Danish she'd bought for the road.

"You had the machine on, and you were like, 'I can see his reverb, it's so much clearer than the other one.'" Camille mimicked wearing his goggles.

"And you said, 'yeah, I can see him too' and screamed and ran, you got him with the Confiner."

"He wasn't even dying," Camille's throaty laugh echoed out over the water. "I think he's still alive, actually."

The old friends were quiet for a while, lost in their own recollections. Finally, Camille started walking again.

"Seriously, what is going on with Lord King of the Bounty Hunters?" Remy asked.

"I know that Cody can be pompous, but I think he means well," Camille answered defensively.

"Did you see his face when we were walking around downtown with the viewer?" Remy made an exaggeratedly stiff face and bugged out his eyes. "Seriously though, he'll give me my power supply even though we didn't find her, right?" Remy worried.

"Yeah, you'll get your juice." Camille laughed, "Cody isn't good for much besides agitating people and paying people."

In another half an hour they were entering Camille's sparse office front.

"Wow, you cleaned up your act," Remy said, and then, "Oh, I see," once they passed through the fake office and entered the rest of her flat.

Once inside Camille apartment, Remy set his box of equipment down by the door and looked around.

"This place is awful, Camille," Remy said. "I'm guessing you're spending most of your time in Prioria."

"No, I'm here in Zeta, I haven't been back home in a while." She typed distractedly on her wrist. Remy wandered into her kitchen, opened and closed her refrigerator, open and closed her cupboards, and then wandered back out.

"What are you doing?" He noticed that Camille was still typing on her wrist and he hovered over her shoulder.

"Trying to ignore you making more noise than the reverb I had in here earlier today."

"On your wrist RAP."

"I'm checking my Node Points to see if Toy's virus has wiped them out."

"You might as well just check the news. I'm sure people would be losing their minds if, all of a sudden, they lost all their points," Remy said as he read her wrist RAP and saw the number of Node Points in Camille's account. "Holy shit Camille, you have more than enough Node Points for an entire lifetime."

"Yeah, well, it's still not as much as I need; I need enough points for two lifetimes." She glared at him, raw and hurt. Remy realized he had touched on one of her few sore spots and was instantly sorry.

"Even a billion Node Points wouldn't bring him back, Cam." Remy reached out for her hand, but she pulled away.

"I don't remember asking you for life advice. I asked you over for a coffee and to catch up." She pushed at his reaching arm, "and get off me."

Remy took a few steps away from her. "Fine. Whatever. Make me coffee then," he said, and then quietly, "even though we just had some."

Camille got to work in the kitchen a few paces from the living room area. Remy leaned over the back of the sofa to talk to her.

"Do you think Cody's really an NBO?"

"Cody again? I don't think about him enough to care."

"Because, if he was, he would bust you for the Confiner."

"Not if it was making him a ton of cash." Camille shrugged. She sat back down beside Remy while the kettle heated up. She silently slid next to him, an act that showed that she forgave from his earlier misstep.

"But seriously, does Cody seem the type to only be interested in money or points?"

"No, he does not. But, I learned a long time ago that people have their own reasons. There's a whole hidden world behind each little choice and there's no way to see that world."

"No, I agree," Remy said, and Camille's kettle started to whistle. "But, what if it's a world of lies?"

They both startled at a loud noise from behind her office door.

Camille grabbed the hot kettle off the stove and held it up menacingly as she headed toward the closed door.

"Is it the reverb?" Remy wondered.

"I'm not taking the chance." Camille swung the door open and thrust the hot kettle in front of her. It narrowly missed Cody's chest. Cody took a calm step backward, unconsciously brushing off the new, sweat-free, charcoal gray suit he had changed into.

"So, you're breaking into my apartment now." She stared plainly at Cody.

"This is supposed to be your office; I was going to wait in the designated waiting area." He gestured toward the single, white, plastic chair pushed against the wall, next to the door. "Who's in there?" Cody nodded toward her living room.

"Remy."

Cody shook his head, "I need to have a confidential discussion. Can he hear us talking?"

Camille stared at him coldly.

"Can you shut the door to your apartment?" Cody asked again, afraid that he'd been misunderstood, "Camille?"

She continued to glare at Cody, Remy's suspicions swimming around the back of her mind. "Just spit it out man, I'm not closing the door. After what he did for us – for you today, Remy is with us."

"Fine," Cody said, verging on enthusiasm, a rare moment for the man, "we may have another chance to stop Toy and the virus."

"Whatever," Camille did not match his excited energy, "You know the deal, I'm a thousand dollars a day plus three thousand NP."

"I know how much you cost, and this will include travel."

This piqued Camille's interest. She had never had a bounty take her outside Zeta City.

"Where to?"

"I'm bringing you to Elworthy Asylum," Cody said with a slight flourish as if he were presenting some great treat.

Remy, who had overheard this, called "No!" from inside the apartment, and was promptly ignored.

"Never heard of it. What Net is it under?" Camille walked back into her apartment, leaving Cody in her office to talk to her through the open door.

"It's not under any Net."

Camille took a surprised step back. "That's not funny."

"He's not joking," Remy offered, flatly as he entered the office.

Seeing that he was losing Camille, Cody spoke faster, "Elworthy the town isn't under a Net, but we'll mostly stay in Elworthy Asylum, which is under a small, minor Net."

"A job in a no Net zone?" Camille looked at her wrist RAP, reflexively wanting to check her Node Points.

"I'll make sure you are safe," Cody said plaintively.

"Bullshit. I know what they're doing there," Remy said.

"Oh really," Cody said, finally paying mind to Remy, "What is it that you think they're doing at Elworthy? And how do you know, exactly?"

Remy took an aggressive step toward Cody. "I'm on to you."

"I highly doubt that," Cody retorted.

"Guys. Please." Camille caught herself and toughened up. "Yeah, whatever Cody, I'll go. I need another five hundred a day plus an extra five thousand NP, for the extra danger of being un-netted."

Satisfied, Cody stood up, straightened out his suit, and headed for the door. "Of course, whatever you need."

"What are they doing at Elworthy Asylum, Remy?" Camille asked the second her office door closed.

"Nothing that you want any part of, trust me." Remy had made his way over to Camille's living room window and was craning his neck around out of it.

"What are you doing?" Camille tried to see what Remy was looking at.

"Trying to figure out which way he's walking."

"I don't know. Probably toward the train station. Why?"

"I've got to talk to him. I'll be right back."

Remy caught up to Cody a few blocks from Camille's office. Remy grabbed him hard on the shoulder and pulled him back. This wasn't the best idea, because, when drawn up to his full height, Cody was over a foot taller than Remy, and considerably more muscular. Cody usually stooped, in part out of habit, but also as a tactic to conceal his size.

Remy was certainly caught off guard when Cody stood tall, spun around, and grabbed him by the throat. Seeing it was Remy, Cody instantly let go and drew back.

"What do you want?" Cody asked.

Remy rubbed the sore patches that Cody had left on his neck. "I know all about the experiments they're doing under small Nets in outside zones like Elworthy. I know why you want Camille to go."

"Enlighten me. Why do I want her to go?" Cody asked with pure disinterest.

"Because you're after me. You can't get me to go, so you're using her as bait. Just like you used her to find me," Remy said remorsefully.

"You think quite highly of yourself, Remington." Cody said, "Why would I go to all of that trouble to find and entrap you?"

"You may think Camille is just some low-life bounty hunter, but she's not. You don't know who she is. You don't know who her parents are," Remy continued, ignoring Cody's questions.

"Oh, I know who she is. Her parentage does not matter to me, so long as she does her job and I do mine."

"You're leading her to her death!"

"That's not true. I don't want anybody to die. I was telling the truth when I said I'd keep her safe."

Remy searched Cody's eyes, but couldn't tell if he was sincere.

Remy turned and walked away, muttering, "She won't go. I won't let her."

Cody shook his head, "Anything you say to her is just going to make her want to go more. I'm surprised you haven't realized that about Camille."

Remy stormed away, knowing Cody was right.

Camille's eyes were on her wrist RAP again when Remy wandered back into her apartment. A mute, holoprojection of the news broadcast hovered six feet from her face. An endless loop of Toy's advertisement played behind a panel of supposed Node experts.

"Any change?" he asked her.

"No, my points are all still there," she said, not looking up.

"I wonder how many other people are doing what you are right now? Looking anxiously at their wrists and watching the news?"

"Probably a lot," Camille muttered. "What was that about with Cody?"

Remy shuffled his feet a bit, then sighed and joined Camille on her worn out maroon sofa. "Would it make a difference if I told you there were some dangerous experiments going on at Elworthy? Would you still go?"

"No, it wouldn't make a difference. I'd still go. Believe it or not, I'm not just doing this for myself, or even for … never mind." There were so many thoughts going through Camille's mind at once, she just grasped the nearest one. "I'm doing it for everyone else too," she said. "I understand what it means to die without points."

"I've got a friend. Deanna Grant, at Elsworthy – " Remy started.

"I'm not surprised. You've got a friend wherever someone's doing something spooky and illegal with technology."

"I have my hands on some of that technology, and it is more than spooky. It has the ability to shake up this whole thing."

"What is it? More ghost viewers – ones that actually work more than half the time? Or is it some ultra-realistic virtual reality," Camille said snidely, "that lets you fuck cartoons or something?"

Remy didn't respond to her snarky remarks. He looked down, almost bashful. If there was some dirt, he would have kicked it.

"What? What is it? Was I right about the cartoon sex thing? Because it's not a big deal," Camille laughed.

He halfheartedly shook his head *no* and then conspicuously changed the subject, "I don't trust Cody at all. I'm afraid they're going to take your RAP as soon as you get there because the place is top secret. You tell my friend Deanna if you get in trouble and she'll get in contact with me. Okay?"

"I've never trusted Cody either, but his money spends, just the same as everyone else's." Camille looked up from her RAP to meet Remy's wide, dark eyes. She saw them brimming with anxiety. "I'm going Remy," she said. "I have people in the Node who need me."

He answered gravely, "That's why he wants you to go. He knows who you are and how far you'd go to protect the Node."

Camille sighed. "He's right. I would do anything," she said, and went back to staring at her account on her wrist RAP. "Did you figure out if he actually is an officer for the National Bounty Hunter's Association?"

"No. I don't know what he is, but I do know he's not one of us."

16
NORA

Nora piled clothes from her half of the dormitory room closet onto her bed. She picked up some of the clothes and held up various items against her body while she looked in the mirror. Most clothes looked good on her tall, slim frame, and her dark complexion enhanced almost any color; but that day nothing was quite right. She ultimately chose to wear a wispy tan cardigan over a plain black tank top and trendy jeans.

She left the women's dorm, leaving the pile of clothes heaped on her bed, and walked across the campus quad to the bookstore. A little bell on the door signaled her entry to the young, probably freshman, cashier. In the back of the store, past the rows of tablets, wrist RAPs, and a few scraggly-looking actual books, there were clothes racks featuring her school's snarling tiger mascot. She picked out pink tiger-striped sweatpants and a matching hoodie, went to the cashier and paid for the set, left the bookstore, and trekked back to her room to change into the clothes she just bought.

Fifteen minutes later, Nora met her friend Alexis in front of her dorm. He gave her a quick nod, and she followed him to the parking lot.

"I ordered us a car," she said.

"Cancel it," Alexis replied.

Nora took out her handheld communicator and began to type. "Why am I canceling it?"

"Because I have a car," Alexis said, and Nora started to laugh. She stopped abruptly when she realized that Alexis was not kidding.

The Amos Roth University parking lot held a fleet of shiny autos that stood waiting for orders. Alexis's car, parked toward the back of the lot, was not shiny. It was grungy and, in Nora's mind, it had a strange shape. She stood next to the back door and waited for it to open for her.

"No," Alexis instructed her, "go around to the other side, in the front, and open it yourself, like this," Alexis pulled a handle on the door to demonstrate, and got in.

Nora made her way around to the front passenger side and did as Alexis instructed. As she slid into the passenger's seat, she was a little alarmed by the large wheel that jutted out of the dashboard on the driver's side and watched with close interest as Alexis slid his key into the ignition, lifted the parking brake, and used the wheel to steer the car.

She knew that there were some manual cars out there, and she had sensed that they were quite dangerous, never imagining she would ever be in one. Alexis ignored Nora's curiosity until she encroached so far into his space that she endangered his range of motion.

"Can you back up off of me?" he asked. "You're not going to be able to see how it works anyway. You'd have to try it."

"Can I try it?"

"Not today."

With no onboard screens, Nora was forced to watch the landscape go by. There were no poor neighborhoods in her home under the Omega Net, but she knew that there were areas of Gamma that were underdeveloped. Some people even called them slums.

As they drove from their college town deeper into the Gamma Net, wide stretches of suburban lawns grew more and more narrow until they disappeared, replaced by endless front porches hung over concrete or the occasional junk-covered dirt patch.

A hand-painted sign that read "Point Pawn" hung above the rickety steps that led up to one of these porches.

Alexis parked the aging auto in front of the pawn shop and waited. Nora almost said something once or twice, but she knew that she would be told to wait and watch, so she decided to just wait and watch without being told. She congratulated herself: she was the New Nora, who could wait and watch on her own volition.

Twenty minutes into their wait, a battered van pulled into what could be called the pawn's driveway, but was actually a badly-cracked cement slab in the narrow space separating the pawn's junky porch from the next house's junky porch. The driver, an elderly, portly woman, swung the sliding door open and stepped out of the vehicle. Another woman, wheelchair-bound, sat inside of the van. The woman in the wheelchair looked frail, gaunt, and lost. The driver, who took enough care that Nora guessed she was likely a relative, used a hover pad to lower the chair out of the van and to guide the woman and her chair up over the rickety steps and through the door of the pawn.

"Well, that's sad," Nora noted, sure she had gotten what she needed from the encounter.

"Why is it sad?" Alexis asked.

"Because the woman obviously needs to buy some points before she dies. She might not have enough," Nora said innocently. Alexis looked at Nora like she had sprouted a second head. Realizing that she had said something wrong, Nora scrambled to come up with the right answer. "Or she might not have any points," she volunteered.

"It's not as sad as it could be. At least she has money to buy Points. Or at least she has something to trade. And it's about to get even less sad for her," Alexis smiled.

"Why?" Nora asked.

"Because you're going to go in and sell her your Node Points," Alexis said.

"But it's a pawn shop. Someone has to pawn their Points to the shop and the shop sells the Points," Nora said. She knew that Alexis was smart enough to understand this concept, so she began to wonder what she wasn't getting. Then she realized before Alexis could respond.

"Oh. You can't give your Points to companies. Only to people. The pawn shop must take a cut of whatever they pay the person selling their Points."

Alexis nodded, "Except it's called a donation. You can't sell your Points."

Nora considered for a few moments. "Alright," she said, "I'll donate."

Because the pawn was in what was clearly someone's home, the door opened into a foyer. To the right was a front room that had been converted into a waiting room. One end of the waiting room was scattered with obviously outmoded, but plush, sofas. At the other end, there was a long desk, behind which sat a middle-aged man with slick, black hair, presiding over a small congregation of ill and angry people. Behind him, a large archway led into a kitchen no one had bothered to convert to modern times.

A half-dozen haggard faces turned toward Nora and Alexis when they entered. The waiting room inhabitants brightened when they saw that neither of them looked sick or injured. Nora scanned the hopeful faces, searching for the woman she had seen enter a few minutes ago.

"Hello sir, madam." The slick pawn shop owner had noticed the pair's relative health as well and had silently sidled up to them while they were surveying the room. "Are you donating or receiving?" he asked.

"I'm donating," Nora said.

"Wonderful!" He clapped his hands and extracted a card from his jacket pocket. "Here's a list of 'Thank You' gifts offered by today's donation recipients," he crooned as he left her to peruse the list of items that included electronics, jewelry, even houses and lots of cash. Some of the gifts were grand, and some were paltry. Nora found the gift with the least value, a diamond ring and $10,200. It wasn't that much to her, but still a small fortune to the people in the pawn shop.

"How many points are they asking for this one?" Nora asked.

"For something like that," the owner sounded disappointed, "ten points. Maybe a dozen if you're feeling generous."

"And how many points do you have, Nora?" Alexis asked.

Tears clouded Nora's eyes. She hadn't ever checked before in her life, but she had before she had left that morning. Between what she had been given at birth and earned as a student, she had a little under 400,000 Points. She had never worked for them or even cared about her Points. They had always just been there.

17
CODY

Cody stalked away from Remy with his hands shoved in his pants pockets and his ire shoved down his throat. Of course, he cared about Camille, they'd been working together for almost a year. Plus, she was another human being and Cody held life sacred, but he had to pretend to be hard. He didn't want Remy to think he was weak.

Cody had been doing a lot of pretending lately. He pretended to not be wounded when Camille said mean things to him. He had been especially hurt when she had unleashed on him about knowing she had a secret partner who could locate ghosts. He hadn't been planning to exploit Camille's relationship with Remy, but he knew they might have to use him someday.

Why couldn't Camille see Cody as a partner the way she had once seen Remy as a partner? They had worked together on dozens of projects. Cody always showed up on time and paid her promptly. He took a great professional risk – at least it would look that way to Camille – by refusing to divulge the existence of her illegal Confiner to the National Bounty Hunters.

Sweltering in his suit, Cody trudged through the streets of Zeta. He could have taken a train, but he was procrastinating. He was not looking forward to the video call he was going to make once he got back to his temporary housing. As always, he was oblivious to the giggling whispers of onlookers wondering what he could be thinking, dressed like that in Zeta City.

Cody's temporary housing was in a neat row of townhouses, one of the few new, clean-looking homes in all of Zeta, although the row backed up to the river, which babbled noisily and sometimes disturbed Cody's focus. There was a downstairs kitchen with a bar that faced a small living room. He didn't notice the furniture was hard and sparse, but if he had noticed, he would have liked it for its economy of space and lack of fuss. Upstairs, there was a cozy bedroom and a bathroom with a shower, but no tub. Overall, the apartment was dark, and Cody liked the dark because it was concealing and inert.

Cody took a shower, changed into a fresh suit, and puttered around the kitchen until the sun had completely set over the gulf. He settled down into a stiff desk chair, set his briefcase onto the desk, and opened it. The briefcase held an ancient laptop that Cody opened and booted. His face was bathed in blue light as the computer came to life.

"Call Anita Bourbeau," he commanded with apprehension.

The United Net's government's gray and gold logo spun on his computer screen. He hoped that Anita wouldn't answer, but he knew she often took her time answering his calls. She was a busy woman.

A chill of apprehension shook Cody when Anita's face popped onto his screen. She was a severe woman, in her early fifties, with dyed, chin-length, bobbed red hair and lips to match. Cody realized he was in luck when Anita did not move. He was looking at her "away" message screen, which was just a still photo of Anita, superimposed with printed directions on how to leave a recording.

Cody shuffled his notes and prepared to leave a message, hesitating a few times before punching the commands into the computer.

"Good evening, Dr. Anita. This is the second message on date designation 1119. As I was unable to reach you earlier as well, I have instituted a set of actions that fulfill Initiative One, based on Protocol Seven with Initiative One being to protect the Node at all costs and Protocol Seven being to act in the best interest of the Node when management is indisposed.

"Further, I have determined that the best course of action would be to activate the dormant Elworthy investigations and to utilize the project technology. This fulfillment of Initiative One is to be carried out by the current team that I have assembled, so as to not create any undue stress in the average population. I look forward to receiving updated correspondence. End Transmission."

He got up and paced the room. A yellow flowering plant had collapsed from thirst in the window box. He rummaged through his rental paperwork to find the instructions on caring for the plant. It said to "water when the leaves began to wilt," but it didn't say how much water. Cody grumbled and measured out a half of a cup, hoping it was enough.

He sat down at his desk and called Camille. She answered after a few rings, heavy-lidded and disheveled, and glaring at him.

"What?" Camille asked angrily.

Why is everyone always so mad at me? he wondered.

"I'm just checking to make sure we're still on for the trip to Elworthy Hospital in the morning."

"Yes, Cody," she rolled her eyes, "I'll be ready." Her hand hovered over the disconnect button.

"We'll have to take a car, which means we'll need to rent it outside of the Net."

"I figured."

"Will Mr. Nakamoto be joining us again?"

"No, Remy's not coming."

"Okay, I'll bring us each a breakfast sandwich. Just two then," he said.

"Fine."

"What kind do you want?"

Camille had already hung up. Satisfied, Cody settled in and began to write his report about his recent encounter with Nakamoto's reverberation viewing technology.

18
CAMILLE

"Why do you do this?" Remy had asked Camille several years ago when they were newly acquainted and his technology was precarious enough that he often needed to accompany it on bounties. "There are other ways to rack up Node Points," he said pointedly.

At the time of the question, Camille had been standing next to the emaciated body of a young man. She had used a Confiner to hold his consciousness just long enough for him to say goodbye to a lost love that he had forsaken at the onset of his illness. A few moments ago, Camille completed releasing his mind, and the woman had left, her soft cries fading as Remy shut down the equipment he had been testing.

"There's a dark cloud over this work," Remy said.

"There's a dark cloud over *me*," Camille said sardonically. "Seems like it's been there since the moment I was born. I know myself, and I know people. I am good for people in times of crisis."

"You are good at seeming calm," Remy said.

"I am calm. But I'm also never going to tell anyone to calm down because I understand. Life is a bloody cunt, and we should all be in a constant state of panic."

"There's the vulgarity I'm coming to know and love," Remy had said, half distracted by a whirligig on his machine that had randomly decided to beep and spin.

"See," Camille said, "your doohickey knows what I'm talking about."

Camille thought about her early days as a mercenary as she successfully staved off panic, while she and Cody stood several yards behind the painted white line on the pavement that denoted the end of Zeta's Net. The road was desolated on both sides because no one wanted to build, or even wander, that close to the edge of the Net.

Camille's current companion never seemed to care why she did what she did. And he was certainly not fond of her profanity. Cody had bought her a bacon and egg sandwich, which she gratefully chewed, and hovered around her as they waited for the rental car.

Cody had also bought himself a new, slick, black wrist RAP on his way to the rendezvous. He was now typing furiously upon his wrist with an air of self-importance, making sure that he was in Camille's visual range.

She refused to take his bait, there was no way she was getting drawn into a long annoying conversation about his new tech. Instead, she started off, past the Zeta line. She had only ever been outside a netted area briefly, to travel between Nets. She imagined dying outside the Net, her life bleeding away uselessly instead of being pulled into the next world.

"I'm using this RAP to talk with Doctor Winter, head of the Elworthy experiments," Cody announced, tired of waiting for Camille to ask.

"Good," Camille said flatly, hoping that was enough to end the conversation.

Cody waited exactly one minute before attempting to engage her again, "Did you like your breakfast sandwich?"

"The car's here." Camille nodded up the road. A maroon sedan crept toward them. Camille bit her lip and stepped over the Zeta City boundary line. Cody followed her, too absorbed in his new RAP to notice he had done anything out of the ordinary.

The car pulled up to them and its doors and trunk opened. Camille tossed her one, lightly-packed backpack in and Cody shoved it aside to make room for his three-piece luggage. After a few seconds of jockeying, Camille slid into the back seat, and Cody sat in front. The car's long dashboard console had once been a slick innovation, but now it was a scratched and warped screen flanked by large, red, Emergency Stop buttons.

"Elworthy Community Asylum," Cody barked at the car's computer. The dash screen lit up, showing a digital map of their route.

A set of warnings scrolled across the bottom of the screen: *Caution Route Net Deficient. Caution Destination Net Deficient.*

"Will it still take us to the hospital?" Camille wondered aloud.

"Yes," Cody answered her and then said, "Override," to the computer.

The car started moving, creeping along at first, but it was soon speeding along at about 60 kilometers per hour.

Cody turned to Camille, "Do you want to watch a movie on the way? There are screens in the dashboard and in back of the seats too."

"Put on whatever you want," Camille replied.

Cody chose a documentary about the impact of desalinization plants on orca whales, which Camille promptly turned off on the seatback screens. She was left to watch the countryside roll past the window. There wasn't much to look at for the most part: abandoned towns with rows of decrepit buildings that propped each other up as if removing one would collapse the next, reducing the village to dust. She occasionally spotted one of the old kinds of cars that had to be operated by the passenger, and sometimes she would see a lone person, or a pair of people, wandering these towns as if they were lords of forsaken dry rot.

Then there were the farms: miles of vast farmlands overseen by a few brave growers who were compensated extensively for their work in areas impossible to cover with Nets. Those farmers and secluded townsfolk came to Zeta, or to small Netted hospitals like Elworthy, to die if they were lucky enough to make it. If not, they would suffer certain mortality, the most feared of all the fates.

After a few hours of Cody's boring documentaries and the eerie landscape, the car drove up to the Elworthy hospital complex. They pulled up just short of the painted line that marked the edge of the hospital's Netted zone. Camille felt the palpable lifting of the weight of dread that she hadn't realized she had been carrying.

A message scrolled across the bottom of the car's dash screen: *$342 has been deducted from your account, Thank You.* Cody and Camille stepped from the rental and scanned the scene before them.

Elworthy Asylum was a compound of three red-brick buildings with a central courtyard. The middle building was four stories tall, and the flanking buildings were each six stories tall. The buildings were ancient by Camille's standards, with odd architectural additions like mostly-intact stone arches graced with carved gargoyles and mermaids that mocked or beckoned visitors from above.

"Cheery," Camille noted sarcastically as she studied a particularly gruesome-looking gargoyle.

The whole Elworthy compound was ringed by a faint, painted, blue line that marked the edge of the hospital's Net. Grabbing her backpack from the trunk, Camille stepped over the line. The inside of a Net never felt any more different from the outside, except for a sense of palpable relief.

Once up the two sets of low stone steps and inside the front hall, Camille and Cody signed in at the first building's reception desk, which was manned by a drab looking woman with a perpetual scowl.

"We have a one o'clock with Doctor Winter," Cody exclaimed to her, much too excited for what the situation warranted.

"Conference Room B," the attendant said, so apathetic she bordered on comatose.

The halls of Elworthy were laid with smooth, stone tile so even the softest footfalls resounded. Camille and Cody encountered few patients on their way to Conference Room B. They were wheelchair-bound, for the most part, although one woman with long, ghostly white hair walked upright, clinging to the staff of an I.V. fluid line. Camille realized that this place was no different from Zeta City, both were refuges for those awaiting death.

Dr. Winter was waiting for them in a startlingly modern conference room, considering the age of the buildings. It was carpeted with a long, faux wood table and a half-dozen peach-colored swivel chairs. Dr. Winter was a wisp of a man, small of stature and with bright, white, shoulder-length, hair, apropos of his name. He vaguely reminded Camille of the sickly woman she had seen on the way to the conference room. He spoke in short clips with little inflection, and it was hard to tell when he finished speaking.

"Obviously, we'd like to get this started as soon as possible," he said as he stood and shook hands with both of them, "with prudence – vetting and all – leave nothing to chance."

"Yes," Cody agreed resolutely, not realizing that Dr. Winter had more to say. When he realized that he had interrupted the doctor, he said "sorry" and made a gesture for Dr. Winter to continue.

"The race is not to the swift, and the battle not to the warrior; for time and chance overtake them all," Winter finished.

"I like the sound of that," Camille said.

Dr. Winter nodded in response, then turned and spoke to her directly.

"You'll begin by taking initial rounds of medication tonight, and we'll send you in there tomorrow, mid-morning," the doctor continued.

"Whoa! Medication? In *where?*" Camille was confused. "*Where* am I going? We just got here."

Winter looked surprised. "Into the Node, of course." He looked from Camille to Cody and back again. "I'm sorry, I didn't realize you hadn't been briefed."

Camille glared at Cody with open rage as he stared downward, avoiding her eyes. She had been under the impression that he was talking pure speculation back in Zeta, but Remy was right about the dangers here. They were going to try and send her into the Node alive – at least she hoped she would be alive.

"I thought it was best if we get you here first, and then explain the full nature of the mission," Cody said tentatively.

"You're going to kill me!" Camille shouted as she turned on her wrist RAP, intending to call Remy, hoping he'd be able to extricate her.

"No, no," Winter reached out and grasped Camille's RAP arm, "please don't call anyone and tell them about what we're doing here. We're not going to kill you. We're going to offer you an opportunity." Camille allowed Winter to lower her wrist. Cody and Winter watched her closely, she wondered what they would do if she reached for her RAP and completed her call. They might try to restrain her, but she was fairly sure that she could take down an old man and thin, stiff Cody.

She weighed her options. Remy had warned her against Elworthy altogether, but Remy was a chronic worrier with a penchant for the dramatic. He would come for her if she called, but he would be unforgivably smug about it. On the other hand, Winter was offering her a glimpse at eternity and a path to meet her deepest longing.

Winter spoke again when it seemed that Camille would neither make a move nor say a word, "We're going to send you into the Node and bring you back out alive. We've done it before, I promise. Trust me."

"We only met a few moments ago."

"Who seeks, and will not take, when once it's offered, may never find it again," Dr. Winter said and spread his arms wide.

"Knock it off," Camille snapped. "I'm not swayed by your phony enlightenment, and I didn't come here seeking anything but a payday."

Winter walked over to a window, unlocked it, pushed it open, and leaned on the sill. They were several stories up with a view showing Elworthy's scraggly lawn and the Net line beyond it.

"A hornet flew into my office the other day, through an open window," Winter said. "So, I opened all of the rest of the windows in the hope that it would fly out on its own accord. The hornet remained and became more and more agitated, bumping into walls and buzzing around. I thought I might take a paper and gently guide the hornet out of one of the windows, but it stung me in my benevolence and, of course, it died shortly afterward, just curled up in the corner. Had it trusted me, for just a few moments, it would be out there flying."

"I am not a hornet, Doctor," Camille said.

"We shall see," he answered.

19
CODY

Cody was not sure why Anita was angry with him, but he could tell, by reading her body language, she was livid. She leaned forward and glared into the camera lens at Cody making her furious face take up even more of his computer screen.

"Agent Prilio," she growled, "you're looking as twitchy as ever."

"Yes," Cody acquiesced.

"Didn't go well, I take it."

"We were unable to apprehend the hacker, Bowen."

"Yes, we assumed she was the person who died on the Neaveau Street tracks. We were able to keep the media from making the connection. Good thinking on your part – getting her to the tracks – the body was unidentifiable."

"It wasn't me that got her there; it was my partner," Cody said.

"The civilian mercenary?" Anita made a strange face Cody couldn't read. "Anyway, I want you to shut this down. Consider it case closed."

"We brought in a specialist with the ability to detect reverberations! We almost had her. The mercenary was able to watch her enter the Node – this is a very exciting technology!" Cody pressed on despite Anita's finality, but she was resolute.

"Even more reason to terminate the project. We have proof that Bowen entered the Node and the Point System is still intact. The media will drop it to sensationalize the next bit of gossip."

"Alright Ms. Bourbeau," Cody said, using her formal name in a gesture of deference, "but have you had a chance to listen to all of the briefs that I sent you when you were incommunicado?"

"No. I consider this the debrief. I'm giving you a few days off of field work, but I want a report on the technology that allowed you to view those reverberations. I'm wiring you funds and Node Points to pay the mercenary and this new tech specialist."

"The man who created the reverb viewer requested to be paid in electricity," Cody remembered.

"Fine," Anita said dismissively. "I don't have to remind you that you're not actually a bounty hunter and the girl isn't really your partner, do I? You are just a boring old government technical officer. Focus on identifying new underground technologies and destroying whatever you deem dangerous."

"Okay, I'll –" Cody began to respond but Anita had already disconnected the call. He slouched in his chair and stared at the black computer screen for a few moments, before taking in a deep breath and sitting up to take in his surroundings. The otherwise desolate wall of the hospital room was graced with a single painting of a pot of purple flowers. This would be his resting place and base of operations for now.

He considered calling Anita back and telling her what was on the briefing tapes she considered too irrelevant to take up her precious time. He wanted to let her know he would *not* be taking a few days off of field work because he was in the middle of saving the Node because there was no one else to do it. But he decided not to make that call.

20
CAMILLE

Camille was moved into her hospital room and tucked onto her hospital bed that night even though she still hadn't fully agreed to the experiment, but that didn't seem to matter. Dr. Winter had carefully explained how the procedure worked and how safe it was. Cody, a witness to the explanation, was encouraging.

Winter explained that he would induce the coma slowly – "something like being put under hypnosis," he said. They would put her into stasis by winding down her mind, thought by thought, cell by cell, deeper and deeper until she was on the brink of death. Winter would hold her in that precarious twilight, tricking the Net into thinking she had died. He also explained this was why the experiments took place at the nondescript Elworthy Asylum: any place within a city-sized, sophisticated Net would never be fooled, but a tiny, hospital-sized Net, such as that at Elworthy, could be manipulated.

Cody remarked for the third time that the procedure was safe, to which Camille replied, "Did *you* try it?"

Cody opened his mouth to respond but shut it again. He admitted that he had not tried it himself.

"Well, why don't *you* go in, since it's so damn safe?" Camille sat up in the hospital bed and held her arm out stiffly so Dr. Winter could draw some more blood.

Cody's face went red, and Camille knew she had him. "I thought you'd want all of that extra hazard pay," Cody retorted. *He's not wrong*, Camille thought.

Eventually, both Winter and Cody disappeared into the inner workings of Elworthy leaving Camille in the care of an army of uncharacteristically muscular nurses and technicians.

Her heart pounded. Her first instinct was to run, but she dismissed that option, considering she had nowhere to run to but a wide swath of unsafe, Net free territory. She looked over a particularly rough-looking orderly and decided that she did not want to tangle with him. Even if she did, what would she do? She devised a plan to wait until she was alone, perhaps in the bathroom, and then clandestinely use her wrist RAP to call herself a car. The car would have to sit at the edge of the Elworthy boundary, close but not close enough to be seen from the hospital, waiting for her escape. What she barely considered was the possibility her paranoia was unfounded as a result of a life lived on the edges of society. She may very well have been free to come and go as she pleased.

She decided to stay quiet and observant, allowing herself to be wheeled from the room and into a second room with the same unremarkable floral art as the first. She was greeted by a woman whose name badge read "Deanna" and "Nurse Technician." It also had the designation, SPECIAL VISITOR, in bright blue capital letters.

Once the nurse left and the door was closed, Deanna addressed Camille, "I knew when I saw that ad from that Nirvana hacker, that they were going to send someone here," she said excitedly. Deanna was a tall woman, with curly brown hair and a spatter of light freckles. Camille took a moment before she realized this was the friend that Remy's had told her about.

"You mean Toy Bowen?" she asked.

Deanna had to back up a few steps for Camille, who was always a bit larger than life. "Yes," she answered breathlessly. "That blonde hacker from Nirvana. I knew that people were going to start to come here – because of our experiments."

"Right. Winter says they are sending people into the Node and bringing them back out – allegedly alive," Camille said, realizing the burly orderlies were absent and that she could easily take out this nurse who was a waif compared to her.

"Not allegedly," Deanna said. "I've been in there."

Camille gaped at Deanna as she continued: "I've been in the Node. I was the first one from here to go in, and – so far – the only one."

Camille put the brakes on her escape plan. There were a million things that she wanted to ask, but all that came out was, "What was it like in there?"

The landscape of the Node, its functions, and physical, or actually, digital conditions were one of the great mysteries of life. Writers and philosophers speculated, artists sketched and painted, and everyone else dreamed of the next world. But, no one could say, with even a tiny degree of certainty what it wonders the Node held. Here, this normal-looking lady, stood several feet from Camille, prepared to unravel the Node's enigma.

"Different from what you think," Deanna said.

Camille wanted to ask her in what way, but she reserved her questions as Deanna went on.

"Then Remy said they were sending you here with an NBO agent and I thought, 'that's them.' One of them is going into the Node."

Camille looked Deanna up and down. There did not seem to be anything particularly special about her, at least not special enough to be chosen as the first person to go into and come out of the Node.

Camille had been mulling it over since Dr. Winter had first told her what she was to supposed to do; and she was sure she, Camille, an occasionally-sleazy bounty hunter, was definitely not good enough to be one of the first people to journey in and out alive. She was also sure this, nice-enough, want-to-be nurse, was not good enough either. *Perhaps it isn't special people who get do great things,* she thought to herself. *Maybe all it takes is someone who is willing to jump in at the right place at the right time.*

While she listened to the not-good-enough nurse, Camille surveyed the technology in the room. It had many normal hospital room items: vitals monitor, IV drips, and drawers full of sterile pads and towels; but, it also had a projector and a massive screen, and a mini-fridge. Deanna opened the door to the fridge, and Camille saw that it was stocked with several of her favorite foods: turkey and bacon sandwiches, powdered donuts, iced tea, and candy bars. Camille figured she had eaten around Cody too often, and wasn't sure if she should feel touched or creeped out that he had memorized her favorite foods. Deanna continued to bustle around the room, opening cabinets and checking supplies while Camille kept asking questions.

"Did you spend any of your Node Points while you were in there?" Camille asked.

"No," Deanna laughed nervously and glanced up at the security camera mounted in the celling's corner. Camille couldn't tell if the glance was a warning or an unconscious tic.

"What about your family? Did you see them?" Camille pressed on.

"No. I didn't want to cause any problems," Diana said, but this time she did not look at the camera.

"Hey, can you hand me an iced tea and a marshmallow candy bar from that fridge?" Camille asked.

The bed where Camille sat was to the far side of the camera. When Deanna handed her the candy bar, Camille dropped it, and both women bent down at the same time to grab it.

Hoping she was hidden from the security camera, Camille whispered, "Wanna tell me what the fuck is going on here?"

"Nothing," Deanna hissed back.

"Something fascinating on the floor, ladies?" Dr. Winter asked as he walked in the room.

"A marshmallow bar." Camille held it up with a cheerful smile.

"Uh huh." The doctor eyed them both. "I'm here to give you a rundown of tomorrow's procedure. Please, enjoy your candy while we chat."

"No," Camille said, her voice filled with steel, "I've been waiting to talk to you and you've been putting me off while you and Cody are running my life here. I haven't technically agreed to do anything you know. I haven't signed – " she said before Dr. Winter cut her off.

"We don't have time for you to waffle around young lady. Someone could be destroying the System as we sit here and chew. From what I understand, you're being well compensated for your work and, like everyone else, I'm sure you have people in the Node you'd like to check in on." Winter's cool presence had melted and had been replaced by one of authority.

"Deanna said she didn't get to see her family," Camille interjected. She glanced over at Deanna who was looking downcast and guilty.

"Well, Deanna's experiment parameters were different from yours. I'm attempting to lengthen the amount of time that we can keep someone in the Node. Your mission, while important, is not my main objective. As long as you fulfill your primary duty, you can do what you like. I see no reason you can't pop in on grandpa."

Camille sat and listened while Dr. Winter and Deanna explained Camille's responsibilities during the procedure. After being uploaded to the hospital's Net, Camille would then have to make her way out to the hospital courtyard to find

Elworthy's Node Gate. Once inside the Node, Winter could keep Camille in a twilight state for about 300 hours. Camille had to use those hours to discover if the Node Point System had been compromised, find Toy, and deactivate her if needed.

"You're going to keep me almost dead for three hundred hours." Camille typed the calculation into her wrist RAP. "That's, like, twelve days. Deanna said she was only under for a few days."

"And Deanna was fine, more than fine," Dr. Winter soothed, "There are several experiments that we need to conduct with your digital body, and many of them take several days."

"Excuse me." Camille pulled herself up out of the hospital bed and shoved Winter aside with her shoulder. "You're going to have to find someone else's digital body to experiment on. I'm out."

Camille prepared herself to make a run for it if they decided to ignore her refusal. With Winter momentarily stunned and knocked to the side, Camille moved toward the door. Once she was through the door, she bolted down Elworthy's tastefully decorated and painfully clean hallways. She ran past the burly orderlies, and past the doped-up patients shuffling to nowhere. A few people gaped at her, flying by fast, powered by her strong, thick legs.

It wasn't until she ran outside and down the front steps that she realized no one was chasing her. Camille slowed, but still jogged to the very edge of the Elworthy Net. She stood on the edge of that blue, painted circle that separated real safety from absolute danger. She turned back to the hospital double doors, realizing that no one was going to come after her. It seemed the choice to enter the Node truly was her own.

Deanna came out of the hospital's ornately carved double doors. She wasn't rushing, and she was alone. When she reached Camille, she put her hand on her shoulder reassuringly.

"I'm not afraid," Camille told her. "I just don't want to be forced into anything or get fucked over by experiments."

"That's not what we're about here. We're just Node scientists learning the truth about the Node," Deanna gently explained.

Camille narrowed her eyes. "What do you mean truth?"

"All the things we don't know about the Node: what it's like in there, how the Points buy things, how to find our loved ones. You'll be an explorer, like the first man on the moon, well, the second man on the moon." Deanna smiled.

Camille answered after a few moments, "I don't need answers or fame. I just want Node Points, lots of them."

"I'm sure you'll get those too."

Twenty minutes and one lunch order later, Camille was back in her hospital room eating a tuna salad sandwich and listening to Deanna describe her experience entering and moving around inside the Node. According to Deanna, movement in the Node was almost instantaneous, but only from specific access points.

Dr. Winter crept into the room, closed the door behind him, and stayed to the edges as if Camille might run again if he got too close to her.

"How do I come back?" Camille asked through a mouth full of tuna, addressing both Deanna and Winter, "How do I get back into my body?"

Deanna deferred to Winter's expertise, and he stepped in.

"You'll already be in your body," Winter answered. "When you die, the Net makes a digital copy of your memory and neural paths. That copy is what passes into the Node. All we have to do is wake you up. The Net can't reconcile the new neural pathways for your awakened body, and your presence in the Node dissolves."

The rare feeling of panic crept up on Camille, making her neck tingle and her face flush. She swallowed hard.

"Don't alert anyone in the Node that you're actually alive either. We don't want word getting back to the Founders," Winter warned. "They have the power to remove kings and establish kings; to bestow wisdom upon men."

"Do you keep quoting Shakespeare?" Camille wondered aloud.

Without answering, Winter pushed a few forms and a pen into her hand, she looked them over dripping crumbs on the pages. One of the forms was a waiver denying the hospital any culpability should the procedure go awry. The second was a nondisclosure agreement assuring that Camille would tell no one of the hospital's experiments. The last document was a family contact and next of kin form. After some thought, Camille listed Remy as her next of kin, and both he and Cody as her family contacts. She handed the doctor the signed forms, and he cheerfully shook of the tuna sandwich crumbs.

"Yes, well, that'll do," he muttered before leaving the room.

On her way out, Deanna turned to Camille, "The courtyard is a great place to walk in the evening," she tried to give a reassuring smile, "if you're nervous."

Camille was reluctant to admit her nervousness. It was not a common feeling for her, but she still took a stroll at dusk to clear her mind and brighten her failing spirit.

The hospital courtyard was not the best place for an evening walk. It was average, without much of a walkway. Paths from all four corners of the hospital converged in the center, and there were a few, spare, copses of bare, ornamental trees. She ran out of walkway to stroll upon in one turn around the courtyard. She mused on her suspicion that Deanna's suggestion had been a veiled request, then gravitated toward a cove made up of three trees, and leaned against one with her arms folded.

Eventually, Deanna stole through the doors of the middle building and made her way to where Camille was.

"Can you please just tell me what your deal is?" Camille growled as Deanna approached. "Why couldn't you just talk to me alone before or just tell me to meet you out here. This whole 'trust us' *shtick* is wearing thin."

"I was waiting until I knew for sure you were going to go into the Node. I didn't want to talk to you and then have you run either." Camille started to shake her head and huff. "Listen," Deanna demanded impatiently ignoring Camille's huffing, "after you come back, I need you to talk to me before you talk to anyone else."

"About what?" Camille asked indifferently.

"You'll know. Just pretend to be out of it when they ask you questions, don't answer them, I didn't. Then, I'll come to you and we'll talk about it."

"About 'it'? Come on, what is this 'it'?" Camille demanded.

"I told you already – you'll know," Deanna said.

"Hey. I'm about to basically die, and you're being a weird creep. It is the opposite of reassuring." Camille drew closer to the woman so she could lower her voice.

"I'm sure the whole thing will go fine, that's not what the issue is. With me, I went to sleep, woke up like a ghost in the hospital. I found the gate – it's right here in the courtyard – and went into the Node. I was cared for by a greeter who offered to bring me to my family. I said 'no, then I hung out in a city for a few days. Then I woke up, just like from a dream."

"But there's something you're not telling me."

Deanna smiled, her curls caught the moonlight, giving her a bluish halo. "Yeah," she said with a shrug, "when you come out of it, we'll talk."

"Talk now," Camille insisted.

Deanna was nearing the end of her rope. "I'm not smart. But, since I've been in there, I know more than any other person alive on this planet. Knowledge itself doesn't make you better if you're not intelligent enough to know what to do with it. I know just enough to realize that I know nothing."

"And you think that I'm intelligent to use what I'll learn in the Node?" Camille asked.

"Maybe not, but at least there'll be two of us then." Deanna signaled the end of the conversation by abruptly heading back to the asylum.

Cody was waiting for Camille when she returned to her hospital room. He was sitting in one of the plush visitor chairs, watching his wrist RAP.

"I heard you named me next of kin," he said trying to hide his rapture.

"You're just one of my contacts, we're not going to get married or anything," Camille said, anticipating some outlandishness.

"Why not list one of your family members?" Cody looked at her pointedly.

Camille glared at him, choking back sad rage. She had never mentioned any family to Cody, so he was either investigating her or attempting to poke around her personal realm.

"This is a bit dangerous. Don't you want your family to know if something happens to you?" Cody continued when she didn't answer.

"I spend my life hunting people on the edge of devastation. This is no different. There'll be no calls home."

PART II: GHOSTS IN HEAVEN

21
CAMILLE

As Camille lay on the hospital bed, hooked up to several machines and with an I.V. drip in her arm, she imagined making another desperate run that would involve ripping herself from the bed and running headlong into the no-mans-land outside Elworthy, trailing blood the whole way. It was one of her last thoughts before Dr. Winter injected a sedative into her I.V. while he intoned, "Behold the mystery. We shall not all sleep, but we shall all be changed – all in the twinkling of an eye."

Pretty words. Camille thought. Or said. She wasn't sure if she had spoken aloud.

"Count backward from 100, and you'll be out before you get to one ... the last trumpet."

What was that he said? Camille declined to count backward. Instead, she let her mind wander back into to her past, an indulgence she otherwise wouldn't have allowed herself. She soon found that she was unable to hold onto her thoughts, they slipped from her mind and faded into a wooly mental silence. Then, her thoughts gradually faded back, but they were a different kind of thought, mechanical and sharp.

As she regained consciousness, she realized she had, what seemed to be, a new mind in a new body. This new body and mind existed alongside her previous mind and body, and she learned she could control them like a remote-controlled car.

The reality that she was in looked grainy, like a roughly pixelated photo. *This must be what looking at the world through the Net is like*, she thought. She could see her corporeal body on the hospital bed, her eyes were closed and her arms rested by her sides, the I.V. still attached and all the wires leading to the machines. Dr. Winter leaned over her body as Deanna stood nearby, watching the machines. Camille was aware of pixelated sunlight streaming low through the windows, indicating that hours had passed since she had been in her other body.

Memories of who she was, and what she was doing now, began to creep into her new mind. Forming whole thoughts was difficult at first, but then the thoughts came easier. Time seemed to skip ahead, and Camille now noticed Deanna standing in the hospital room's doorway, beckoning around the room, motioning for Camille to follow her.

I'm here; I'm going to follow, Camille thought, but when she tried to speak it came out as, "I-I-I."

When Deanna did move, Camille followed, but as soon as she did, she realized she wasn't walking as she had in her body outside the Net. She looked down and saw that this new body had no legs – it seemed to fade out below her pelvis, and she realized she could just float along like a ghost, steering herself with her eyes and mind. She trailed Deanna through the hospital halls, a few yards behind, careful to keep her eyes on the woman's pixelated tuft of red hair, which was now made a dull maroon by the muted colors of the Net.

I'm trying to save the Node, she thought. The memory was shaky and far away, but Camille held onto it as desperately as if it were a life raft in the midst of an empty ocean. Deanna led Camille to the hospital courtyard, where there was a tall blue arch that wasn't there before. As it radiated twisting bolts of electricity, Camille was struck by the lack of sound. Something as big and vibrant as the gate should be making a tremendous noise, but everything was dead silent. As Camille made her way to the arch, the bolts reached out for her like long tendrils, enveloping her and pulling her in.

There was no pain. She felt nothing, except the gentle pull of the gate. She knew she could resist it and it was frightening enough to run away from if she had forgotten her purpose for going through into the Node. *No wonder there are so many ghosts,* she thought as her digital form kissed the surface of the gate, and in that instant, she was through.

Less than a second later, Camille found herself standing in a vibrant, green meadow on the cusp of a hill overlooking a vast moor. Aside from a single, massive oak on the hill's crest and a lonely shed nearby, there was nothing visible, but long grass and flowers. Her wits had returned to her at the same moment she had jumped through the gate. She was grateful for the ability to think without a thick layer of fuzz over her thoughts.

She took stock of herself; she had a solid form, and she ran her hands over her arms and belly, then she touched her face. She was glad to see that her legs were back in place of the eerie mist that had been there before. She also noticed she wasn't wearing the hospital gown she had on in the hospital. Instead, she was dressed in her typical outfit – a black tank top and gray cargo shorts. She reached up and touched her hair. It was still short, and still there. The only thing missing was her reality augmentation pad. *Why am I wearing what I always wear and not have my wrist RAP?*

All of these thoughts were overshadowed by the realization she was inside of the Node.

From Deanna's descriptions, she knew travel in the Node happened via a system of internal gates, which were also used to locate individuals. Camille didn't see any gates near her. She briefly considered wandering out onto the moor, but there was no gate in sight and the shed next to her was her only glimpse of civilization.

The shed was old and weathered, but not decrepit. It was about 250 square feet with brown siding, a red roof, and a red a door. It looked like some of the storage sheds in the countryside where she had grown up.

She knocked on the door and, finding no answer, entered the shed. The floor was hard, tightly packed earth and it was entirely empty except for a pedestal, on top of which was a large, green button. Camille strode over to where the pedestal stood and pressed the button, but nothing happened. She pressed it again, several times, in rapid succession but still, nothing. Frustrated, she sat down on the dirt floor, prepared to give up. Looking around the room a little more closely she noticed a frame mounted on the wall. Inside the frame was a large letter. Camille stood up, walked over and read:

Greetings Newly Deceased

Congratulations on making it into the Node.

I'll be 'round shortly to pick you up.

If you desire anything in the meantime, press the green button, speak it aloud, and the Node will deliver it to you.

Enjoy!

Moses

Camille thought for several minutes. Finally, she pressed the green button and said "Santos." Nothing happened.

"Axia Industries D9 wrist communicator and reality augmentation pad," she tried again. Her wrist RAP materialized on the ground next to the button's pedestal. She picked it up gingerly and inspected it. The RAP looked just like her old one, white with black accents, and a long gray screen. She strapped it on her wrist and initialized it.

As soon as the RAP booted up, Camille said, "Call Santos" into it. Nothing happened. Next, she tried directing it to her Node Point account. The screen flashed "Unable to Access." Camille wondered if that meant Toy was successful, or if Node Points were accessed differently inside the Node. She also wondered whose Node Points had paid for the wrist RAP: her own, or the ones belonging to this absent benefactor, Moses.

She leaned against the shed wall and slid down to the dirt floor again. After sitting there for a few moments, she scrambled back up and walked over to the pedestal and pushed the button one more time.

"A sofa. A large comfortable one," she said pressing the button. A plush, cream-colored, rose-patterned sofa appeared at the opposite side of the shed. Camille reclined on the sofa and fiddled with her new wrist RAP.

"Call Remington Nakamto," she commanded the RAP, but it blinked an error message instead of calling.

"Call Cody Priolo." She received the same error message.

"Project Zeta City News Network," she commanded, and the RAP's projector sputtered on, but what it projected on the shed wall was not quite ZCNN. The peppy, brunette news reporter who appeared on the screen was presenting the same story on Toy she had seen before, complete with the virus jacking video being replayed in the background, but the reporter's words were muffled as if by static or a broken connection. Sometimes the screen would blink out entirely, but the newscast had occasional stretches where she could understand what the reporter was saying.

"Now, our Node expert, Doctor Ian Rames, will discuss the possible ramifications of an NP breach," the reporter crackled, then the projection cut out entirely. In a couple of seconds, it started over at the same point it started at before, with the reporter speaking in a muffled voice while Toy's video played.

After it looped a few more times, Camille realized she wasn't watching the news; she was watching her last memory of the news. The transmission was spotty because she hadn't paid much attention the first time. The Node did not, or could not, access any new information from ZCNN, so it was using her memory. Camille wasn't going to be able to watch anything she couldn't remember all the way through. This meant any source of entertainment must either come from before the Node was created, or it was made by people living in the Node.

"The book, *The Time Machine*, by H.G. Wells," she said, mashing the green button. That was the only pre-Node book that Camille could recall the name of at the moment. An ebook reader appeared next to the sofa, the same weathered one that Camille had used to read all of her books in high school.

Camille read until the sky began to darken and she returned to the green button to order an end table and a lamp that glowed without being plugged in. She wandered outside to watch the sunset over the moor. The sky was red, orange, and purple. The purple bled from the sky and settled in the grass. The peace and beauty unnerved Camille.

Her thoughts turned toward food. She hadn't eaten since she arrived in the Node. She tried to feel if she was hungry. Where there should have been hunger, there was emptiness. Her stomach was hollow. *More like ... nonexistent,* she thought to herself. After much deliberation, Camille decided she was not hungry, she wasn't even sure she was capable of hunger, but she was restless, so she thought she might try to eat. She conjured up one of her favorite hometown foods, one that was not available under the Zeta Net.

"Real strawberry rhubarb pie," she told the green button, "and a fork."

A bag of flour, eggs, butter, a bag of sugar, a jug of milk, a pint of strawberries, a fork, and a few stalks of rhubarb popped up, a few yards from the button.

"Does this mean the Node doesn't know how to make pie?" Camille groused. She conjured herself up a pie tin, an oven, and a counter and set to baking herself a pie.

An hour and a half later, Camille lounged on the sofa reading *The Time Machine* eating a poorly-baked strawberry pie directly from the tin. She looked up at Moses's note on the wall.

"I'll be round shortly," she grumbled. She came to understand that Moses's idea of "shortly" was relative and highly subjective.

22
TOY

After several days of communication errors and transportation slip-ups, Toy's Node guide located Toy's grandmother and together they made the journey to the Node's version of the Wild West. Byron led Toy through the dusty streets of a crumbling town, with every shop and residence sepia-toned, every serape draped horses led by men in spurs, and cowboys who walked next to tourist-heavy boardwalks, tipping their hats to the passerby.

"I suppose it takes death to find out who you are," said Toy's grandmother from behind the bar at her Wild West-styled saloon. She had named the bar *Toy's Island*, after her granddaughter and her favorite place on earth. Toy had always harbored mixed feelings about her grandmother since her life of poverty was the catalyst for Toy's life-ending crusade so, she was not entirely sure what to think about her posthumous bar ownership. The bar seemed indulgent and lavish, but when Toy saw her own name carved roughly into a wooden sign hung on rusty chains over the door to the bar, she gave temporary precedence to the warm thought that her grandmother would preserve her memory in such a precious way.

But, when she saw her grandmother, she was young, busty, and scantly-dressed – a thirty-year-old pin-up version of the grandmother Toy knew. Toy fell into her arms nonetheless and they both started crying.

"You're here too early child," Marion lamented.

"I know," Toy said regretfully, "and I'm so sorry." Toy started to say more, but the words were caught in her throat. She shook her head and tears welled in her eyes.

"It's alright dear." Marian reached out for Toy, and she felt her grandmother again, even under the layers of corset and corn whiskey.

Byron left them, and they spent the next few hours discussing the arc of life that had brought them together again. Marian talked about how she spent a few years in Paradise trying to re-create her old life, but it never felt right. She visited the Wild West with a friend and fell in love with the setting and the people. Toy was careful not to touch on her own experiences as a rebel hacker; she wondered if they'd tie the Node communication disruption to her and she hoped the disruption was just the first link in a chain that would topple the Point System. Instead of sharing her devious thoughts, Toy spoke about her own time at school and her experiences with her friends.

"Any special friends?" Marion asked with a twinkle in her eye.

"No," Toy replied, shrugging, "I've been busy grandma, really, really busy."

Toy settled into her bar stool while her grandmother insisted on serving her a sarsaparilla, whatever that was. She was planning to lay low and in the Wild West and wait for the other shoe to drop when, hopefully, people's Node Point accounts mysteriously began to drain, if it wasn't already occurring. Toy contemplated how her grandmother might react if the virus was traced back to her. Idle speculation ended though, almost as soon as it had started when Marion grasped both her granddaughter's hands and began to delve into the secrets of the Node.

23
CAMILLE

By the next morning, Camille had made a pleasant little apartment for herself inside the shed. She had ordered a few rugs to cover the dirt floor, a refrigerator (which she stocked full of simple snacks that didn't require assembly), and an old-fashioned television set that tapped into a station playing TV shows from before the Node was created. Most of the shows were from before the war and Camille marveled at the opulence; everyone had a car and a huge home, and everything was clean and spacious. She tried sleeping, but she realized that, just like hunger, it was possible to sleep but the drive was just not there.

Every once in a while, Camille emerged from her den and wandered around the hilltop. She never went out of sight of the shed, for fear of missing the elusive Moses. She was reading, sometime around noon according to the clock on her wrist RAP, when she heard a familiar noise outside the shed, and the memories of a thousand days of her childhood marched along in stride with the sound of hoof beats.

She left the shed, and the door slammed behind her, which attracted the attention of a galloping chestnut colt. The startled horse barreled down on her, chased by a man with long, black hair who waved his arms and yelled, "Hey! Get out of the way!" to Camille.

Camille ran back into the shed and waited for the galloping horse to pass. She was about to step back out when the door swung inward and the man strode in. He was short and quite thin, but not gaunt: he was a fit thin. He had straight black hair that hung down his back, a round, delicate nose, and bright green eyes.

"Sorry about that. I like to break wild horses, but you know, it couldn't have hurt you anyway," he chuckled, "we're indestructible here."

"I know a little about horses," Camille said. "Are you Moses, finally?"

"Yea." He looked around at the living area that Camille set up for herself. "Nice digs!"

"I've been here for a day. Where were you?" Camille demanded.

"Don't worry about it, you have all the time you could ever want. People don't show up here very much, you're supposed to arrive in the orientation station in New Zeta City, but for some reason, a few stragglers arrive here. Must be some kind of glitch. I don't check up here very often. It's a long walk from my home."

"I thought travel here was instantaneous," Camille noted.

Moses examined Camille, his green eyes turning steely, but only for a moment before turning to his default calm. "Who told you that?"

"No one, I just thought."

"Well, movement here is instantaneous to and from specific points, but, aside from those points, we have to move around normally. Although, I suppose I could make an extra fast hovercar to bring me here, instead of the horses. But, then I'd have to figure out how to make a hovercar unless someone else has already... I didn't catch your name."

"It's Camille."

"Well Camille, let's get you back to my place. We'll look for some of your relatives and get you home."

Camille nodded. Moses pressed the green button in the middle of the shed and said, "Revert." The sofa, television, rugs, and kitchenette all disappeared.

"You should have left that for the next person," Camille admonished.

"I like to see what people create when they first get here before they realize how unlimited they are. One guy made an incredibly realistic sex doll. It wasn't fun coming in on that." Moses shuddered as they left the shed and started down the hill.

"It could make a sex doll, but it couldn't make me a strawberry rhubarb pie when I asked for it?" Camille was getting winded walking down the slope, trying to keep up with Moses. Then, she realized she didn't have a physical body so she couldn't get winded. She held her breath to see if she could go without breathing, which she could, but the concentration it took to focus on her breathing caused her to stumble down the decline.

"Careful there, careful," Moses said. "This digital body will do whatever you want, but you still have to control it."

"Like getting on a manual bicycle after you haven't ridden one in years," she said. "I know how to move, but it's like I forgot, just a little."

"No, it's more like riding a bicycle on the moon. All of the parts are here, but the environment is different," Moses responded. "Take a wrong turn and you'll be tangled up, floating away."

Moses seemed both morbid and wise, and Camille liked him immediately.

"About your pie," Moses went on, "the Node has a bit of a personality – some quirks, you know. It's not as good with organic type items like food, and sometimes you have to be very specific. You might have asked for a certain brand of strawberry pie, and had it made for you."

"I ordered a wrist RAP, but it doesn't work right." Camille held up her wrist.

"What is it supposed to do? May I?" Moses gently lifted Camille's arm and examined the RAP. "Who were you trying to communicate with?"

"No one. My real one outside the Net did a bunch of stuff besides video and holo-chatting. I was trying to check my Node Point account to see if the stuff I ordered in the shed cost me any points."

Moses did not respond; he was looking ahead, seemingly lost in thought.

Camille ignored his reverie. "You want to know something weird? I tried to watch the news, and it played my last memory of the news." They reached the bottom of the hill and Camille was able to walk and talk with greater ease.

"That's because this whole place is made up of memory. Well, memory and imagination. We're nothing but bits of advanced computer code writing other bits of simpler computer code. Once you jack your pad into the system, you can play the news and television shows created by Node residents – entertainment that's much more amazing than anything you'd ever see while living."

"What about Node Points? How is that calculated?" Camille asked.

"I'll let you handle that with your family, once I get you to them. For now, enjoy the scenery, it's my version of heaven."

Camille and Moses walked on for about an hour through exquisite scenery. The pastoral moor gave way to a few sparse orchards of fruit and beech trees. A path appeared, starting as thin grass and evolving into a dirt and pebble lane.

"What about your horse?" Camille asked dreamily.

"It wasn't my horse, it was just a wild horse. I may or may not see it again," he answered casually. "You can see my house – just there – " Moses pointed to a large, blue and white gabled house that appeared about a quarter of a mile up the path.

"It's nice," Camille said.

"So, this part of the Node is in a territory called the Summerlands – a land of eternal summer. It borders on another territory called Elysium, very close to the shed where you landed. There are ten main Node territories and hundreds, and potentially thousands of sub territories. This is all information that you would have learned had you come through a Node Gate and gone to orientation," Moses explained. "Those gates connect centers designed to help people transition from living to dead. They help you find your loved ones and choose what territory you might want to live in."

"What happens to me? I came in the wrong way."

"The same thing that happens to everyone else; you go through a gate and find your family. The gates correspond to entry points in the Node so major city centers have sprung up around famous gates – none bigger than New Zeta City, which corresponds to the Zeta gates. However, smaller city gates led to less grand entry points and even smaller gates led to towns, or sometimes nothing. My shed wasn't always there, there used to be nothing until I noticed that people kept on showing up there and wandering around, so I set up the shed to keep them from wandering and until I could get up to there to show them the way out."

"That was pretty nice of you," Camille noted as they neared Moses's home, which was much bigger, grayer, and even more gothic than it had seemed from a distance. It had a wrap-around porch complete with deck chairs, tables, and a long wooden bench. Camille climbed the steps to the porch and waited at the threshold of Moses's screen door.

"Who do I need to get ahold of for you?" he asked. "Who has come here before you? Family? Close friends?"

Camille thought of her body lying comatose on an Elworthy hospital bed. She thought of the hacker with her damn head hole. She knew what she was supposed to do, but somewhere along the line, perhaps when her mind transcended matter, the hacker had become less important. She pushed all thoughts of Toy and her mission from her mind.

"My brother is in here. His name is Santos."

24
CAMILLE

Moses gave Camille a few books and pamphlets about the Node so she could read while she waited for him to contact Santos. He also offered her a glass of lemonade and some chocolate chip cookies, which she readily accepted.

"Lemonade number 72 and chocolate chip cookie number 12 please, make that two of each," Moses said to the air and two frosted glasses of lemonade along with plates containing two large cookies appeared on his scrubbed, wooden kitchen table.

"You didn't press a button," Camille noted.

"You don't actually have to press a button. I put that in the shed because you newbies can get confused, living people are used to doing something to get something else. Really, the Node is like a never-ending genie in a bottle."

"How much does everything cost?" Camille asked.

"As I told you before, I'd rather have you discuss Points with your family members once you're reunited. It's not my place. Eat your cookie," Moses said, and he went into the next room leaving Camille alone with her reading material. *Gee, lessons for the newly dead,* she mused as she glanced around.

Moses's kitchen was sparse, with a few cupboards, an old gas stove, and a white refrigerator so old it had rounded corners instead of being shiny metallic with angular lines. Camille thumbed through the thick pamphlets and thin books, picking up assorted facts about her temporary home. She learned that, because reality in the Node was so malleable, people who wanted the same reality gravitated toward one another. They had drifted into what made up the ten main territories and thousands of tiny sub-territories that made up the Node.

The one exception was the area around the Zeta Gate, which was technically known as "Orientation," but colloquially termed "New Zeta City." That area was full of people who were either new or broken, or just stubborn and simply refused to move on. It was like an encampment with a jumble of warring realities. There were similar encampments around smaller city gates, but none were as vast as New Zeta City. Camille knew that's where she would eventually have to start on her search for Toy.

Citizens moved between territories using gates called "docks" that allowed them to jump from place to place. There were official docks marked on maps, and then there were unregulated docks that disappeared after a short time. The territories did connect with each other and shared "soft" borders; so, if one wanted, one could walk through all the territories of the Node.

Camille thought she would most like to settle in a gun-slinging, outlaw territory called the Wild West. She was picturing herself as a corseted salon owner when Moses strode back into the kitchen.

"I found your brother, he's in Maybury," he said as he sat down opposite Camille.

Camille scrunched up her face. From what she had just read, the Maybury territory was a series of rural farm towns.

"Yea, not an especially fun territory, but let's go. I sent him a message, and he'll be waiting for you at the Maybury dock."

"Right now?" Camille asked with nervous excitement.

"Yeah," Moses said, and smiled for the first time since they'd met. "Right now."

Moses loaded Camille into a horse-drawn, covered carriage. As they traveled to the dock, Camille marveled at the extreme irony of the whole situation. She had grown up in an area limited to horse travel and hated it so much she ran away to Zeta, vowing to never come near a horse again. Now she was with a man who could travel any way he chose, and yet he chose a simple horse and carriage. At least the horses drove themselves, leaving Moses free to sit in the carriage opposite Camille.

"Why not a car?" Camille asked him, once they were settled and on their way.

"I like horses. They're old-fashioned and noble," Moses answered.

While they rode through the countryside, Camille's thoughts drifted toward the last person who took this trip with Moses.

"I've been meaning to ask you about my friend Deanna. She died in the same hospital that I died in. Did she show up in your shed?"

Moses leaned forward to study Camille's face in the dim light of the carriage. "No. But, I could look her up for you."

"No, that's alright."

They rode the rest of the way to the dock in bouncing silence. Moses's demeanor had chilled since Camille mentioned Deanna, and she wondered if he suspected the truth. *Impossible, how could anyone guess that I'm alive ... if I'm still alive.* That last thought shook her, as much as a fake body could be shaken.

The parking lot for the dock had several vehicles, including a slick sports car, a hover car, more horses, ancient motorcycles, and a floating bubble. The line to use the dock stretched out into the parking lot.

"Don't worry," Moses assured her as they queued up behind a large, bald man and his tiny brunette wife, "it'll go fast."

The man swung around and shook Moses hand vigorously. "Hello Moses, go ahead if you'd like." He gestured to the spot in front of him in line.

Moses declined.

"The wife and I are headed on a trip," the man squeezed the woman next to him, hugging her to his massive chest, "Wonderland."

"Have fun and be careful there," Moses warned cheerfully. "It's a crazy territory."

"We know!" The man's wife beamed.

The line for the dock snaked through a park. Every few minutes, people would walk away from the dock area and head toward the parking lot. Camille figured they were arrivals. The dock itself wasn't visible until they were several yards from it. It was made up of two stone archways on a platform in the middle of a field. Small computer screens with a few buttons were attached to the arm of each archway. People were stepping in through one archway and arrivals came out of the other.

As they neared the dock, Camille could feel her excitement stir. This excitement was an unusual emotion for Camille, whose normal moods were a mix of boredom, anger, and hunger. This odd feeling of excitement snuck up on her, making her heart tingle and flooding her mind with hopeful joy. Visions of her brother danced through her mind. She used this time to allow herself the hundreds of thoughts she had banished from her daily life: memories of Santos playing with his wooden cars and laughing; his funny stories and jokes, and, finally, the last time she had ever seen him. He was eating an apple and heading out the door with a smile on his face that spread all the way up to his light brown eyes.

This gave way to yet another set of thoughts that involved her presenting Santos with the millions of Points she had saved up for him as a physical representation of how sorry she was he had to die so young. She could march him away to their own private Paradise, packed with an eternity of jokes, smiles, and apples.

A little tug at her mind reminded her it wasn't quite real. She would have to leave Santos and find Toy, but she pushed that from her mind in the same way she had banished the thoughts of Santos from her mind in her daily life. There were places she could send thoughts she didn't want: she had a network of basements, caves, and burial plots in her mind.

After about a half hour of waiting, Camille climbed the platform stairs with Moses at her side. She stood in the archway, looking around.

"What now?" Camille asked before she noticed Moses programing her destination into the archway's console for her.

"Goodbye Camille," Moses said stiffly. "It was nice to meet you. I'll see you around."

"You too," Camille said distractedly, as she watched the world in front of her: Moses, the line of people coming and going from the gate, and the green expanse of Summerland all dissolved into mist.

She felt a disjointed rush, similar to the feeling when she had left her body at Elworthy. A moment later she stepped through the opposite side of another stone archway. Again, she was standing on a platform but, instead of in the middle of a park, she was in a town square.

A steady line of people fed into the archway next to her, a few groups milled around the base of the platform. Camille shielded her eyes against the sun and scanned the groups waiting for travelers to appear at the gate. There was an older couple, two men in suits, and a creature that might be described as a wolf-fairy. Then she saw a tall, dark-haired man standing with a beautiful woman and two children, a boy and a girl. The man tentatively broke from his daughter's grip and walked toward Camille.

"Camille?" the man asked.

"Santos!" she half asked, half exclaimed, before rushing toward him.

25
CAMILLE

Camille cried hard and clung to her brother. He was so big, but it was still him. Though he was tall and broad-shouldered, he had the same heart-shaped face and twinkling eyes that relentlessly danced through the back of her mind.

She cried in long, heavy, cathartic sobs that wracked her digital body. Santos cried too but in calm streams of tears.

"You're here much earlier than I expected," he said.

"Things happen. You know." Camille pulled back from him, smiling. She felt softer than she had in a long time as if all of her rough edges had been smoothed.

"Camille, this is my wife Mary Ann, and my children –"

"Children?" Camille momentarily ignored Mary Ann and looked over her niece and nephew. The little girl looked Asian, and the boy had deep, brown skin and curly, black hair. Camille wondered if they'd been ordered from the Node like a glass of lemonade in Moses's kitchen.

"Daisy and Marcus," Santos finished introducing his family.

"Are they real?"

Mary Ann looked annoyed, and Camille knew she had said something wrong.

"The Node can't make people. The closest you could get would be, like a realistic looking robot. But, you would know it wasn't real, just from talking to it. Daisy and Marcus passed over when they were very young, and we adopted them. They like to give the children to people like me, who also passed over young."

"Hello little sugars," Camille smiled and patted the children on the head in turn, "sorry I asked if you were real." She was heartened by the idea that her Node Points would be going to support her brother's family.

"They didn't tell you how it works in orientation?" Marcus asked.

"Shhh. Maybe she wasn't paying attention because she's sad that she died," Daisy offered.

"I didn't go to orientation," Camille said.

"Everyone goes to orientation, that's what they say in school," Marcus said.

"Okay kids," Santos's wife stepped in, saving Camille from further explanation. "Let's get your aunt home where she can tell us all about it."

Santos led Camille to his red and blue hover car. Camille saw that it seated four. She looked at her brother questioningly.

"Van style addition, please," Santos said to the car, and the vehicle stretched, with an electronic *whoosh* and *click,* to include another row of seats.

On the way to their home, Santo's wife and the children watched while Santos and Camille volleyed questions back and forth: *How are mom and dad?* (good, but I haven't seen them in a while) *Who took care of you when you first got to the Node?* (a lovely couple –Sandra and Diane) *What was your job before you died?* (um…acquisitions).

Santos's ranch was flat and sprawling with a yard for cats, cows, and chickens, but Camille noticed there were no horses. The ranch house itself was decorated with warm tones and rustic touches like longhorn skulls and cowboy outlaw "Wanted" posters. It was much like the home their parents were trying to build when Santos had died, and almost identical to the home they had finished just a few years ago. It was lovely and a little haunting at the same time. Santos and Camille settled into chairs in the family den while Mary Anne whisked the kids into the kitchen to give Santos and Camille some time to talk.

"How did you get the Points for all this? Did your wife have all the NPs or did your Node parents give them to you?" Camille asked once they were settled. Camille was bursting to tell him how many Points she had saved up for them. She was picturing his wide-eyed shock and then joy at the new and nearly unlimited future he'd be able to give his family.

"So … I don't want to overwhelm you," Santos hesitated, bringing his hand up to his mouth and dropping it back down to his lap, then reaching out for his sister, and repeating the process again. He finally said, "Node Points aren't real. They're just a trick the Founders set up."

Camille stared at him in silent disbelief. She thought he had to be joking. Maybe this was a joke they played on all the newly deceased. Although, it was a cruel joke and Santos didn't seem inclined to meanness.

"I'm sorry," Santos said. Camille grasped the realness of Santos revelation.

Before Camille could ask any questions, Mary Anne swept in and placed a bowl of fresh fruit on the table. Camille stared morosely at the Red Delicious apples, purple plums, and golden pears in the dark wooden dish.

"Oh dear," Mary Anne said to Santos as she shook her head. "Is it about the Points then?"

"Yes," Santos replied.

Mary Anne sat down next to Camille and put a reassuring arm around her. Camille looked closely at her for the first time and saw that she was a rare mix of earnest and self-assured.

"It's awful, but you'll forget about it soon enough. It's wonderful here; your old life will just fade away like a bad dream. Did you play her The Story?" Mary Anne asked Santos.

"No," he said, "but that's a good idea."

The Story was a holo-movie depicting the creation of the Node – not unlike the movies played for every school child. However, this story had a few added elements. It introduced and explained the reasoning behind the Point System deception. It also starred the Founders themselves instead of actors.

"The Founders thought that it would be important for them to deliver the message to us personally. It makes sense because they *are* all responsible," Mary Anne said.

"They're awful actors though," Santos added.

Camille patiently sliced and ate some apple while she watched the part of the Story she already knew. There had been a shortage of water that caused the great Water War between the states. One woman, Edith Cole, was on the verge of creating an instantaneous method of safe desalinization, but Edith's mind was slipping into oblivion, eaten up by the early onset of Alzheimer's disease.

Then they introduced the teams of engineers, scientists, and doctors who had set out to digitally repair and preserve Edith's failing brain. This group would become known as the Founders. Once they successfully digitized Edith's mind, they realized it could be done with anyone, but more than one mind in the system would cause it to close off to the outside world, ending communication between Edith and the other Founders.

The repaired and digitized Edith completed her instant desalinization project with ease, and her team began work on the Node. That was when they called in the last member of the Founders: Amos Roth. Amos was an ethicist and philosopher. While the rest of the Founders were deciding how to create the Node, Amos was pondering whether it should be created at all.

"Pause," Camille said when the hologram introduced Amos. She knew she was supposed to know what the Founders looked like, and she was never one to pay attention in school; but this small, wiry, long-haired man was burned into her recent memory.

"If you can look like anyone you want here, what's to stop someone from making themselves look like a Founder and going around scamming people?" Camille asked.

"Well, there's nothing to stop you from looking like whoever you want, and there's nothing to scam except for art and original creations, which are easy to track. Everyone has a designation though. That's how you were able to find me. Someone could make themselves look like a Founder all day long, it's not going to change their designation," Santos said.

"How do you find out a person's designation?"

"The computers on the arches that we use for travel. They record who and where everyone is. Are you ready to go with this?" Santos asked. Camille nodded, and he continued the hologram.

Shortly after Amos's induction into the Founders, the story diverged from what Camille had learned in her history classes. She had been taught the Node could hold a finite amount of data and that the data had to be allocated, and so the Founders came up with the Node Point system.

In reality, Amos had determined that, if given the option between mortal life and immortality free from pain and imbued with lavish, infinite choices, people would choose death. He devised the Node Point system as a way of keeping large numbers of people from killing themselves just to get to the Node. That was why everyone earned an annually increasing amount of points on their birthdays. The concept of earning points for positive work was Amos's own push for morality. It never seemed to occur to anyone that people would, or could, start illicitly trading the Points.

The holo-movie ended with a rotating galaxy and a deep voiceover: "The entire Node is altered, and held together, by our minds and what we create with them. But this is also true of the world beyond the Node: the world that we all came from. In this world, just like the last, we should never stop discovering, and defining, what it means to be human."

Camille's mind was swirling as much as the galaxy in the movie. This was the great secret Deanna had gone on about. No wonder she had been so terrified.

"I'm going to set you up with a room," Mary Anne said, and spoke the word "door." A door sprung open on the living room wall as a stylish oak sideboard jumped out of the way to make room. Mary Anne shut the door behind her, but Camille could hear Mary Anne's muffled voice ordering furniture for the new room.

"It's sort of a skill to change the Node," Santos said when Camille had been quiet for too long. "You can say something and it might appear, but you have to remember or picture it right, or won't come out right. You can alter your body and surrounding in the same way. You can also just think something and it will appear. People do it both ways, watch."

Santos grabbed one of the Red Delicious apples from the bowl. He held in his palm, level to Camille's eyes. As Santos focused on the apple, the base turned green and the color crept up the apple, overtaking the red until it had changed from a Red Delicious to a Granny Smith.

"Cool, right? That takes practice though," he smiled. After a few moments, he realized Camille hadn't said anything since he revealed the secret about Node Points. He added, "You had a lot of Node Points, huh?"

Camille nodded. "Millions."

"Millions? I thought you said you were in acquisitions, not a surgeon or something."

Camille looked around Santos's hotel-clean living room, desperate for something to look at to distract her from her own, spiraling thoughts. Her eyes were tearing up, but she hardly ever cried, not while alive. She wondered if something of her mind had got mixed up in the upload to the Node. Maybe she was a crier now. Maybe her digital body liked to cry.

"You were getting them for me too," Santos said with slow realization. "I'm sorry."

"It's my fault, I should have known it was a trick. Everything's a goddamn scam," Camille said bitterly, wiping away the two tears that managed to escape before she hardened up.

Santos patted her on the shoulder, and then pulled her in for a hug. His life in the Node was simple and picturesque. He would never know anything like the raw, dirty, suicidal world Camille had fought through to be by his side: the same world she would be going back to shortly.

Mary Anne opened the new door and popped her head in. "Your room is done," she said cheerfully. "I think of myself as a bit of an interior decorator," she chuckled, "so I hope you like it."

Santos rose and made an *after you* gesture, and followed Camille to the door of her room. Mary Anne had created a room that was all in black, white, and silver, with the only splash of color coming from a tall, leafy, green plant. There was a plush, white carpet, a black accent rug, and a cabinet with black-and-silver checkered cupboards. The bed was huge and soft with a black frame and piles of white and silver bedding.

"Thank you, Mary Anne, it's beautiful," Santos said, and Camille nodded.

"Add whatever you like to it, a four-poster bed, a kitchenette, a TV, whatever," Mary Anne said. "And, of course, stay as long as you want. I mean, forever even – but, you'll probably want to, you know, explore the territories."

"I'm not really good at manipulating the Node yet, Moses had me use a button." Camille stood up and headed off to her door in a dreamy fog.

"Moses who?" Santos asked with an edge of alarm.

"Oh, I died in a hospital outside of any Nets, so I landed in this field where there was just a shed," Camille said, seeing Santo's mounting confusion. "I'm kind of glitch," she explained. "Moses is the guy who found me and brought me to you."

"Do you stay outside of the Nets very often?" Santos asked.

"Just the once."

26
CAMILLE

Camille tried to furnish her new room in Santos' ranch by thinking of an item and ordering it out loud, but she found she had to imagine things exactly as she wanted them and focus fully in the item or it came out wrong. She tried to order a down comforter but ended up with a wooden frame full of a massive pile of feathers.

She opened the door and called to Santos, "How do I make this go away?"

"Imagine that it's not there," Santos hollered back.

Finally, after several hours of trial and error, Camille had added a sitting area that was complete with a holographic television, as well as a bathroom with a whirlpool tub.

"You know, you don't have to use the toilet ever here if you don't want to," Santos said when Camille showed him her handy work.

"I know, I haven't used one since I got here. It just appeared when I tried to add a bathroom. It wasn't worth the effort to try and make it go away," Camille explained.

Once her room was set up, Santos showed her how to connect her television and wrist RAP to the InterNode. She was able to watch movies and television shows created and broadcast by the Node residents. Some of the programs were stranger and more marvelous than anything Camille had ever seen while among the living because they were made by intensely creative people who had no restrictions on resources or time. The resulting productions were vast in scope and rich in content.

There was one show about a woman who traveled the universe, searching for the cure to her unique condition, a disorder that caused her to randomly change form into anything from a duck to a cactus. Many of the movies were abstract. She saw one that was nothing but whorls of color, thumping, and the occasional sound of rushing water.

Camille became quite engrossed in a vampire drama set in an erotically lush underworld, where the sky seemed at perpetual twilight and everything was draped in black velvet. She was drawn to all aspects of the show, the blood red and jet black clothes, the sexy, melodramatic bloodlust, and she was entranced by a building central to the show's plot, an ornate medieval church called the Cathedral of Light, which was used to cleanse vampires of their wickedness. Camille noticed the same set of numbers periodically flashed across the bottom of the screen and she asked Santos about it.

"That's a reality show." He put the word 'reality' in finger quotes. "It's recorded in a place called Nightshade and those numbers are coordinates for the Nightshade dock. You could go live there if you like, but you won't get any airtime. You'd have to be way over the top."

"Nightshade might be a cool place to visit," Camille said. "I need to learn how to use the docks."

"It's kind of complicated, and there are a lot of rules because we *do* have criminals you know, and their access is restricted. Plus, there are so many destinations."

"Criminals? How?"

"Crimes against other people, assault, forcibly changing the environment. People don't automatically turn nice just because they've died."

Camille thought of all the slimy bastards she had guided into the afterlife. "I'm sure," she said.

"There's an ongoing, sort-of class for people who've just died. It teaches you how to use the docks and takes you around to the major places. You might want to do that."

"Yeah, okay," Camille said hopefully.

Still, she spent that first night sleepless at Santos's ranch, which wasn't a big deal because no one needed to sleep in the Node. She didn't need to eat either, or even wash up, because if people were dirty, they could just imagine the dirt away.

But people often made themselves sleep and eat. Some even imagined themselves to be sick, just for something to fret over. For all that they could create, most people just re-created being alive with all its glorious tedium. It turned out, many of the dead had spent their mortal life clawing their way to more of the same.

Camille used her new access to the Node's version of the Internet to look up Moses. She wondered why he hadn't told her he was a Founder, or if he wasn't Amos, why was he trying so hard to look like the Founder? She thought that perhaps he figured she was stupid for not recognizing him right away. She certainly felt stupid.

Moses didn't run any television shows, but he did write books and essays. Camille scanned through his writings, which were mostly about the philosophical nature of the Node. A week ago, she would have found his writings tedious. Now, she thought they were fascinating. One of Moses's passages, from an essay on the dual nature of living death, struck her as extremely potent:

> We are not who we were when we were alive. We are not even the same creature or species. We are digital representations of our minds at the moment of death. Is the representation authentic? How can you tell? You can't. Neither can you tell if you are learning or progressing as a person. We are programs. Nothing more. Forget poetic dreams of ghosts in machines. We are the machine. We donated our souls to it.

He's wrong. Camille thought. Deanna was proof the digital mind was the same, and it could learn and progress. Her mind had passed into and out of the Node intact and as a single stream of consciousness, just like Camille's would in several days. Camille wished that she could tell Moses he was wrong. *Maybe on my way out of here, I'll stop by and see him.*

•   •   •   •   •

Camille decided to take the "newly dead" classes Santos had suggested, partly to keep up appearances and partly out of curiosity. Santos walked her to the town dock, and they took the time to talk more. Between Santos's family duties and Camille's obsession with Node media, they did not often get a chance to talk alone.

"Can I ask you a strange question?" Santos asked.

"Yeah."

"I don't know how I died. When you come to the Node as a child, they take the memory from you."

"I didn't know they could do that." Camille began to doubt her own memory. What if she *wasn't* being kept alive by machines in an off-Net asylum?

"If it's too much for you, you don't have to tell me," Santos said. He had misread her deep thought as hesitation.

"No, it's okay." She paused for a moment, searching her memory, then continued, "You were killed by one of mom and dad's horses. She kicked your head. We had a bushel of apples and you wanted to feed them the bruised ones. You were too young to feed them, but I did it at your age. I didn't think …"

Camille let out a quick sob that took her by surprise. She disliked the weepy nature of her digital self, and she felt wounded by her recollections.

Many subcultures are tuned into the needs and whims of their children. The children of these cultures are born to piles of soft toys lovingly placed by parents who've read scores of child-rearing books. Their childhoods are filled with activities chosen to provide a balance between entertainment and education – day trips to amusement parks and vacations to historic sites.

Then there are children, like Camille and Santos, who are born into an adult world. These children are no less, and perhaps more, cherished than children from a child's world. Their toys are beloved heirlooms freed from neighbors' dusty attics. When passed in the street, everyone knows the child's name because she is the only ones for miles. Yet, the same child may sit ignored for hours while her parents conduct business.

Sigma Net was the newest Net in the world at the time when Camille's parents moved there. It was created to ease some of the overcrowding under the other Nets and was a sprawling, wild territory almost no one had inhabited for over fifty years. The first people who moved there were pioneers, and like many pioneers, their bravery was repaid by vast wealth.

Sigma did not have the complex railways system of the other Nets, and the ancient roads were overgrown and often unpassable, even by motorbike. Camille's parents had brought horses to help them get around. Horses bred by Camille's family are still the main mode of transportation under the Sigma Net.

Camille was the first baby ever born in what would eventually become Sigma's bucolic capital city of Prioria, but at the time, and for most of her childhood, Prioria was just a convergence of a few streets in the middle of nowhere. Her home was a farmhouse and livery on the outskirts of town. Childhood toys for her were few and far between and had to be shipped in special to the town's general store. There was no schoolhouse, so she attended school on a computer, overseen by a digital teaching aid. She spent most days alone, playing in worlds she fashioned in her imagination.

Prioria had a scattering of other children by the time Camille's brother, Santos, was born, but still not enough to build a school or a proper toy store. Camille was nearly a teenager when Santos was born, so he was like a doll to her, a new and special treasure.

When he died, his reverb haunted the livery for weeks, spilling troughs and banging on walls. The farmworkers, and eventually even Camille's parents, had to abandon the building, but Camille stayed. She would sit on hay bales and speak softly to her brother's ghost, telling his favorite stories and singing sweet songs. Every evening, as the sun set, singing and talking, Camille would walk the three and a half miles to the nearest Node Gate, hoping to lead him into his eternal resting place. But she would wake up every morning for weeks to find that Santos's ghost had remained in the barn, as troublesome and obstinate as ever.

Then, one morning, months into her vigil, his ghost was gone.

Unlike some of the older, wealthy families, Camille's was not in the practice of siphoning off the family's excess Node Points to children. Santos died with about two thousand Node Points – one for each day of his little life. Camille imagined her baby brother, dead and alone, without the means to comfort himself.

In the Node User's Guide, the Founders wrote that a team of loving volunteers would care for dead children, aging them up as the years went by if the children chose to age. But Camille worried about how her brother would survive with so few Node Points. She imagined a desolate orphan begging in the streets. Her worry gave way to obsession, and her obsession is why she was now walking beside Santos, on her way to the Node orientation class. But Camille told Santos none of this. She just thought it and cried some more.

After a long break, Camille composed herself and changed the subject. "The names of so many of the territories sound like they look the same – Summerlands, where I started out, here in Maybury, and Elysium – all rolling fields and loose woodlands like in summertime," Camille noted, gesturing around to the light-flooded forest they were currently stepping through.

"I guess a lot of people have the same idea of heaven, but that's not quite true. The Summerlands are all the same, but there are parts of Maybury that are desert – even tropical – because Maybury doesn't describe the location; it describes the idea of small towns and close-knit communities. And Elysium is a set of islands and granted, many of them look like this, but Elysium is where many of the supernatural settle – the angels, the mermaids, satyrs and the like."

"Why didn't you choose anything like that?" Camille asked, "Why are you just … normal? Living in a place that's so much like the one where we grew up."

"Well, I didn't grow up," he said and his voice broke a little.

"Sorry," Camille said quickly.

"I didn't mean it like that. I didn't grow up there … I was adopted by my Node parents who lived on the edges of New Zeta. I gravitated here, once I was old enough to start a life of my own."

"Your life is so much more … wholesome than mine," Camille said sadly and halfway to herself.

"Well, that can change now. The Node is a new beginning for a lot of people."

Camille was so appreciative of Santos' consistent refusal to ask questions about her life that it was easy to forget she wasn't a permanent resident of the Node.

Santos took her expressive silence to mean something different. "I mean, you don't have to be wholesome, trust me, there's a whole lot of unwholesomeness that goes on here too."

Camille laughed. Their conversation became less and less cumbersome as they chatted, and when they reached the dock, Santos sent Camille off to her "newly dead" lessons with a bright smile and a wave.

Camille arrived at a dock in the heart of New Zeta City. The dock was on a raised stone platform, much different from the small wooden one she'd departed from. She was overlooking a small park with a few patches of grass and two weak trees. Around the dock and the park, the city bustled with hundreds, maybe thousands of people, on foot and in all manner of vehicles.

Camille's gaze darted around, and she felt apprehensive and lost until she was approached by a woman whose bright purple tee-shirt marked her as a guide.

"Are you here for the classes?" she asked. She was a middle-aged woman with shoulder-length brown hair, and she struck Camille as the type of person who would try and talk to you in line at the market.

The guide led Camille off the platform, through the park, and across the busy street. Crossing the street was an issue because, as Camille soon found, there was no discernable traffic pattern. Everyone drove and stopped and walked whenever and however they pleased.

"What would happen if you got hit by a car?" Camille asked once they were safe across the road.

"If your avatar – you know your body – were damaged enough, which it would be if you were hit by a car, your program would reboot to the nearest load point – that dock across the street." The woman pointed to the dock on the stone platform where Camille had just materialized.

"It's like a video game," Camille marveled out loud, "a game with infinite lives."

"Yes, okay, you wouldn't be alone in that line of thought," a note of haste had entered the guide's voice, "but we're going to be late for the next class. You were one of the last to arrive this hour."

She ushered Camille into a large, warehouse-type building that was split into large rooms. The bright purple tee-shirts turned out to be designations for the instructors carrying out orientation. The purple-garbed instructors each stood under tall signs that specified their subject. Each set of a sign and an instructor pairing were ringed by different-sized crowds of newly dead.

The largest crowd was gathered around the sign that read, "Beginner Orientation" in large letters with "Movement," "Docking," and "Deadiquette," written in smaller lettering underneath. Other signs boasted tours of all the different realms of the Node. Camille noted that Wonderland and Elysium were the most popular.

"What the fuck is 'Deadiquette'?" Camille asked, looking around for her guide, but the woman had rushed out of the warehouse door to meet another straggler who had appeared at the dock across the street.

After a few moments of internal debate, and while the prospect of Wonderland was enticing, Camille eventually sauntered over to the Beginners Orientation group. The guide for this group was an elderly man with a long, gray beard and deep-etched wrinkles. His appearance surprised Camille, as he was one of the first people she had seen who had aged themselves or made themselves look unfit.

"These docks are transporters that double as security measures," the old guide explained in a rich voice that shook with age. "The Node has no jails; instead, we restrict movement throughout the Node using the dock system. If someone is restricted from an area, the dock simply will not allow that person to access that area."

A hand shot up from the crowd, and the old man nodded to indicate it was okay for the owner of the hand to ask his question, "What would someone do to make you restrict their access?"

"Mostly, we restrict movement because someone is harassing someone else. The victim files a petition to have the harasser barred from their area. If the petition is granted, the harasser will not be allowed to travel to the victim's location in the Node." The bearded professor said this in a drawling tone that suggested he had said it thousands of times before. "Are there any other questions?"

"What about the soft borders?" Camille asked, recalling Moses had said that a very determined person could walk from one end the Node to the other, but she was interrupted by someone who shouted out "Who reviews and decides on the petitions?" at the same time.

"Excellent question," the old man said, nodding at the interrupter and ignoring Camille's question. "The reviewers are made up of a group of about a hundred volunteers, who are chosen every year by the members of the last year's group. There's information if you're interested in volunteering to become a reviewer."

As Camille listened to his trembling, old man voice droning on as he instructed them on the docks' location numbering system, she found him less and less charming. The seminar reminded Camille of learning about latitude and longitude lines. *Interesting*, she thought, *but unnecessary knowledge.* Anyone could just look up public location numbers and private locations were handed out at the discretion of their inhabitants.

The class was practicing entering coordinates on a fake dock in the back of the class area when an early tour group returned from their destination. They were headed back from the Node area known as the Wild West. Many of them were dressed in cowboy hats, boots, and chaps.

A helpful young stranger stopped Camille as she backed away from the droning old man. "You didn't get your turn on the practice dock yet," he said when he noticed Camille's attempted departure.

Camille did her best to conjure up some Western clothes fast so she would match the next Wild West tour group. All she could manage was a mildly racially-insensitive sombrero, but it was just enough to allow Camille to blend in with the party well enough to receive an informational pamphlet from the Wild West tour guide.

According to the pamphlet, the Wild West realm was made up of dozens of small towns. Each had two intersecting main streets surrounded by a sprawl of about a hundred buildings. Everything was made to look authentic with horse-drawn carriages, a saloon, tumbleweeds, and dust. The buildings were made of aged plywood held together with rusty nails. Men walked around with shiny, Sheriff's badges on their puffed-out chests, saloon girls and other ladies of questionable repute spilled out of their bustier, and unfortunate outlaws hung their hands outside of the iron bars in the town's jail.

Camille loved everything about the place, and briefly considered settling down there, but she had to remind herself she wasn't dead yet.

Well, maybe when I'm here for real, she thought as she set out from the gate.

27
CAMILLE

Camille wandered around for a while, investigating the Wild West closely. She found that the pamphlet description of the location was not quite accurate. Although some of the elements of the old West were in place – the sun warmed her without beating down, and insects buzzed yet never stung – the Wild West was not the romantic place she had imagined all her life. This place was just overly dusty with lots of drunken shouting, punctuated by random bursts of pistol fire.

The digital environment of the Wild West was a lot more unstable than other areas of the Node. Walkways would change from wooden platforms to hard, muddy streets, and back again while you walked on them; a mountain on the horizon would morph into a plateau, then opening to a mine, then a snow-capped peak, on and on. Animals appeared and disappeared in a flash. Manmade structures – saloons, bathhouses, and hotels – seemed to be the only areas where the environment stayed stable. The rest was up to the whims of the inhabitants.

Camille looked around at the tour group she had gone through the dock with. No one seemed unnerved at all, so Camille figured she must have missed some key bit of information about the place.

Camille walked past the areas of the most commotion. As the crowd thinned out, the areas of chaotic flux lessened, and the Wild West theme remained the only constant. She was just about to duck into a saloon when she heard someone call her name.

"Holy crap. Don't tell me that train got you too." The voice belonged to Toy, who was standing on a platform across the dirt road. Her smooth blond hair flowed from under her dusky, brown hat.

Camille thought fast while she crossed the road to greet the woman who had recently offed herself. "Yeah," Camille lied to her, "I went over right after you and then – splat."

"Wow, I'm surprised that you were able to climb that fence at your size." Toy looked Camille up and down. "You know you *can* make yourself thinner here," she said, not unhelpfully.

A dead bitch is still a bitch, Camille thought, annoyed. "Did you come in with Wild West tour?" Camille asked, keeping her cool for the moment.

"I live here now," Toy said. "This is where my grandmother settled."

"It seems a little too exciting for an old lady."

"She's not old anymore."

They stood side by side for a moment, contemplating the strangeness of the exchange. Finally, Toy broke the silence. "Do you want to get a drink?" she asked.

"God yes."

Several minutes later, they were both belly up to a raw wood bar, grimly staring into two tumblers of whiskey.

"You can get drunk here?" Camille asked Toy, nodding at the whiskey.

"They do a good job at faking the memory of it, if that's what you want. But you don't have to drink to feel it – all you have to do is remember what it was like to be drunk and will yourself to feel it," Toy said, raising her glass.

"People must just choose to stay wasted all day forever," Camille wondered out loud.

"Some people choose to stay wasted all day when they are alive. Doesn't much change after they die," Toy answered. "On the other hand, some people choose to spend their lives exploiting others." Toy looked pointedly at Camille.

"Was that a shot at me? Because of the Confiner?"

"You killed me," Toy said tersely.

"You killed yourself –" Camille echoed Toy's tone. She wasn't going to get angry, but she was curious to see where the conversation might go. "— for nothing. Node Points are just stupid made-up shit."

"They're *not* made up. They are real enough to the people who use them and collect them. I gave my life for them. You sold your life them!" Toy's voice was strong and clear.

"How's it feel to know that you died for no reason?" Camille knew she shouldn't prod, but she went there anyway.

"How's it feel to know that you lived for no reason?" Toy shot back, looking pale and ridiculous under her Stetson hat. "You must have made a fortune in Node Points, chasing victims around and capitalizing off of their deaths!"

Toy's raised voice attracted the unwanted attention of nearby saloon patrons and Camille twitched nervously.

"Well, I didn't really 'capitalize' did I?" Camille said, lowering her voice in the hopes that Toy would do the same.

"Yes! You did!" Toy's voice rose higher in defiance of Camille's social cues. "You got money and the peace of mind that comes with knowing that your soul will be eternally happy. You won and everyone else lost! And how many more people are starving and scraping just to have a chance at a better afterlife? They will always be scraping – they will never know the truth – that we are all headed to the same place and that place is only just as good or just as bad as you care to make it." Toy pointed her finger dramatically at Camille.

Camille glanced around to see how many people had noticed Toy's tirade. Her eyes locked with a young man wearing chaps and a tan, fringed leather jacket. He was holding up a sign that read "Wild West Tours."

Camille rubbed her brow and watched the barkeep stoop and shuffle to avoid eye contact or any signal that might extend the tedious conversation Toy always insisted on repeating. He was tall and gruff, wearing clothes made out the same sepia tones that seemed to permeate everything in the Wild West.

Camille gave up and let loose when Toy continued to scowl. She stood and rounded on Toy, gesticulating with her whiskey hand so wildly her elbow hit the edge of the bar. In a terse voice, she said, "I didn't *choose* to chase you down, I got assigned to you, just like I get assigned to every other fucker hell-bent on dying. And you and your little team of self-important nobodies think you can decide for everyone else what happens to our Points. Because you think you know better. Well, fuck you!"

Toy shrank back, thinking she was about to get hit, and shielded her face while Camille continued her tirade, the thick-scented whiskey soaking over her fingers and splashing on the dirty floor. "You're not here because of me; I'm *here* because of *you* – so much more than you know."

The barkeep sidled up to them. "If you two ladies are going to brawl, you might take it outside. You can have a high noon gunfight if you'd like."

"Is he real?" Camille asked, maintaining her angry tone. "Like, is he part of the scenery or is he an actual dead person?"

"Sure as shit, I'm a person," the salty barkeep grumbled. "I think that you two should call it official."

"What's official?" Camille asked.

"No." Toy shook her head at the barkeep.

He was already removing a set of ancient pistols from a rack on the wall. He slammed them on the bar in front of Camille and Toy.

"Duel!" he shouted.

"Duel!" a few other voices echoed from around the saloon.

"Duel! Duel!" rapidly turned into a chant and it seemed like the bar was full of dozens more people than minutes before. The crowd surged, pushing Camille and Toy into the street.

"I've never shot a pistol before," Camille called to Toy.

"Me either."

"What happens if you shoot me and I die?"

"You're body rematerializes at the last gate that you went through. I'm not surprised that you didn't pay attention to orientation."

"I didn't go to orientation." Camille noticed that the group was trying to line up Camille and Toy in the street, and they were being joined by other merry-makers. "I can't risk this."

"Why not? It's a fun way to get out some of or aggression toward one and other." Toy pointed her pistol at Camille.

Camille, careful to stay out of the line of fire, pulled Toy into a nearby alley. The crowd groaned, and the barkeep said, "I'll have those guns back, then."

"If I have to pick between a duel and you shoving me around all the time, I'm going to shoot you," Toy huffed.

"Please don't shoot me," Camille said sincerely. "I'm not dead."

28
TOY

"You have to tell the world the truth when you come back," Toy said, voice agitated, almost shouting, her eyes wide.

Camille had explained everything to Toy: how her body was very much alive inside the walls of Elworthy Asylum, Dr. Winter's project, the whole thing. Toy had not taken the news well.

"I knew that would be the first thing you'd say. I already thought about it, it can't be done." Camille moved closer to her, forcing Toy further into the alley.

"Please," Toy spoke with a mixture of pleading and sarcasm.

"No, your stupid idea of saving the world is why you're standing here right now wearing a lame hat." Camille knocked Toy's flourished cowboy hat off her head. "I thought it through: people would find out that there's a way they can visit here without dying, which would cause problems. Second, the Founders had a point: people are already killing themselves to get here. Imagine what they'd do if they found out the Node is a genie who grants unlimited wishes."

Toy picked her cowboy hat up from the ground and slapped it against her thigh to shake off the grit. Having her hat knocked off seemed to have steeled her resolve. "Node Points make the world miserable," she said. "That's why they want to die. If you told the truth, life would be better for them. You'd be freeing people." Toy's face had begun to glow with a feverish animation that made Camille squirm. "Think about it," she continued. "No one would be grubbing around for NPs, everyone would be free to live a peaceful existence. Free from NPs, people would be able to pursue their own lives instead of slaving over their own deaths. Please." Toy's voice rose just as the gaggle of reveling cowfolk trouped by them, casting nervous glances at the odd tableau that played out in the alleyway: a woman close to tears and pleading, another woman who looked nonplussed, and a bored-looking horse.

"That's why I died! To free people from the system!" Toy went on, ignorant of the onlookers. "Now *you* have that chance. Don't waste it."

"That's your fight. I, very literally, do not give a flying fuck." Camille turned away from Toy and walked up the alley. She looked up and down the town's main street. "People are still gathering for high noon. Are they still expecting us to gunfight, or will there be another duel?"

"It's always high noon, they do it like seven times a day," Toy grumbled, but she followed Camille onto the street where a crowd gathered around two men dressed in full Old Western garb, down to the wide, silver buckles on their belts and spurs on their heels. One had a bolo tie. Camille and Toy joined a clump of people watching from the sun-shaded area under a general store awning.

The cowboys turned their backs to each other, and the crowd hushed. The men walked in measured paces away from each other.

Toy whispered something about a duty to humanity and Camille told her, firmly, to give it a rest.

The men stopped walking away and turned to face each other. Their right hands hovered over their hip-holstered guns. Across the road, a woman in a tight corset fainted. Camille chuckled, and a more sensibly-dressed woman near her leaned in and said, with no uncertain glee, "She does that every other time."

Both cowboys pulled and pointed their guns at the same time. A gunshot blasted through the air, but Camille was not sure whose gun it came from until the man in the bolo tie fell onto the dusty road, blood blooming like a red flower on his chest. Four men appeared with a stretcher made from two planks with linen hung between, but the body disappeared before they could reach it.

Camille used the confusion after the duel to attempt to escape, but Toy followed Camille down the wide main boulevard, past the people crowding back into the saloons, past the bathhouse and the livery. They wound back into the overgrown and wild area on the edges, where the dimension broke apart and there didn't seem to be any rules.

"If you come back to life and don't tell people about Node Points, then you are pure evil," Toy continued as a small dust storm full of glitter and fishes twisted past them.

"I bet you were fun to hang around with when you were alive," Camille grumbled, not looking at her.

Camille spotted a Node Gate in another wide alley. The area around it had been altered since she left, but one of the guides stayed nearby. He was leaning on his tall, purple guide sign instead of holding it aloft. Camille approached him, and, to her surprise, Toy hung back.

"Had enough?" the guide asked with false worry and a smirk.

Camille nodded. She had to ignore the impulse to turn around and look at where Toy had gone.

"This whole horse and pony show isn't for everyone." The guide tried to urge a smile from Camille, but she would not play along. "Alright, where are you going?" he asked at last.

"Maybury," Camille said flatly, after giving and craning her neck around. Toy had deserted the street.

"Right well you have to do it yourself. You're supposed to learn."

The guide led Camille up to the Wild West's dock and watched over her while she input Maybury's coordinate.

"Good," he said when she used the correct input.

"Are you coming back tomorrow? I'm guiding Antiquity. It's a little like this place, but not so corny and weird."

It took a moment for her to comprehend what he was saying. "Maybe," she said before rushing through the dock and back into the world of Maybury. Within moments, she took a deep breath of the Maybury air, which was fresher and much moister than the air in the Wild West. She could taste the trees. She wondered if she was breathing in her own memory of country air, or if someone else's recollection had infringed on her inhalations. She began to dwell on the act of breathing, and she began to wonder why her digital body still hung on to this remnant of life.

She purposefully held her breath. She waited for the natural heaviness and dizziness that came with refusing to respire, but none of it happened. The freedom to choose not to breathe struck her. She decided to stop breathing and wander around the landscape instead of heading directly to Santos's home.

Maybury was suburban, on the edge of rural, with homes close enough to walk to your neighbor, but far enough so that you didn't have to see them. Camille thought of her childhood home in Prioria, with everything overgrown and sprawling. She would rather be in a city, living in cubes stacked on cubes, the air full of congestion and sweat.

There was an inch of Zen here though. In walking down dirt lanes arched with trees and listening to birds babble, Camille realized she hadn't taken a breath for miles. She circled back to the town square so she could find her way to Santos.

Thankfully, not all of the houses looked the same, and she was able to locate Santo's stretched ranch, made even longer and uneven by the addition of Camille's rooms. She walked into the ranch feeling calm and in control.

All of that fell apart when she saw Toy, still in her cowgirl outfit with its ridiculous plumed hat, sitting upright on the sofa next to Santos. Ever the gracious hostess, Mary Anne had laid out a spread of teacakes and lemonade.

"I've just been chatting with your friend." Santos looked at Camille with amused suspicion. "She says you two were hit by the same train in Zeta, which is weird because you said you were in a hospital outside of the Net."

Toy turned to Camille, took a bite of teacake, and said casually, "Are you going to tell him? Because I will if you don't."

29
MOSES

The brown horse crested the hill at a full gallop and then slowed to a trot. Eventually, he paused to take in his surroundings. He munched on some grass and thought a few horse thoughts about the flavor of the grass and quality of the air. He also realized, with some resignation, it was time to think human thoughts again. Over the next hill was a little hut, so he struck out in that direction. The closer he came to the shack, the more human his thoughts became, until, at last, he was back in human form, a thin man with dewy features and long black hair, who was preoccupied with self-reflection and worry.

Moses trudged the rest of the way to his farmhouse, muttering to himself and neurotically running his fingers through his hair. Once he got there, he went into the kitchen and sat down at the long, wooden table. He got up again and set his old-fashioned, black, hook-and-dial telephone on the table in front of himself.

"Screen," he said, and a floating screen appeared before him, bathing him in its teal glow. "Please list the names of all of the Founders who are willing and able receive contact from me," Moses said to the screen.

A short list of three names appeared in white on the screen. Moses studied them for a few seconds. "Chalk," he called, and a piece of chalk appeared next to his hand. He picked it up and began to copy the names from the screen directly onto the surface of the wooden table. He waved at the screen, and it disappeared.

Moses sat staring at the list of names. He used the chalk to draw a line through two of the names, leaving just one: *Anita*.

Moses held the chalk over the name as if he were going to cross it off as well, but he changed his mind and wrote *contingency* next to her name.

He left the kitchen and went downstairs to the basement. He looked around at the bookshelves, worktable, and load-bearing pillars as if it were the first time he had ever seen them. He ran his fingers through his hair some more and then paused.

"Three metal clamps, on chains," he said, "two wrist-sized and one waist sized." He thought for another few moments, "large waist sized," he added.

Two shiny metal clamps materialized on his work table, their jagged clasps open like an angry shark's maws. He slid one clamp around his wrist. "Seal," he said, and the clamp sealed around the zigzag pattern. It was smooth as if there had never been an opening. His hand was stuck tight, and the heavy metal chain trailed down his arm and onto the floor.

He concentrated for a moment, and his hand slipped through the clamp, which clattered to the floor.

"Screen," he said, after surveying the clamp. Another teal screen appeared before him.

"Call Anita Hasan," he said.

A woman appeared on the screen. She was sharply dressed and had shoulder-length, styled red hair. Her hands were folded over a mahogany desk.

"Moses," she said this in a cold tone, neither surprised nor welcoming.

"Anita, you could sit anywhere in the universe, and you're still sitting at your desk," Moses observed.

"Yes, well you seem to be in some sort of dungeon," Anita retorted crisply, "and us bureaucrats like our desks. It's a nice big separation from ourselves and the masses." Her lip curled in something that might have been an attempt at a smile.

"Anita, how do I contain someone who doesn't want to be contained? In the Node I mean," Moses asked, his voice betraying uncertainty.

"You don't," she replied, her lips pursed harder than usual. "You let them out, and I deal with them later. I'm sure that you're familiar with the arrangement since you set it up yourself."

"I'd like to keep her for a little while."

Anita's brow furrowed. "What are you up to? Since when do you go around jailing the Node broachers?"

"I'll tell you when and if you need to know." It was Moses's turn to exude cold indifference.

"I always need to know," she said.

There was a long silence.

"I'll work it out for myself." Moses reached toward his screen.

"I'll tell you," Anita said. "You'll need to use a firewall to code in your materials. Contain her like a virus."

"Yes, go on," Moses said eagerly. "That's exactly what I need."

30
CAMILLE

Santos was the genial sort of person who would take just about any piece of news fairly well. He took the idea that his sister was not truly dead in stride. The idea that he'd seen her, and would be able to see her again whenever she decided to die for real, soothed some of the shock. Of course, he wondered how many living interlopers were wandering around the Node. When Camille assured him, as far as she knew, there were no others, he began to harp on her about the mercenary work that had landed her in the Node. He accurately surmised her work had been on his behalf, because how else would a young lady from a respectable family end up on the dark fringes of society?

"She wouldn't have been bounty hunting if it weren't for Node Points. She was trying to give you a good afterlife," Toy wheedled from the edges of the tense conversation between the siblings.

"And if you weren't pushing your agenda than she wouldn't be here, risking her life," Santos shot back, clearly not having any of what Toy had to say. Before this, Camille couldn't have imagined the docile man her brother had become acting angrily, but his stern and quiet anger seethed. She almost felt sorry for Toy, who was dumb enough to keep going.

"I came here to convince her to tell the truth about the System when she goes back to being alive. We're all in this together now."

Santos prowled around his cozy den. This was the first time Camille saw any family resemblance between herself and her brother, who normally held the same sort of well-rounded, small-town composure her parents had used to help found Prioria.

"We are not in anything together," Santos growled.

Toy ignored Santos. "Don't you want to save everyone else from being a slave to Node Points?" she asked.

"Stop it," Camille said at the same time that Santos said, "Enough!"

Santos calmed himself and continued, "Obviously, the Node system works, the Founders knew what they were doing, and we should just leave it alone," Santos said coldly. "And I think you should leave us alone too."

Toy shook her head as if she could not believe anyone would dare defend the Node System in her presence. Before she could speak, Santos went on while Camille silently enjoyed her brother's rampage.

"If you keep this up I'll file a petition to keep you out of Maybury." Santos spoke in stern, fatherly tones. "You'll be forced to leave us alone."

"If you do that, I'll tell. I'll report that she's not dead." Toy got up and walked toward the door.

"Who are you going to tell?" Santos laughed and scooted her out, shutting the door behind her.

Then he turned to Camille. "I'm glad that you're not dead. I was expecting to see Mom and Dad here before you." His smile loosened the knots that had been tying Camille's stomach and threatening her throat.

"What do you think about the things Toy said, really?" she asked her brother. "What do you think I should do when I get back?" Camille felt their roles had been reversed and that now Santos was the older, wiser sibling, instead of her.

"Just what I said. Do nothing. I trust the Founders," he said automatically, as if it was a rote memory.

Camille wondered if she felt the same. She had never thought too much about the System, besides how to game it. The fact that there might not even have to be a System at all had loomed over her since Santos had told her the truth about Node Points. The thought of a world without Points lurked in the periphery of her mind, but she still couldn't quite grasp the totality of the idea.

Camille spent much of the rest of her stay in the Node either in her room watching unbound creations on Node television or with her family, and found she enjoyed basking in the simple warmth of domesticity and children, which had always been abstract ideas to her.

She got to know her niece and nephew. Marcus liked wizards and hoped to live in Wonderland someday. Daisy liked boats and writing long stories, which she would read to you quietly if you coaxed her with the promise of a trip to the seashore. In the evenings, Camille played poker with Santos and Mary Anne and ribbed them both on their lack of skills.

She had no desire to explore the Node's realms any further, aside from quick trips at the children's request. She was still rattled by her encounter with Toy. She also felt like an interloper. All of these places, with their endless marvels, were not for her – not yet. Someday, she would have an eternity to traipse through them; but, she thought, today was for Santos.

Camille became adept at using her newly-honed Node powers to idly recreate odd items from her life; her favorite doll from when she was a child, a quick potato peeler she had seen advertised on television and had always wanted; then she had to conjure up potatoes and a wastebasket to hold the peels. One afternoon, she created a black and red cocktail dress she had coveted but never bought because she would never have a place to wear it.

Once the dress was on, she stood in front of her vanity mirror and forced her body thinner, using what she had learned in the "Body Alterations" section of the Node's user's manual.

What would my life have been like if I looked like this? she thought, smoothing out the dress along her newly-meager curves. *Would it have been easier or harder?*

"No thank you," she said, and puffed herself back out to her normal size. She turned on her television and sat down on her bed, still in the dress, to watch her favorite vampire program. The red and black dress made her feel at one with the dark and bloody goings-on. She made herself a heaping plate of nachos, complete with warm creamy yellow cheese sauce from a can, sour cream, and fiery jalapeno peppers.

Without warning, the room dissolved around her. She was overcome by the same feeling she had when she stepped through one of the Node Gates. A moment later, she found herself standing in the meadow she first appeared in when Dr. Winter put her under, complete with Moses's moor and shack nearby.

They must be reviving me already, she thought sadly. She must have lost track of time, and she consoled herself with the knowledge that Santos now knew the truth and would understand why she had disappeared. She also felt some sadness for his children, who would not understand why, and then she held a moment of silence for her perfect plate of nachos, left forever uneaten.

The fluffy black and red skirt of her dress rustled in the calm, false breeze while she stood waiting to wake up in an Elworthy Asylum room, possibly with

Cody hanging over her like a nervous, sweaty mobile.

Standing alone in that grassy expanse, Camille felt like the only person in the Node, as if this place had been created just for her to stand in. Then, Camille saw a figure in the distance walking over the hills, toward her, at a fast pace. The wind picked up, and as he moved closer, Camille recognized Moses, with his long, black hair whipping behind him.

She had barely thought of him her entire stay in Node, but now she remembered. Moses has made himself look like, or possibly even was, Amos, the philosopher Founder. Amos was the odd creative among a room of scientific minds. The Node Points were his fault. The whole world lived in his fever dream.

"Hello there," Moses said, when he was within shouting distance. "Are we going to a party?"

"No," Camille said self-consciously smoothing the cocktail dress, "I just wanted to wear something fancy that I wouldn't wear at home."

"Are you almost ready to go home then?" He closed the space between them. "Or, at least, back to the hospital that's hosting your body?"

"What?" She recognized that now would have been the time when she would have felt a sinking feeling in the pit of her stomach, if she had a stomach; she might have lost her nachos, but she used her Node powers to block any effects of fear.

Before she could fully react, a huge, metal clamp on the end of a thick chain sprung from Moses's wrist and clasped tightly around her waist.

"What the fuck?" Camille yelped. If she had been alive, the clamp would have caused her massive pain, but all she felt was tingle and a tug as Moses, ignoring her question, started to drag her down the hill, toward his house.

"I was just doing my job," Camille explained. "I was trying to save this place," she justified.

"You were trying to save yourself," he said, his voice calm and steady as if he were not using a clamp and chain to drag a woman down a hill.

He pulled her fast, but she was able to keep on her feet so he couldn't drag her across the ground. She tried to make herself thinner, to slip through the clamp, but the clamp shrunk as well, staying tight around her waist. She tried to pry the clamp off her, but it wouldn't budge. Running her hands along it, she found the clamp and chain were coated with a small, raised pattern of lines and circles.

After several minutes of struggle, they reached Moses's house across the moor. Once inviting, the farmhouse now seemed dark and ominous, like someplace where pigs were butchered and secrets kept in attic trunks. Dragging Camille behind him like a particularly cumbersome, reluctant pig for the slaughter, Moses walked up the steps, onto the porch, and started through the front door.

Camille braced herself against the porch railing's newel post and hugged it tightly. Moses gave another tug and pulled Camille through the post as if it was not even there. She turned and looked behind her to see the post perfectly intact. *Of course*, she thought, *he knows every trick in the book. He wrote it.* She was convinced that this Amos look alike must truly be Amos the Founder.

He force-marched her through his house and down his basement stairs, but Camille had given up her futile struggle by then.

The farmhouse basement was supported by wooden columns that ran from the floor to the ceiling. Stretched between two of the columns was a long, polished mahogany table. The walls were lined with bookshelves. The most prominent item, by far, was a four-foot-long, thick log suspended from the ceiling by the same sort of chains and clamps that held Camille. Another set of wrist-sized clamps hung from it.

"No," Camille shouted, realizing what the ceiling clamps were for moments before Moses reached for them. Ignoring her, he used his superhuman strength to hang Camille from the log, by her arms. The other clamp stayed tight around her waist and Moses wrapped the end of that chain around a nearby column.

His furious work complete, Moses stood back and looked over the helpless woman.

"Why?" Camille asked tiredly. "Are you a torture weirdo? Because I can get you off. It's not a big deal. You don't have to do all this."

"This isn't about sex. You are a mystery. I need to solve you."

Camille noticed regret etched into his tight lips, and lines of his face, and there was guilt in his eyes.

Camille resigned herself, realizing there was no way out besides, possibly, cooperating with Moses.

"Fine," she said, "solve away."

Moses began his story to his captive audience: "There was once a man who died, came here, and spent eternity as a wine glass."

31
CODY

Normally, Camille radiated raw strengths and nonchalance, tempered by an undercurrent of a basic respect for humanity. She was warm, almost hot, delivering rough language with disarming delicacy. None of this life or complexity shone through her cold still body, lying prone and terrifyingly still on the hospital bed.

Cody, holding tight to his briefcase and slightly ruffled from a hasty journey, stared at Dr. Winter's lips, watching as he formed the words, "We can't wake her."

"I don't believe you. What else have you tried? She likes food, put a chocolate near her mouth."

Winter said, "For a dream comes with much business and a fool's voice with many words."

"I don't understand what you mean."

"Why would you doubt the words of a physician? I'm quite an expert at knowing when people are sleeping and can't be awakened."

I don't want it to be my fault, Cody thought, but wouldn't say out loud. Cody had left the Asylum two days after Camille went into the Node. When he left, she seemed safe and stable. During the car ride home, he had received a call from Anita.

"You might have bothered to tell me that you put the woman in the Node," Anita said crisply. Cody had his briefcase laptop balanced on his knees in the back of the car.

"What woman?" Cody stiffened and adjusted his collar in case it was crooked. It was not crooked.

"You are a poor liar. I suggest you end your attempt at dishonesty."

"Was sending her in not the next step?" Cody choked a little when he asked.

"Knowing who you are, I'll assume that you tried to tell me what you were doing and couldn't because of the technical communications issues we've been having; which is not an excuse. I can't see you acting against your better judgment, faulty as it might be."

"Am I fired?"

"No, you'll keep your job. But, you have cost the young woman her life."

Cody blinked rapidly at his screen.

"Your next assignment is again in Zeta." Anita reached forward and tapped the screen indicating that she was sending him files. "A gentleman receiving manipulated Node Points. Don't bother about him, but see if you can find the original point of manipulation."

Six long days later, Cody was in the company of Tanner Varner, who, he was positive, was responsible for the manipulated Points. However, he wasn't quite sure what to do with him. The revelation that the Node Law Enforcement Bureau killed people was new to him, and he was guilt-stricken over his hand in Camille's impending death. He did not want more blood on his hands.

Mr. Varner was a short, olive-colored man with elaborate facial hair and a twitchy smile. He vacillated between oily and earnest, and Cody was hard-pressed to guess the true nature of the man. Mr. Varner claimed to be able, for five thousand dollars, to turn a half-dozen Node Points into several hundred thousand Node Points.

"How?" Cody asked him. They were sitting in Tanner's narrow living room, and Cody was watching Tanner scratch his basset hound's head.

"What I do, I do for love – not to sound cliché," Tanner spoke quickly and deeply, too deep, it seemed to Cody, for his small frame. "I want everyone to have security. It's my warm hug to the world."

"You're a lovely man," Cody conceded. "Is it hardware? A machine? Software?"

"It shouldn't matter how, as long as you get your Points. And, they *are* real Points," Tanner said.

Cody's wrist RAP lit up with a call from Dr. Winter. He declined it.

"If you've got better things to do." Tanner nodded toward Cody's buzzing RAP.

"No. I'd like your bank code, please. I'll send you over the five thousand dollars."

Cody's wrist lit up again, this time accompanied by an emergency tone. An urgent message pushed through and displayed in a small hologram floating above his forearm:

You are listed as Camille's emergency contact.

●   ●   ●   ●   ●

Upon arriving at Elworthy Asylum, Cody paced around outside, hesitating to go in. He was relieved to find out he was called as next of kin – not because Camille was dead, but because she was comatose – comatose is salvageable, dead is not.

There could be two reasons why Camille was in a coma. Either Anita had covertly come after her while Camille lay prone in her bed, or Winter's experiment had failed. Cody hoped the latter; his culpability was a hard pill to swallow. But Cody wasn't ready to see a lifeless Camille, so he met Winter in his small, cluttered office.

"We have some decisions to make," Dr. Winter said, placing a reassuring hand on Cody's. Winter's pale fingers contrasted with Cody's dark skin. "Go see her tonight though. I'd like you to get together with the team tomorrow morning."

Cody nodded and then allowed a young nurse with an angel tattoo on his forearm to lead him to his lodging. The room was in a wing that served as housing for the Elworthy staff. It could have been a hotel room if it were not for the vestiges of oxygen hookups and nurse call buttons that still hung on the wall. As soon as the nurse closed the door, Cody flipped on his wrist RAP. "Call Remington Nakamoto," he ordered.

Remy answered, but didn't turn on his video chat, so Cody heard his voice without seeing Remy.

"Hello Mr. Nakamoto, this is Cody Priolo. Camille is having what you may call … some issues."

"Ugh," Remy moaned. "What did they do to her up in that place? Did they put her in? Is she in the Node?"

"She's … I don't know," Cody stammered.

"Oh, you know. You know way more than you let on," Remy said, his agitation mounting.

"Well, they can't … they can't seem to wake her up. He sent her into the Node alive, and now he says he can't bring her back." Cody trembled, he wasn't prepared to say the words.

"Do you mean she's *dead*?" Remy sounded on the edge of despair.

"No, she not dead – yet. Not technically. There's a meeting tomorrow about what to do about her. She's listed me as her family contact. However, you're listed as well and I don't think I should make these decisions by myself." Cody hesitated.

"Decisions," Remy scoffed.

"Will you come?"

"Yeah, I'll come."

"Do you know Elworthy Asylum?"

Remy sighed, "like the back of my hand."

32
MOSES

"He tried living in all of the realms, and hated every one of them," Moses went on. He looked Camille in the eyes, avoiding looking at her bound arms and waist. "With all the endless possibilities that this life offers, he wanted nothing. He came to me, as a Founder and as a philosopher – "

"I knew you were Amos pretending to be Moses," Camille interrupted.

"—and asked me what he could do to relieve his pain." Moses nodded in acknowledgment and then continued, "We have the ability to shut off here. Just turn off our programs. That's true death unless you ask someone to turn you back on. I turned him off for twenty years. When I turned him back on, to him, it as if not even a second passed. He found it unsatisfying.

"He didn't want to be off; he wanted to be nothing. I advised him to try being an object. For a while, he lived as a tree, which he liked well enough, but he wanted to be around people. He tried to be a chair, which was fairly unpleasant, so he settled on being a wine glass. He's spent all of the past decade intoxicated by his favorite drink and being pressed to ladies' lips, and never having to make a single choice for himself," Moses finished.

"I don't see what this has to do with my being chained up in your basement," Camille sulked.

"First, this is an elegant story with a moral; and second, it demonstrates that anybody can be anything in the Node. For instance, in the service of following you, I have been a lamp, a book, a rock, and a horse. I know what you are, why you're here. And, in service to the Node, I suppose that I can't let you leave," Moses said.

"You'd kill me?" Camille asked.

"You're already dead; we're just letting the clock wind down." Moses turned and walked up the basement stairs, leaving Camille alone.

Camille tried pulling at the chains a little more before giving up. She tried to make a television appear so she would at least have something to watch while in captivity, plus she was curious to see what was happening in Vampire world, but the chains also prevented her from manipulating the Node.

She examined the chains more closely and realized the lines and circles were ones and zeros. She surmised that the chains were made of computer code, apparently able to suppress some of the Node's functions.

Usually, if she wasn't working, she was distracted by her wrist RAP or her television. Now, she was alone with her own mind for the first time in a long time. She wondered what she would do with her life, granted she survived the current situation, now that she was no longer bound by Node Points. She could do nothing, which had been a dream of hers for quite some time. She had gained millions of dollars as a side effect of gaining millions of Node Points, and she never had to work again.

These thoughts lingered in her head as Moses came back down the cellar stairs.

"Can you give me a TV or something down here?" Camille asked before he had time to talk.

"What do you want to watch?"

"The vampires."

"Nightshade?" he asked, raising an eyebrow.

"Yeah."

"I might let you watch it." He paused and looked Camille over. "But I am not trying to torture you."

"Then these chains are a little misleading." Camille shook her arms, letting the chains rattle.

"Well, I'm not sure what to do with you, and I can't let you go," Moses said. "They're trying to pull you back, and I can't let that happen, yet."

"I promise I won't tell anyone about the fake Node Points, okay?" Camille said, "I just want to be alive again."

"What? And forsake all of this?" Moses swept his hands around the room. "You have had a taste of the Node's freedom and wonders, yet you still want to be alive?"

"Yes."

"I think that's how most people here are," Moses said with a sigh. "They enjoy the Node, but they would rather be alive if they could," he concluded.

Moses sat down on the table across from Camille. He folded his hands and looked at her earnestly. "I wasn't supposed to be a Founder, you know. I don't know what they teach you in school now, but the Founders were Engineers and Scientists; they weren't even trying to make the Node or anything of the sort."

"They were trying to find a low energy way to take salt out of water, to end the Water Wars," Camille said, recalling her recent orientation video as well as her decades-old schooling.

"And Edith Cole, the head engineer, and most brilliant mind of the century, was rapidly deteriorating from Alzheimer's disease. They took – not me, I wasn't there yet – an experimental technology designed to help preserve memories and used it on Edith. The only problem was, she couldn't enter it alive. In order to use the program to restore her mind, she had to die. The Founders had to figure out a way to refine her consciousness and keep her mind alive. She volunteered to die. Some might argue that she was too far gone to make that decision, but the Founders were not ones for morals over progress.

"Edith became the first resident of the Node and its first suicide victim. She was able to continue her work from within a digital node, obviously, the low energy instant desalinization that she invented from inside the Node is still in use in the world today, but Edith was bored and alone.

"So the other Founders devised a program to give her a digital body, and then a furnished house, and finally they developed a way to allow her to control the program from inside. They realized that most everyone would want the same treatment: the assurance of eternal life instead of the wobbly promises of religion. That's when they called me.

"I was no one. I was a not-even-tenured philosophy professor, but I was cousins with Wade Maillia, one of the scientists on the desalinization project. He called me in to discuss the moral implications of the Node technology. The Water War was over, so the team was free to focus on the Node.

"They had concluded that some people, perhaps many people, would kill themselves to get into the Node, either to see loved ones or to experience the Node's endless, mutable cosmos. I thought, 'what keeps religious people from killing themselves to get to heaven?' aside from the thought that heaven may not exist, because we know for sure that the Node does. The concept of hell is what keeps people from committing suicide. But we couldn't, in good conscience, create a real Hell, so we created the next best thing – a fear of eternal poverty."

"That's awful," Camille said, giving Moses a very dark look. "You purposely created Hell on earth."

"Is it? You may be poor in life, but if you are a good person, you will reap eternal rewards. Sound familiar?"

Camille took a moment to compose herself. "That's not a good excuse – "

"Not an excuse. A reason!" Moses interrupted with a sudden rage. He banged his fist on the table, signaling his anger was not directed at Camille, but at everything. "We took the historical tenets of religion and made them *real*, for the same reason that religion has always existed; to *guide* people to what's *right*. To keep people happy and safe!" he finished and leaned back in his chair, rubbing his forehead.

"Well, I can tell you that it's not working," Camille growled. "People are confused and angry. A *ton* of people kill themselves to get here the second they've got what they think are enough Points – do you know what my job was before I got here?" Camille's anger rose to meet Moses's.

"A bounty hunter of some sort, I gathered."

"Not just a bounty hunter. I was an angel of death. My job was to find people who were about to kill themselves and keep them alive long enough to pay off debts or see their loved ones." Camille did some mental math. "But mostly it was to pay off debts."

Moses was shocked. "I knew it was a problem, but I didn't realize- why would you do that? Was it a lot of money?"

"It was Node Points, Moses. They were paying me in Points, and money. So much that I am rich in both. And, I was doing it so that I could get enough Points for my brother, who died when he was eleven. I spent my whole life picturing him poor and alone, and he was fine," Camille said, "more than fine."

"I'm sorry, we knew that children would be a problem, but when is a child's death not a problem?" Moses said sadly.

"You're defending yourself and the Node Points. But you don't believe what you're saying. You know it's wrong," she accused. "I read your book." Camille quoted: "Forget poetic dreams of ghosts in machines. We are the machine. We donated our souls to it."

Moses paused for a long time. "Of course we were wrong. Every person that walks through those Node gates and finds out the truth knows that we were wrong."

"Does that mean that you're going to let me go, alive?" she asked.

"Maybe. I'll won't let you go until you agree – *truly* agree – that the Node system is wrong. I've trapped you here—" he said with an exasperated sigh, "—not to kill you, but to convince you to help me."

"And?" Camille rattled her chains impatiently. "What am I supposed to do for you?"

"They won't let me have a voice. You have to be my agent out there in the world. The real world. The *living* world."

Camille didn't say anything. She kind of wished she hadn't heard him.

"Please," he said. His hands shaking, Moses reached up and undid the clamp around Camille's waist.

33
REMY

Remington arrived at Elworthy just as dawn broke. He knew the hospital well, even in the blue light of early morning. He had engineered half of the technology in the Asylum and consulted on the other half. Elworthy was his prodigal offspring, but he was the one returning with his hands empty and his eyes full of tears.

A tall, perpetually-bothered woman named Doctor Margret Crespo met him in the large conference room. She was doing quite a bit of hand-wringing.

"We weren't expecting you this morning, Mr. Nakamoto."

"Or any morning, I'm sure." He sipped his cafeteria coffee.

"What brings you?" Dr. Margret asked crisply.

"It seems you've killed a friend of mine. Or nearly killed her."

"I don't follow."

"Camille. The woman that your Doctor Frankenstein has hooked up to our monstrosity."

"Well, I had no idea; but I can't discuss her case with you. Only the next of kin." Dr. Margret shuffled some papers on the table in a half-hearted effort to look less idle.

"I'm listed on her contact sheet," Remy said.

"So you are. But Mr. Priolo is listed as well," Dr. Margret said.

"He's a prick. Have you met him?" Remy scoffed.

"I have not, but I'm expecting Mr. Priolo and Doctor Winter shortly."

"Actually, you two will probably get along." Remy rolled his eyes.

If the conference room had had windows, the mid-morning sun would have been beating into them by the time Cody and Dr. Winter arrived. Dr. Margret was long gone and had to be called back in, which took several more minutes.

"Deanna Grant is missing," Dr. Winter explained their tardiness.

"You know that she's probably dead, right?" Remy asked.

"Of course, that's a possibility," Winter said.

"Did Deanna know that possibility? Did she know before or after you hooked her up to that machine?"

Dr. Margret swept into the room and saved Winter from answering Remy.

"Why don't we all sit down?" Dr. Margret said, when she noticed she had walked in on a tense scene. Remy, Cody, Dr. Winter, and Dr. Margret sat around the conference table giving each other grim stares.

"We have three possible courses of action," Dr. Winter announced. "We can do nothing, and hope that Camille wakes up on her own."

"That may not be feasible," Dr. Margret cleared her throat, "monetarily. To keep her body alive indefinitely."

Remy glared at her. "Camille is a very wealthy woman, from an even wealthier family. Don't worry, you'll get your money."

Margret shut down, folding her arms and biting her cheek.

"Yes," Winter continued, "Let's assume that money is not an issue. The second option is to try and shock her awake, to pull her more forcefully from the Node."

"Why haven't you tried that already?" Cody interjected nervously.

"It's an aggressive technique. It could harm her. We needed permission from the next of kin." Winter gestured toward Cody and Remy huffed.

"Actually, Mr. Nakamoto, we could use your help on this item as well." Dr. Margret turned to Remy. "Is there any possibility that shocking her back to life could somehow damage the Node?"

Remy thought hard before answering, "Normally reverbs enter through large, established gates. When you set up a small gate, like the one here, it's like a backdoor. If she can get in and out through a back door, we have to assume that other things can too."

"What does that mean?"

"There is a whole universe in there, several universes, in fact, but it's still just a computer program, susceptible to viruses, bugs, irregularities …"

"I'm less concerned about the health of the Node. The Founders are in there, supporting it from the inside out," Cody said, turning to Dr. Winter. "What's the difference between this aggressive shock technique and what you've tried already?"

"Well, we've only tried to lift her out of her false death by gradually reducing the dose of medicine we used to put her under. The more aggressive treatment requires a shot of a medical concoction that includes adrenaline and amphetamines. A quick, potent boost to her system," Dr. Winter said, miming giving a violent injection.

"What's the third option?" Cody asked.

"Does he have to say it?" Remy shook his head.

"Well, the third option is to disconnect her and let her die," Dr. Margret said.

"Obviously, that's not an option." Remy stood up and stalked out of the room, signaling the end of the conversation.

Cody followed at Remy's heels. "You might have mentioned that you worked here. Or did you just design the Node entry equipment?" Cody whispered.

"You knew I worked here. I'm not giving you any more information. I'm not stupid." Remy tried to push past the much taller man.

"They seem to think that you're pretty clever around here," Cody said.

"In the land of the blind, the one-eyed man is king."

"Well," Cody said, "my eyes are wide open."

"You enjoy that." Remy maneuvered around him and headed down the hall toward where Camille's body lay, while the rest of her was in the Node.

34
CAMILLE

Doctor Winter hovered over the unconscious Camille. He held a large, fluid-filled needle poised to inject into her heart. Cody stood in the back corner of the room and fidgeted with his wrist RAP while Remy stared out the window and tried his best to look stoic.

"No!" Camille opened her eyes and shouted. "Don't do it! I'm awake! I'm awake! Holy Hell!" She pushed Dr. Winter's hand away.

Startled, Winter put down the needle and tried to regain his composure. He was not expecting Camille to awaken on her own. "Oh, well, good …" he said, trying to look casual.

"What were you doing? Trying to put me to sleep like someone's old cat?" She glared accusingly at Remy and Cody.

"We were unable to wake you," Winter explained. "We were going to give you a special shot to shock your system."

"A 'special shot'?" Camille looked the needle up and down. "What would happen if … oh, never mind." Camille struggled up to a sitting position and swung her legs over the edge of the bed. "Get me out of here," she said as she prepared to stand.

"No! Your leg muscles – " Dr. Winter started, but it was too late. Camille attempted to stand and crumpled to the floor, "—have atrophied," he finished. Remy rushed to her and Cody started to make his way out of the room.

"Fucking lame," Camille mumbled, as Winter and Remy hauled her back into the hospital bed.

"Plus, you have a catheter in," Dr. Winter added.

"How long will I be stuck in bed?"

"A few days – a week or so – while we work on some physical therapy with you. You should bounce back fairly quickly. You're a strong girl." Winter patted her legs. "We have a lot of Elworthy Asylum LLC-mandated questions for you, but we'll leave you to your, um, friends for now." Dr. Winter nodded curtly toward Cody and Remy before leaving.

"I'm so sorry," Cody said in a rush. He seemed about to burst.

"Yeah, well, I'm fine," Camille said, "or I will be fine in a few weeks. You heard him. I'm a strong girl."

"The mission," Cody said before Remy could get a word out, "what happened with the hacker?"

"Absolutely nothing," Camille said, as if she had been accused of something, then she relaxed. She took a moment to form her response. "She didn't do it. Or it didn't work. The Node was fine."

"So, you went through all of this for no reason. You almost died for nothing!" Remy said angrily.

"No," Camille soothed. "I saw my brother, and he was good. He was great," she said smiling, her words catching in her throat and her eyes welling with happy tears. "I mean, wonderful."

"You must be tired," Remy said, not accustomed to this new, emotional Camille. "You need some rest."

"I don't feel like I ever want to rest again," Camille smiled again. Remy and Cody exchanged uneasy glances.

"Are you sure they put the right one back in there?" Remy pointed to Camille's head.

Camille laughed. "Yeah, it's me," she said, chuckling, and then she added, "Maybe you two losers should leave me alone for a while. Go find something else to do."

They left with promises to bring back food. Camille sat in her bed, touching her own arms and running her fingers along the bedspread. *Is this place any different from the Node?* She asked herself. *Doesn't it feel almost the same?*

She wondered if she was more alive, or less alive, than she had been in the Node. The Node had looked so vibrant; now that she was back, the colors of reality seemed muted. She sat by herself for a long while, just touching and feeling everything within her reach. She tried to will something into existence in front of her, but nothing appeared. Everything was so ordinary.

Then, she started to cry in earnest. Everything she had seen and felt for most of her life came pouring out of her at once, out of her eyes and spilling down onto her hospital gown. *This is what was missing in the Node*, she realized. For the entire time she was in the Node, there was never *this* acute of a feeling, or a rush of emotion. She wondered if the Node's lack of these feelings – or sincerity of feeling – was due to a download error. Perhaps the threat of death, and the limits to the time that we are alive, gives an imperceptible urgency to our feelings making every moment more precious and more painful by death's inevitability.

Camille cried for about half an hour, both from relief and sadness, until there was a light knock on the door and Remy entered, carrying her wrist RAP and a plate of mashed potatoes.

"I bet you missed this," he said, purposefully ignoring her red nose and tear streaks when he handed her the wrist RAP. He set the potatoes on her bedside tray.

"Actually, I had one in the Node," Camille said, surprised she had already forgotten the constant pressure on her wrist, even for the brief time since she had awakened. When she slipped the RAP back on, it felt like she was reattaching a missing limb.

"Cool," Remy smiled. "How many NPs was that?"

"How many NPs was what," she asked, distractedly buying herself some time to think up a lie.

"The wrist RAP inside the Node." Remy shook his head and laughed.

Camille considered for a minute, "not a lot," she said.

Remy watched her. "You've been wearing your wrist RAP for almost a whole minute, and you haven't checked your Node Points. Don't you want to see how much you spent while you were in there?"

"I guess it doesn't matter so much anymore, after being in there. You know?"

"I don't know. Enlighten me." Remy curled his hand under his chin.

Camille was saved from explaining by the worrisome intrusion of Cody and Winter, who edged their way into her room. Winter was looking as if he were about to vomit.

"We were able to contact Deanna's family; no one has heard from her in over six days."

"They won't find her alive," Camille said, with as much authority as she could muster through a mouth of mashed potatoes. She hadn't realized how starved she was for real food.

"How do you know that?" Cody momentarily forgot himself.

"The same way you do, slick," Camille said, after she swallowed her potatoes. "I got someone on the inside."

"In where?" Remy asked.

Camille ignored him. "Or should I say, Agent Slick,"

Cody stood cold and still.

"What do you mean, 'Agent'?" Remy said, looking back and forth from Camille to Cody. "There's no Service anymore."

"There's the Node Taskforce though." Camille started eating again.

"I *knew* that he wasn't from the National Bounty Hunters! And you named him your next of kin?" Remy exploded.

"Oh, come on Remy. Are your little baby feelings hurt? This was Cody's project. He was around. I didn't think anything was going to happen to me."

Winter, realizing that he'd been forgotten, felt the need to make an announcement. "I'm leaving," he said.

"I'd like an update on any news of Deanna," Cody said to Winter.

"I meant I'm leaving Elworthy altogether. I'm returning the control of the equipment to you, Mr. Nakamoto, for the time being. Ms. Eko, I've arranged for you to begin physical therapy immediately. Your muscles will be very weak."

"Um, thanks?" Camille mumbled.

Remy folded his arms and waited for Winter to leave. As soon as Winter shut the door behind him, Remy demanded Camille check her Node Points.

"Why?" Camille asked him.

"Because I've seen you watch a guy kill himself by stabbing a pen in his eye, and then check your Node Point balance. I've seen you check it the first thing in the morning and the last thing at night. You watch over that account like it was your child," Remy said.

"Fucking fine," Camille said. She logged into her account and waved her wrist at Remy. Seven figures blurred as she waved. "Are you happy?"

"No," he said. "You still haven't told me the truth."

Camille paused, "I will," she said, "but not yet."

A tall, brawny, blonde man entered the room without knocking. His hospital-issued name tag labeled him "Anton." He narrowed his eyes at Remy and Cody. "She's got her physical therapy," Anton said.

35
REMY

Remy stood outside a small rear service door. He watched as four men and one woman loaded up a massive white trailer with equipment from Elworthy. They were filling it with his inventions: the machines that twice breached the wall between the living and the dead. It was all his now. Proprietary rights had been signed back over.

He had no idea what he was going to do with it. He was hoping Camille's revelations about what happened to her in the Node would bring some insight when he noticed Cody loping down the path toward him.

"You can't have any of it," Remy shouted, "because you are the worst spy that anyone has ever heard of!"

This did not deter Cody. When he was within speaking distance, Cody said, "Deanna has been killed."

"That's not a surprise."

"They found her murdered," he sucked in his cheeks, "about 45 miles outside of the nearest Netted Zone. She's gone. Really gone."

"That *is* shocking." Remy's smugness vanished. He was noticeably shaken. "They're trying to punish us. Send a message."

"We have to warn Winter and anyone else who knows about Elworthy," Cody said.

"I'm sure they already know, as they are long gone. The Asylum staff is wiping away every evidence of our existence, hence all of this." Remy swept his hand toward the equipment loading operation.

"I can't believe they killed her outside of a Net," Cody said, shaking his head.

"It's just so strange," Remy agreed. "There haven't been any other visible, tangible punishments. To kill somebody outside of a Net sends a message … and they're coming for us next."

"Well, they're coming for *you*," Cody corrected. "They think I'm on their side."

"Aren't you?"

Cody's wrist RAP buzzed. When he pressed it, a hologram of Camille's face and neck appeared over his arm.

"They went from telling me that I couldn't move for days to telling me that I have to clear out," the Camille hologram said.

Remy stuck his head in front of Cody's arm so that Camille could see him. "Lucky for you I am the reluctant owner of a metric shit ton of random medical equipment."

Cody turned the hologram so that Camille could see inside of the truck.

"Well, come get me," Camille said. "We've worn out our welcome here."

"We have something to tell you." Cody turned the hologram back to face him.

"I already know. I told you that you would find her dead. I guess I just didn't realize how dead," Camille said grimly.

Remy had the orderlies set up an area in the trailer, among the piles of Node hacking equipment, for a hospital bed. Within the hour, Camille, Remy, and Cody were speeding down the highway toward Zeta. Camille was even more wary than she would usually be when vulnerably traveling outside of any Net.

Remy calmly cataloged his equipment on a clipboard while Cody chewed his fingernails. Camille lay in a hospital bed, draped in white sheets. A bag of saline hung from trailer wall and dripped medicine into her veins. The bed was on wheels, so it rocked slightly when the cab turned, and it rolled during sharp turns.

One of these great rolls almost toppled the bed onto Cody, who was hanging on for dear life in the back of the trailer. He almost fell over backward, but still managed to use both hands to push Camille's bed back into place.

"You just missed Cody being a moron," Camille said to Remy, who failed to look up from his cataloging.

"I'm sure I did, but I'm not talking to you until you tell me why you aren't checking your Node Points." Remy crossed the back of the truck and stood close to Camille.

"I'll tell you once we're inside Zeta," she said with her voice lowered. "I'm not telling you out here."

"It's because they're not real, isn't it?" Remy said very quietly. He set his clipboard down on her bed and looked into Camille's eyes.

"Yes," she said with soft surety.

"I've always known that's the truth. I've always known that you can't buy eternal happiness. I think that's what all of this was about." Remy nodded at his equipment. "Trying to prove what I already knew."

Cody, who had been poking around one of Remy's computers, noticed Camille and Remy looking grimly at each other. "What's not real? What do you know? What are you talking about?"

"Node Point are fake. About as fake as you," Remy said. "Possibly faker," he added.

While the truth set in for Cody, Camille and Remy continued talking. The color drained out of Cody's face, turning it from olive to pale gray.

"So, who do we tell? How do we start spreading the truth?" Remy asked and then paused. "Are we going to start spreading the truth? I know that you're a fairly large supporter of minding your own business."

"I wasn't and then," Camille looked at Cody, "something changed. Someone changed my mind. Guilt and fear and grasping every goddam second for the far-off hope of getting ahead is no way to live. It's torture."

"Was it Santos who changed your mind?" Remy asked.

"No."

"Toy?"

"No," Cody jumped into the conversation, late again. "We're not telling anyone anything."

" *We*," Remy made a circle with his hands, "are just incidental for the time being," he pointed at Cody, " *you* may do whatever *you* please once this truck reaches its destination."

"I have a plan," Camille said. "I had to change it after Deanna was offed. But it's still the same basic idea."

"You can tell me after we drop him off." Remy narrowed his eyes at Cody.

"I can't tell you at all. That's part of what changed when Deanna died; but I can tell you how to help me, when it's time."

"I can't be any part of this," Cody said, partly to himself.

Camille swiveled around in her bed and addressed Cody directly for the first time, after a long, angry sigh. "You know what Cody? You were not asked to be any part of this. I don't know specifically who you work for, but I've got a pretty good idea, which means that you care whether I live or die, because I'd be dead already if you didn't. You can say that you don't want to be part of it, but you started it. You're in it. You are in the shittiest and most dangerous part of it. Here's my question for you: are you going to use your connections to help me out? Or are you going to tell on me and get me murdered in some godforsaken wasteland?"

"Neither," Cody said without hesitation. "I believe in the Founders. Even if what you've said about the Node Point System is true, I believe that the Founders have good reasons for lying to us. They know things that we don't know. They understand the world in ways that we never could, but you're in this position because of me. I did this to you, and I will keep you safe. Camille, I can protect both you and the System."

"The fuck you can" Remy yelled "Stop the truck," and punched a bunch of directions into a console. The three looked at each other warily until the brakes slowed the truck to a halt. When the doors on the back of the truck opened, they revealed a road with nothing but windy cornfields on either side. A teenage boy on horseback halted the beast to get a look at the truck that stopped abruptly. As he passed by, he craned his head around to view a strange little world in the back of the truck: stacks of computers and fancy medical equipment, a woman in a hospital bed, and two angry-looking men.

"Out," Remy ordered.

Cody looked furious but said nothing. He collected his bag and briefcase and jumped off the back of the truck to the pavement and walked away. He never looked back.

"We needed him, you know," Camille said to Remy, as the truck door slid back down.

"When you're doing the right thing, you can do without," Remy said.

"You sound like one of the Nirvana Movement nuts."

"True. Maybe that's who we are now."

"Maybe we are," Camille echoed. "I can't tell you the whole plan, but I can tell you that I'm going to need to go back into the Node."

36
CAMILLE

When Remy and Camille arrived at her apartment, a male nurse was waiting for them. Remy noted that the nurse had shoulder-length blond hair and ripped muscles that glistened in the Zeta heat has he easily carried Camille up the narrow stairs, through Camille's sterile office, and into her apartment where he had already set up a hospital bed and care center in Camille's living room.

"I didn't know that gigolos also provided medical services," Remy said wryly to Camille when the nurse left to fetch Camille's bags from the trailer.

"Anton is not a prostitute. He's a physical therapist I worked with at Elworthy. I can afford the best." Camille settled into her bed and turned on the hologram set, changing the channel until she found the local news.

"I guess I'm rich now too. Now that we don't need Node Points, I can trade all of mine for money or electric; but once people find out the truth, the Points will be worthless," Remy said.

"Well, you'd better hurry and cash in. I already traded a bunch on our way home," Camille said, while intently watching the holo-news.

"Even when you're doing the right thing, you're still a terrible person." Remy shook his head in disbelief.

"And they say, 'you can't have it all,'" Camille said, smiling.

Anton walked back into the apartment, laden with luggage, and headed toward Camille's bedroom.

"Can you cook, Anton?" Camille called after him.

"I can scramble an egg, but that's about it." Anton reemerged from the bedroom and headed toward the galley kitchen.

"Never mind then. Can you order me some food?" Camille said, looking Anton up and down. "Something meaty," she said before going back to watching the news.

"Yikes," Remy said. "I'll leave you two alone."

"Let me know when and where you have your new lab set up. Use code or something to tell me. Be safe," Camille said.

"Are you sure you need to go to go back in?" Remy searched her face. "It could kill you. We have no idea what will happen to you from attempting to go in and out a second time."

"I have to. I made a deal."

"I wish you'd tell me with who."

"Yeah, and get you dragged outside the Net and killed like Deanna. No," Camille said. "Look, I'll explain it when I can. I don't need any more pressure right now. Just set up the lab and be fucking careful."

"What are you watching the news like that for?" Remy asked, realizing that his other line of questioning was going nowhere.

"This is going to sound bad, but I'm waiting for someone to die," Camille said.

"Who?"

"I don't know yet. And if you see Cody, be nice to him."

"I'm willing to go out on a limb for you for this because I believe in getting the truth out. But being nice to Cody is too far." Remy shook his head.

"I told you before, we need him. I'm going to keep in contact with him and hope he comes through. If you see him, it means he's working for us."

"There's nothing he could do to convince me that he's working for us."

Remy started for the door, but had to side-step when Anton burst back into the room said, "I ordered a roast beef sandwich." He was rather proud of himself.

PART III: HEAT AND BONE

37
NORA

Nora didn't sit at the lunch table with Cosmo anymore. She didn't sit with Emma that much either. Sometimes she sat with Alexis, but he was often so quiet it was as if she was sitting alone.

She was sitting alone when she heard the news about the assassination of a prominent member of Nirvana. Nora hadn't thought about Nirvana since the media storm surrounding Toy's attempted hack of the Node Point system had died down. The death of another Nirvana member rekindled her thoughts of the unfairness of the System. It had weighed heavily on her ever since Alexis had taken her to the Node Point pawn shop.

That day, Nora had donated all of the Points each dying person asked for. She didn't want to take any "thank you" gifts for her Points, but the owner was paid by skimming some of the cash from the gifts, so he insisted she accept. Nora went back to college $30,000 richer, her pockets heavy with jewelry and the deed to a house that sat, rotting, outside the Omega net. The man who owned the house was especially grateful and thanked Nora profusely for accepting a home outside a netted territory. In total, her donations set her back a few thousand Node Points.

"You can live there all your life," said the man who traded his home. "I did. Just come into the Net and rent a room if you feel sick. The Net is close enough to walk to if you are hurt bad enough that you might die."

Nora nodded and fought back tears. That day changed her. She was not sure what to do with her new feelings of regret and responsibility. She knew Alexis belonged to some organizations dedicated to protesting the Node System. She considered asking to join Alexis's cause, but she was not at the point of open protest to the system that had protected her for her whole life.

But now the school year was over anyway and it was time to go back home.

Protests could wait until next semester. The news of the assassinated Nirvana member made Nora sure she had made the right choice about staying uninvolved; that was until she saw Alexis's face.

Alexis entered the cafeteria, glanced at the news, and looked at Nora like she was singularly responsible for the death of the protester. He continued to glare as he sat down across from her at the lunch table. He set down his tray but did not eat. He just watched and waited.

"What did I do?" Nora asked.

"It's what you didn't do."

"So, I'm supposed to die in the streets like that guy?" Nora asked.

"At least he stood for something. You know it's wrong, but you don't speak out. You don't care."

"I care." Nora was offended.

"You care in the sense that you feel a certain way, but I need you to physically care. I need you to do the verb care; the action care," Alexis said.

"I could go to the pawn more often. Donate more Points," Nora offered.

"That's just using the System to exploit people," Alexis said.

"Do you want me to go to protests so that I can get followed home and shot in the street?" Nora looked up at the cafeteria holo-screens. They were playing a loop of the Nirvana protester crumpling to the ground after being shot.

"Yes," Alexis said simply.

"So, you do want me to die?" Nora said.

"Yes, to the first part. I want you to protest. Your Points, your money, your status could mean something to the movement."

"I don't know," Nora said. "I'm going home for the summer. Maybe in the fall."

Alexis stood up and left Nora blankly staring at a projection featuring Eli Trent, the fallen Nirvana member, and his newsworthy corpse.

38
CODY

Cody stepped off the moving sidewalk and walked up to a flower vendor, reaching out to buy a bouquet that had caught his eye. The blooms were pink and white with small, spear-shaped petals spiraling out from the center in perfectly symmetrical rounds.

"Lovely choice," the vendor said, reaching out a plump, flower-filled fist. Cody bent over the counter to write out a note on the attached card and felt a cool breeze brush his neck.

When he finished with the card, he thanked the flower cart owner and briefly considered hopping back on the moving sidewalk before changing his mind and deciding to take the slow route home. The regular, motionless, sidewalk was straight and clean. It had little mica chips embedded in it, so it sparkled in the sunlight. Nearby buildings hummed and hovered four feet off the ground, seemingly anchored by stairs and thick railings. Overhead, larger buildings and skyscrapers floated like clouds, occasionally extending tubes to the ground and scooping up pedestrians. Everything was clean and cool in Delta City, and the air smelled like fresh laundry.

Cody climbed a set of steps to reach an oddly-decorated building painted in swirls of star-specked dark blue and bright pink. Once he was through the door, he walked past rows of display cases filled with artisan chocolates. His feet kept time to the sound of the *chocolatier* snapping huge bars of tempered chocolate in the craft house's open kitchen.

He acted like he was perusing, but he knew what he was going to get: a large bag of milk chocolate-covered marshmallows and a small bar of raspberry dark chocolate. His order was the same every time, and he always got the same curt nod from the cashier in response to his purchase.

After the *chocolatier*, Cody decided to forgo both the moving and the stationary sidewalks and take a car the rest of the way home. He gingerly set the flowers and candies down on the car seat, activated his wrist RAP, and started talking.

"I am quite glad to be home. I can wear a suit without sweating, and it only rains when scheduled." He spent several moments looking out of the car window. "My contact with the Zeta mercenaries has proved to be very fruitful. I have discovered the source of both the Reverberation Viewing Technology and one of the systems that was used to trespass into the Node while alive. They are all coming from the same source, and this engineer is also responsible for many of the street Confiners that have been confiscated within Zeta." He paused for a moment, then continued, "However, I am reluctant to name the engineer, because he is a known confederate of my contact and I fear that revealing him will reveal my contact as well, and you have already stated your desire to terminate. I had once seen the Elworthy Asylum experiments as my crowning achievement to be carved into the annals of history – or, at the very least, a feather in my cap lofty enough to impress you; but it has ended in murder."

Cody's car was stuck in traffic. Noting his surroundings, he considered it might be faster if he walked home, but no, he was working. He pressed the record button on his wrist again.

"I feel that my time at Founder United is coming to an end. I will spend the upcoming months looking for my replacement. In the meantime, my mercenary contact is becoming increasingly lawless. I will not give this person over to you, but you can give me the tools that I need to defend the system. This transmission includes images and design specifications for the Elworthy machine," Cody said. Finally, he entered a few more commands into his RAP and then rode the rest of the way in silence.

It was a starlit early evening when the car stopped in front of a medium-sized, boxy, stucco house just outside the densest part of Delta. Two long balconies hung off the back and front, keeping the house from being a perfect square.

When Cody entered his foyer, the house sprung to life. Lights went on, and screens appeared inside walls asking him if he needed anything. A knee-high chrome robot with extendable arms and an oblong head whisked his luggage away before he could even set it down. Cody kept the chocolate and flowers clutched to his chest.

"Daddy?" a young woman's voice called from the hallway.

"Oh honey," Cody brightened, "I thought you'd be back from school, but it didn't look like you were home. All the lights were out."

"I was in my room, conserving energy." Nora hugged Cody around the shoulders. Like her father, the young woman was tall and skinny with olive skin. Her pink tracksuit complimented her skin tone. "Just like how you constantly tell me."

For the first time in weeks, Cody smiled a genuine smile, relaxed and real. He handed his daughter the flowers and chocolate.

"You don't have to bring this home every time," she said. "But thank you." Nora's round, brown eyes darted toward his wrist. "You got a wrist RAP Daddy?" she laughed. "You're not that cool."

"No," he said, "I'm not." Cody unclipped the RAP and slid it off his wrist. "If you want it, it's all yours."

Nora lit up and reached for the RAP. "Are you kidding? I do want it! Nobody I know can afford one."

Cody did not drop the communicator into her outstretched hands, instead, he pulled it toward himself. "I have to delete some sensitive information from it first."

"That's fine." Nora shrugged. "I was about to watch a movie, do you want to watch it with me – oohh does the RAP have a *holoprojector*? We can watch it on that. Hold on, I'll get the download code and some snacks."

Nora disappeared down the hallway while Cody settled into his favorite square, firm, beige sofa.

Several hours later, with his daughter sleeping and his stomach soured from salty snacks and sweets, Cody sat down at his desk, opened his briefcase laptop and slid the Elworthy drive into the computer.

He quietly choked out the words, "Call Anita."

"I'm sorry, sir" the communication center on his end table responded, "I did not understand your last request."

"Call Anita," he said louder and surer.

Anita's flawless head and shoulders appeared on the screen, as always, she was behind her featureless desk.

"I have the complete Elworthy report," Cody said, while plugging the drive into his briefcase laptop.

39
JORDIE

There were not many churches left in the world, and they were even rarer in Zeta City, where every man was a god and the whole world was immortal. Still, sometimes occasions like marriage or death were marked with the same old church traditions. It was the death of Nirvana rebel Eli Trent and the celebration of his life that brought folks to a dilapidated church on a warm, gray morning. Holograms and pictures of Eli, with his short, dark hair and thick-framed, square glasses, filled the room.

Eli's friend Jordie listened to Eli's cousin eulogize "Family Eli" as the Eli who climbed trees and encouraged others to follow. The cousin talked about Beach Eli, floating on the waves in the water outside their seaside summer home.

Jordie thought about *her* Eli. Eli retrieving her, bloody and crying, from her boyfriend Angel's house, telling her this was the last time he'd do so, but it wasn't.

She thought about that stupid rainy winter when she and Eli had spent every moment together because they were unemployed and unambitious.

She remembered getting high with Eli and talking about how to fix broken things: what was broken inside their bodies, what was broken inside their home, and what society had broken out there in the world.

She remembered talking with Eli about his new apartment, the one he'd die in front of, seventy-four minutes later.

Many families didn't have funeral services anymore because death was assuredly not "goodbye," but Eli's family was wealthy so they could afford an expensive "see you soon" sendoff, and this church, as musty as it was, was one of the nicest in Zeta.

Eli's plump cousin finished her perky-yet-somber eulogy, and the funeral director asked if anyone else has anything to share. Eli's grandfather came up and reminisced about them fishing in the Gulf, long before the saltwater reclamation projects had overrun the area. His sister simply walked up to the lectern, started crying, and walked back down without saying anything.

Jordie figured it was her turn. The congregation watched politely as Jordie made her slow way up the podium. Many of his relations knew Eli had lived with a crippled woman, but few of them had met the tiny brunette in person. Most of them saw their cohabitation as a mark of good character on Eli's part, imagining that he was being charitable to a disabled friend. Jordie felt their pity and resented it. Once she arrived at the podium, she waited patiently for the microphone to be lowered enough for it to reach her in her hover chair, but it did not go that low. The funeral director coughed nervously, stood, and bent it closer, toward Jordie's mouth.

"I'm Jordan," she began, surprised to hear her voice amplified in the sanctuary. "I was friends with Eli," she continued. "He was one of the few people who acted like I wasn't disabled. To him, my chair wasn't something to be overcome, it was just a part of me. He didn't pity, or even respect me for it. He saw me how I see me, just as a whole, regular person.

"A lot of people are saying a death like his was meant to be, but I think that's garbage. It was wrong. They say I will see him again in the Node, but I don't know about all of that. I believe there are a million, billion universes and each one is just slightly different from the next. We're just unlucky enough to be in the universe Eli died in. In most universes, he went out for coffee, or rented a different apartment, or did whatever he did to keep himself away from that sidewalk last Tuesday. In most universes, Eli is fine, and he's going on and working and getting older and having a half-dozen babies, or however many it was that he said he wanted. It was a lot." The audience politely chuckled, Jordie continued.

"But there are plenty of universes out there where Eli never existed, was never born. So, at least we lived in one that he lived in. At least we're lucky enough to…" Jordie's voice cracked, and she lost her resolve, "have known him. Thank you." Jordie looked down as she and her chair hovered off the platform. She tried her best to not catch anyone's gaze on her way down.

Most people avoided Jordie after the funeral. They were part of Eli's family and Jordie was not a member of that tribe, but Eli's crying younger sister, Hazel, did approach her.

"You're right, Jordan," she said. "Eli dying is garbage."

Jordie was surprised that, out of everything she had said, Hazel had chosen "garbage" as her focus.

"My name is Jordie, actually. I mean – it is Jordan, Jordan is the name I was born with, but everyone calls me Jordie because it was Jo for Jordan and then it turned to Jordie, which I like better."

Jordie realized she too had chosen the wrong thing to focus on.

"Okay, so I'll call you Jordie," Hazel said, not unkindly, but overwhelmed.

"Thanks," Jordie said, and then she slunk away to find a place where there wasn't a group of Eli's family.

She did not recognize the next person who approached her: a thick woman with short dark hair who wore jean shorts, a tank top, and carried a large rust-colored backpack. She leaned heavily on a wooden cane.

"Nice speech," she said to Jordie.

"I'm sorry, who are you?" Jordie asked.

"I'm sorry, I was going to call you from my business line – it's all professional, and it plays, like, an ad for my services – sort of an introduction. It's totally slick."

Most people wouldn't have been able to follow the woman's monolog, but Jordie also had the habit of speaking her inner thoughts, so she knew mental spillage when she heard it.

"Why didn't you call me from it then?" Jordie asked.

The woman was a little stunned by Jordie's acceptance of her candor. She pushed a little further.

"My name's Camille and I didn't call you because I would have asked you to meet in my office. Eli said you and stairs don't mix."

Jordie furrowed her brow. "When did you talk to Eli?"

"Recently."

"*How* recently?"

"As in after he died."

Jordie started to back away.

"Wait now, hear me out." Camille advanced, persistent. "Have you ever heard of a device called a 'Confiner'?"

"I've heard of it, but I'm not completely sure what it does."

"It's a device that holds a person's digital consciousness in their body, after they die, so that you can talk to them before they go into the Node. I have one of those."

"Well, aren't you awful. Thank you for letting me know that you tortured my friend a little before he died." Jordie began to hover away from Camille.

"I don't just have a Confiner." Camille tapped her backpack. "I also have a machine that allows us to talk to reverbs before they pass into the Node. And Eli wants to talk to you."

"No," Jordie said. "Who the hell are you? You are *so* full of shit."

"He said that the last thing that you spoke about before he died was a missing toothbrush. Please," Camille pointed at the wide doors that led out of the church, "follow me."

She was right about the toothbrush. Jordie turned and promptly followed Camille.

Camille explained as they meandered. "I don't like approaching people like this, but I'm very short on time and Eli said he would help me, but he wanted to speak to you first."

Jordie wanted to put some distance between them and the churchyard, and especially Eli's relations, who already thought that she was strange. She didn't want them to see her speaking with this very inappropriately-dressed woman who was obviously not here for a funeral. Camille hobbled, as fast as she could, alongside Jordie's wheelchair, but she was having a hard time keeping up while relying on her cane.

"I assume you need Eli's help because he was in Nirvana," Jordie said, her chair gliding effortlessly down the sidewalk.

"Yes." Camille tried not to sound too impressed with the other woman's quick deduction. "Can you please slow down? I don't have a fancy wheelchair like you do."

Jordie slowed the pace, realizing she wasn't the only differently abled person in the conversation.

"You *do* know that he's dead because of Nirvana?" she said to Camille, who was breaking a sweat from the exertion.

"I saw it on the news. He was assassinated by an ex Fund policeman with an ax to grind."

"I'm not in Nirvana," Jordie said.

"I'm not in Nirvana either. I think digital terrorism is pointless and obnoxious; it's kind of like running in place while screaming." Camille paused in front of a roadside stand that held ice-packed crates stocked with juice. "Do you mind if I get something to drink?"

Jordie wheeled around to face her. "So, none of us are in Nirvana, but you need Eli's ghost because he is?" she demanded.

"I know. Sounds crazy, right?" Camille picked up a green bottle and scrutinized the label. "Man, this shit is expensive," she said to the vendor. To Jordie, she said, "This isn't a Nirvana thing. I need Eli because he's in Nirvana, but he's not doing the – you know," Camille mimed injecting herself in the head, "– weird stuff. Do you want some juice?"

Jordie shook her head, at a loss for words for the first time.

Camille went on, "Because I'm really rich. I could buy this whole, expensive, lame-ass fruit juice stand." The vendor looked alarmed.

Camille paid for her drink, and the women continued on their way. "I need Eli to get a message to a woman inside the Node. She's from Nirvana, he's from Nirvana, and once you're in the Node you can contact people there if you already know them from, like, life."

"How do you know that?" Jordie asked.

"You know what? This juice isn't even that good and it cost almost seven fucking credits." She turned back toward Jordie. "Look. I know that you're having a rough go of it right now. But this will only take a few hours at the most. You'll get to see your friend before he, you know, goes into the Node."

Jordie pulled her chair in front of Camille, stopping her in her tracks. "I'm not going to help you if you won't tell me the truth."

"What do you want to know?"

"How do you know how contact works in the Node?"

"Because I was in there," Camille grimaced but didn't hesitate. "tTis juice gets worse the longer you drink it. We don't have a ton of time. If Eli was going to hang around instead of going right through a Node Gate, where do you think we'd find him?"

"Didn't he tell you where he was going to be when you used the Confiner?"

"Yes, but reverbs don't think or move like us. Ideas get lost and you just kinda float around until the Node scoops you up."

"That doesn't sound right."

"No, it's not." Camille stopped walking and leaned on her cane. "I should have brought Anton," she said

"Who's Anton?" Jordie grew more agitated.

"You'd love him. But we need to think about where we'd find Eli's ghost."

"Not his new apartment. It's an unfamiliar place and, from what I learned, ghosts like familiar places," Jordie thought out loud.

"What is a familiar place, then?" Camille was losing patience.

"My house. We used to live in it together, but then he got a better job."

"Are you sure? Because we don't have a lot of time to catch him before he goes through those gates."

Jordie nodded. Camille tossed her empty juice container into the road as they caught the next trolley to the city's Westside.

Jordie lived in a green bungalow framed by low-hanging Spanish moss. It was part of a set of over a dozen homes that had once been set aside for disabled people with mobility issues. However, there were few mobility-impaired individuals left in Zeta, so many of the bungalows were now rented out to low-income families. The happy screams of unseen children playing greeted Jordie and Camille as they approached the home.

"That's a big place, just for you," Camille noted.

"They're just happy to be able to give a house to one of the people it was intended for," Jordie said.

"Why are you still alive?" Camille asked.

Jordie laughed, "People always want to ask me that, but no one ever has. Why are you?" Jordie nodded toward Camille's cane. "All of us cripples are supposed to go live a better life on the other side."

"Because I got shit to do," Camille said, "Like find your boyfriend's reverb." Camille walked into Jordie's dining room and set her backpack down on the table. She unzipped it to reveal a tangle of wires, speakers, and mainframe boxes connected to a pair of goggles. She set the goggles over her eyes put the backpack back on, and walked through Jordie's house scanning the rooms up and down.

"He's here," Camille called from one of the back rooms.

"That was his bedroom," Jordie choked back tears and followed Camille down the hallway.

Camille slid the backpack over one of the arms of Jordie's hover chair. She put the goggles over the woman's eyes.

"Here," she said, adjusting the goggles, "Do you see him?"

"Yes," Jordie gasped.

"He can hear you, but you can't hear him unless you press this." Camille held up a pair of headphones and pressed a red button. "Hold it down to hear him," she said, as she placed the headset over Jordie's ears.

Jordie looked a bit like a human-robot hybrid in her hover chair, wearing goggles and headphones with wires radiating from her head in various directions, but she was a happy hybrid, beaming as she first spied the ghost of her friend.

"I'll leave you two alone," Camille said. She was unheard.

Camille raided Jordie's kitchen and was sorely disappointed by all of the healthy foods. She remorsefully ate something called a "carob cookie" that neither looked nor tasted like a cookie.

Jordie looked stunned when she emerged from the bedroom. "He said that he loves me," she said breathlessly.

"Yeah, they usually say something like that," Camille said. "Why can't they say it when they're fucking breathing, you know?"

"Do you think that he's telling me because when I go into the Node, I won't be in this chair anymore? Do you think he only wants to love me whole?" Jordie asked, trembling.

"Probably," Camille said and Jordie looked shocked, "but you should be glad that someone loves you. Nobody's ever going to love me, whole, broken, or otherwise."

Camille entered Eli's old bedroom and donned the reverb communication equipment.

"Okay, you saw her. Can we talk now?" Camille said into the void, and then pressed the headset's red button.

40
CODY

Cody sat in a silence so total he could hear himself breathing. He could hear the sound of nothing in his ears ringing like distant bells. He sat still too; if he moved he would have heard his suit rustling against the soft chair cover. His daughter, Nora, was sleeping on the other side of the flat, but he could not hear her because her door was closed.

In one hand, he gripped his briefcase. He didn't notice how hard he was holding it. His knuckles were white. His communicator was on his other wrist, which rested across his lap and occasionally he looked down at it. He had promised to give the communicator to Nora, but it turned out he needed it once more.

A digital noise pierced the silence. It was just a blip from his wrist RAP. Cody gripped his briefcase even tighter and read the message, then he stood, suit rustling and then shoes tapping, echoing down the hallway as he left his apartment and stepped into the night.

Delta was not a night-life type of city. Windows were shuttered and shops were closed. No neon signs hummed; but the moving sidewalks were still on, whirring and clicking along like blood running through the sleeping giant's veins.

Cody's moving sidewalk deposited him downtown. Shining skyscrapers hovered several stories above the ground and squat, commercial enterprises crouched in their shadows. Cody stood beneath Delilah Incorporated, which hovered over a sleek diner, and typed into his wrist communicator:

I'm here.

Moments later, an escalator descended from the Delilah Incorporated building and bore Cody up like a spirit into heaven.

He was not sure who he was meeting, but seeing as the building had been abandoned for the evening, he figured his search would be brief. A young man in jeans, sandals, and a wildly patterned tee-shirt approached him in the cavernous lobby. The click of Cody's shoes echoed while the man's sandals failed to even muster a squeak.

Cody stretched out his hand, and the man shook it.

"Interesting choice for a meeting place, but I understand why," Cody said to the man.

"Well, I couldn't have you over to my house," the man chuckled.

"I've never met another," Cody said.

"Another what?" the man pursed his lips and shook his head.

The man pulled a knife, quick and quiet. He pulled Cody toward him with a sudden, strong grip and sliced into Cody's throat. Cody's body fell inert. And then, because he considered himself a compassionate man, the assassin swiftly injected a deadly poison into Cody's thigh. Only then did Cody's grip on his briefcase loosen.

The man in the sandals opened the briefcase and looked surprised. He tapped a small device that was clipped over his ear.

"There's no computer his briefcase," he said into the dark lobby. "There's nothing in here at all."

41
TOY

Toy had a hard time getting used to her deceased grandmother. Death had given her grandmother a youthful countenance and it had regressed her temperament. When speaking with her grandmother, Toy often had a feeling similar to one she once had as a sixteen-year-old teenager, being forced to hang out with her younger sister's fourteen-year-old friends. Not that her grandmother was acting like a teen, but Toy felt she was just on a different level – one that felt, at least to Toy, less mature.

In the Node, Toy's Nana was a busty, lusty, young woman. She was as given to fits of drunken anger as she was to all night love-making sessions with random young men. Nana didn't want to talk about anything aside from these suitors and the occasional gossip about Wild West locals, whom Toy did not know, nor care about.

One night, when Toy was watching her grandmother drink moonshine from a glass boot, as part of a bet that revolved around the loser eating a pickled pig's lips, she was overcome by a sudden wanderlust and she, in that instant, removed her cowboy hat from her pretty, blond head, set it down on the bar, waved goodbye to her grandmother, and began a walkabout that would take her to some of the Node's most popular and famous locations.

Toy soon discovered something that she never would have, or could have, known while still alive: she loved to experience new places. Her flesh had been her prison, but so had poverty. The world had so many fresh and precious locations and cultures, but the gift of travel was for the wealthy. Money was the only thing capable of moving one great distances.

In the Node, any distance could be eclipsed in the snap of a second. Toy meandered through tropical jungles and ate street food in urban ones. She laid on the beach while the incoming tide foamed around her legs and drank a latte in a 1940s Parisian café, which is where she found herself when the stranger approached her.

She had been enjoying the weather and breathing in the smoke from the thin cigarettes that all the Parisian women were smoking. The stranger was well built: sporty-looking, but he wore dark glasses and was walking toward her table. Then she faintly recognized him as a member of Nirvana who had been alive when she died.

Toy realized that this also meant that he knew who she was and what she had done, or at least tried to do. He could easily be giving a brief greeting, but Toy was on alert nonetheless.

As he got closer, Toy saw he was tan and had an aura of good health that Toy didn't think had been present when he was alive. His black hair was pulled back into a masculine ponytail, but Toy was sure his hair had been short when she saw him last. He sat down at the wrought-iron table across from Toy and didn't speak a word to her.

"I'm sorry," Toy said questioningly.

"For?" He was inspecting his fingernails in a bored sort of way.

"For being wrong about the Node. Just being so passionately wrong." Toy thought he might be an old follower, out for revenge now that he knew the truth about Points. Maybe she could cut him off with apologetic respect.

"Have you a new passion?" he asked her. Toy could not tell if he was being pretentious or inquisitive.

"I'd like people to know the truth. There's no reason to suffer and struggle," Toy said, hoping that was the right answer.

"People will find a way to suffer and struggle regardless of the truth," he said. Then he said, "Cappuccino, high foam," and a perfectly full, round cup appeared in front of him.

"I'm sorry, I recognize you, but I don't recall your name," Toy said while he sipped his drink.

"I'm Eli. We first met in the abandoned planetarium. When Nirvana was small and all of the Zeta members met there."

"Yes, I remember now. You told me that working for Node Points felt like bleeding to death without dying. I never forgot it. Your words, I mean," Toy said, genuinely.

Eli sighed, "It's taken me weeks to find you. I'd go through a gate where you were registered, search for you, and soon find that you'd gone through another gate."

"I'm on a walkabout," Toy said defensively.

"Unfortunately, it has left us very little time."

"Very little time for what?"

"Camille is reentering the Node. She needs to meet you at a very specific time, in a very specific place."

"Why? Please tell me that she didn't kill you to get you in here to tell me this."

"No," Eli said. "I was already dead when she contacted me. She has a – you know – a thing." Eli mimed tapping his wrist and putting on a helmet. "It sees and communicates with Reverbs."

"Not surprising considering she has a Confiner and can get in and out of the Node alive, apparently."

"Well because I was fading fast, I have limited information. I can't tell you why. All I know is when and where you're to meet her," Eli said, and sipped his cappuccino.

42
MOSES

Moses still slept every night. Node citizens found sleep to be an affectation shared by few. Most had forgotten about sleep entirely, but Moses had not forgotten about that blessed refuge. It was his escape – his short trip into the abyss.

Using computer code, he set himself to sleep and he set himself to feel refreshed upon waking. He methodically made himself tea upon awakening, doing it the old-fashioned way. Instead of just conjuring his tea, he boiled water and filled a tea ball with dried oolong leaves. He steeped the tea in a clear glass mug so he could watch the rich, reddish brown seep from the tea ball's pores and convert the entire cup into amber.

After he drank his tea on his sunlit porch, overlooking his gorgeous, rolling fields, he often had the impulse to hurt himself. This desire for self-injury was not a mysterious voice or fleeting strike of madness. Moses was in possession of all of his faculties, and he knew that he'd done something terribly and purposefully wrong.

He'd heard many tales of the harsh implications of his Node Point System since he'd been asked to oversee the drop point for living people attempting to infiltrate the Node. The other Founders thought he accepted this post out of diligence and duty. They didn't pay enough attention; they were just glad they didn't have to do it themselves.

In truth, Moses manned the interloper access point in order to listen to the stories of those who were reckless and brave enough to attempt to enter the Node alive. He also hoped to attain what he liked to call his "Agents" in the world of the living. The ones who were selfish and uninspired he turned over other Founders, which kept them from becoming suspicious. The clever ones he sent back out into the world with intricate plans to right all of his wrongs.

When it became apparent that his latest agent had failed, he felt like punishing himself. He had methods. Moses turned his digital body's pain receptors up. He might plunge his hands into a fire, or chain himself in the same, agonizing position for hours. Once he made an iron maiden and became trapped for quite a while. After that, he was afraid to try other ancient devices and stuck with his own ideas of physical torment.

Moses had an inclination, but no plans for self-torment on the day that a dark man in a dark suit came shambling over his moor. That morning, Moses was just calmly drinking his tea. It was usual for a stranger to approach Moses. Yes, his farm was the drop site for living people trying to hack into the Node, but his territory was so vast that he was not often found by anyone aside from these hackers. Moses was supposed to be the one doing the finding.

This meant that the man approaching his farmhouse was a friend, a relative, or someone closely connected to either. Those were the only options for locating a person, especially a Founder, within the Node, but this dark man was a complete stranger to Moses. Another option became increasingly more likely the longer Moses thought about the approaching stranger: it could be that the other Founders had discovered his deception and had sent someone, or something, to amend the situation.

The man was far enough away that Moses had time to retrieve the chains he'd used on Camille from the cellar. When the man reached him, Moses was sitting back in his rocker, tea, and saucer in hand, and piles of large link chain at his feet. The man had seemed very purposeful up until just then but stopped short at the base of the porch steps.

"Can I help you?" Moses asked.

"My name is Cody Priolo," he said stiffly.

"I've never heard of you."

"I was Anita's living proxy," Cody hesitated. "Her agent."

That explained it. A close relationship with one Founder was likely to grant you access to other Founders. Moses looked the agent up and down. "And?"

"I believe that Anita had me killed."

"Well, you'll have to take that up with her."

"She had me killed because she thought I was working with Camille," Cody persisted.

"Were you?" Moses raised an eyebrow.

"Yes and no. I wasn't complying with her requests, but I wasn't following Anita's orders precisely."

Moses took a long sip from his teacup. He when he tasted dregs, he flicked the cup and it refilled. "I prefer to brew it in a kettle," he said, "but we may be short on time. I'm going to level with you Cody. I do know who you are. Camille and I had big plans for you and your technology, but you're here. Did Anita's assassin take your briefcase?"

"No."

"Hope springs eternal, as they used to say, before there was an eternity. Who has the briefcase, Cody?"

"How do I know that I can trust you?" Cody asked. He was not a nervous man. He could not recall ever being anxious, not even once during all of his years pretending to work for the bounty hunters. He was not nervous while seeking Node technology, not while watching people die. Not when he walked through the streets of Delta to what was almost certainly his execution; but the answer to this question from Moses bubbled up in Cody's throat and made him full of abrasive anxiety. Perhaps it was his new form; maybe pure consciousness was more anxious by nature.

"Well? Do you trust Camille?" Moses asked. "Because she trusts me."

"My daughter Nora has the briefcase," Cody said after his long silence.

"Okay, that's a good start."

"If you'll permit my communication with her, I'd like to leave all of this up to Nora. It's her world now, after all. I'm no longer a part of it."

"That's fine too, but I hope she makes up her mind soon." Moses continued to sip his tea.

43
CAMILLE

No matter how skillful a nurse Anton was, and he was not, Camille was still very slow to recover. It had been months since her first trip into the Node and she resigned herself to the worry that her second trip into the Node could kill her. She wasn't happy about it. She wasn't Toy. She hadn't signed up to be a martyr.

In order to get to Remy's new lab, Camille had to travel through Zeta and Gamma into a un-netted territory just outside the Gamma Net. Her journey was long and ripe with bitter thoughts. Camille tried to watch television on the car's screen but found it lacking compared to the creations she had witnessed inside the Node. Instead, she twisted her inactive wrist RAP in her hands and watched the scenery change. The area around Zeta was swampy and tropical. There were palm trees, creeping, blue-green Spanish moss, and a soft, fern underbrush. This gave way to grassy fields and then towering elm and oak trees. Finally, forests of thick pine punctured by rolling grasslands told her she was close to the end of the line.

Her car stopped at the far edge of the Gamma Net. It was programmed to go no further. The white line that was supposed to delineate the edge of the Gamma Net was spotty and ill kept. No one lived close enough to it to care about which side they were on, and no computerized cars would run where the possibility of true death was a liability.

Camille stepped over the line and reluctantly turned on her wrist RAP. Her voice subtly cracked when she asked for guidance to the nearest un-netted ranch. It was much colder in this part of the United Nets. Camille shivered under the forest canopy as she walked through leaves and past fallen trees, guided to a path by the robot voice of her RAP. The synthetic sound was dramatically out of place.

Her path eventually led to a large foot and horse trail, which led to a dirt road, upon which, eventually, Camille was hoping to find some signs of life.

The sign of life came in the form of a ranch and a livery, like her parent's ranch, although not as nice. There was a general store across the street that was, most certainly, owned by the same family who ran the ranch.

Inside the general store, the gray-haired owner eyeballed Camille with unconcealed mirth. He examined her shorts, tank top, and wrist RAP and choked back a laugh. Camille ignored him. Her eyes darted around, falling on the shelves of candy jars, the hand-woven parkas, and the chalkboard sign that listed the day's lunch specials: BBQ Pork Sandwich and Mashed Potatoes w/Gravy.

"Do you all take UN Credits?" Camille asked, her accent slipping into a slight Gamma affectation.

"Ayep. But, we'd prefer dollars." He rubbed his fingers together and smiled even wider. "So, UNs are gonna cost more."

Of course. The isolated folks near the Gamma Net would rather have physical money.

"Do you take … anything else?" Camille tapped on the counter and looked the old man in his watery eyes. His expression changed to wary interest.

"Ayep," he nodded.

Camille bought three peppermint sticks, a bag of caramels, a slab of chocolate, a brown and black men's parka (the women's parkas were too small for her), and both lunch specials. She paid for all of it with a generous Node Point transfer.

"You better hope you don't kick it soon," the shopkeeper said when he read the transfer amount from his point of sale screen.

"I need a horse too," Camille told him, "and a saddle, bags, blanket, all of it."

"Sure. That'd be Rand on the ranch across the way. I'll let him know you'll be over," the man paused, not sure how to proceed. "Will you be paying him the same way, then?"

"Ayep," Camille replied, stone-faced.

Before she went out to the ranch, Camille sat on a bench in front of the shop and ate her lunch specials. The meat on the sandwich was good, but the bread tasted old. Nothing tasted old in the Node, nothing there was ever stale unless you wanted it to be. She crumpled up her sandwich paper and wiped her hands off on her jeans before heading over to Rand's side of the ranch.

An hour later, she swayed in the saddle, kicking up dust on the relatively short trip from the trading post to her destination. Maybe, when all this was over, she could take up cooking. She would settle down in Prioria, maybe even buying a cat or a dog who she could put dog sweaters on.

She was riding along the path, considering what she would name her future dog: Peaches or, maybe, Mrs. Havisham. Then she saw Remy riding up the path to meet her. He was having a difficult time atop a dappled old mare, and he was alone. Cody had not made it. A bout of uneasiness was unleashed in her lunch-special-filled stomach.

Camille mentally said goodbye to Mrs. Havisham, the dog she would never settle down with, and the sweater she would never put on her.

44
NORA

Nora's father's briefcase was on the kitchen table. She noticed it when she first came home from her morning jog in the park. She assumed he'd accidentally left it on the table before going into his office. That was unusual; the briefcase never left her father's side. But then, after about an hour, she realized her father wasn't even home.

The briefcase had a note attached to it. It was written on Nora's pink heart stationery. *Please open and boot up,* it said.

Nora ran her hands over the brown, leather surface of the briefcase. It was old. Much older than she had realized before. Nora popped open the clasps. Inside was a very old computer, maybe older than the briefcase itself. Nora had always known there was a computer inside, but she had never seen him use it. The old computer unfolded to open, and it took Nora a few minutes to figure out how to turn the machine on.

Once she located the power switch, a red light flashed and the screen turned to a hazy gray. Nora stared at it for several minutes, pressing keys and tapping the screen, wondering what was supposed to happen. Just when she was about to give up, what looked like a park in autumn appeared on the screen. Then her father's face came into view.

"Hi Daddy!" she said with a squeal of surprise.

"Nora, honey, can you see and hear me?" He seemed more serious than usual.

"Yes. I can see and hear you. Where are you? Why is it fall where you are?"

"I'm going to tell you something very important," Cody said.

"Okay." Nora sat down in the kitchen chair opposite the computer screen that held the image of her father.

"Do you know the story of the Founders?"

"Yes."

"They were trying to save Edith Cole's brain from Alzheimer's disease, but they ended up trapping her consciousness inside of a computer system. The first Node. For the sake of the safety of her program, they transferred Edith to a second Node, one that's both permanent and isolated. They knew she was in there, but communication had to cease for the Node system to hold as many minds as it does."

"Yes, Dad. I remember."

"Well. This is very hard to say, and it is very secret information, that's not entirely true," Cody said.

"What part?"

"They could still talk to Edith, through a computer program. Before the Founders died, they each created one special computer that could speak with people once they were inside the Node. And they gave these computers to people with certain characteristics. These people were called Agents of the Founders. There was one for each Founder, aside from Amos."

"That makes sense," Nora said thoughtfully. "Amos wasn't Founder, initially. He didn't create the technology."

"Right. All that aside, the Agents of the Founders took orders from the Founders from inside the Node and helped to protect it in ways that the Founders could not, anymore. Obviously, the Agents did not live forever. Before they passed into the Node, they gave their computers to another, carefully chosen individual, who would carry on as a new Agent of the Founders. Your uncle Terrance was an agent, I don't know if you recall him. He gave me the computer that you are using right now."

Nora panicked, "Daddy, are you dead?" She didn't need him to answer. She felt the air push out of her lungs. She began to cry and breathe raggedly.

"You've got to calm down, honey," Cody said firmly. He gave his daughter a few minutes more to process and let out her sudden anguish.

"Are you calm?" he asked. "Because I have something important that I need you to do."

Nora nodded, her chest still heaving and tears spilling onto her jogging suit.

"The truth is, I've made a mistake," Cody said. "I don't know what's right anymore, so I'm giving you a choice. You get to pick what you think is right."

"You *are* dead," Nora wailed and started crying again.

"Listen!" Cody said sternly. "You have these two options, I haven't had time to choose a new agent, and we can't have something like this floating around in the world. So, you can destroy this computer."

"Okay." Nora settled down and paid attention as best she could as she struggled to come to terms with the loss of her father.

"If you destroy this computer, nothing changes, and the world and the System stays the same as it always has been. Or, you can end the System and end Node Points for everyone, forever."

Nora thought about her classmates, the ones fascinated by the System and the ones screwed by it. She imagined herself triumphantly recounting her destruction of the System to Alexis, his face stunned and proud. But mostly, she remembered the Node Point pawn shops, crowded with the elderly and dying, each soul desperate to escape eternal poverty.

"How?" she asked her father. "How do I end it?"

"Listen to me very closely. There is a man named Remington Nakamoto. He is hiding in a hospital just outside the Gamma Net. If you choose to end the system, you have to find him first, and you have to find him fast."

45
CAMILLE

Camille walked down the path from the old ranch to the general store. Yesterday, she had ridden one of the horses, but today she didn't need as many provisions.

"Just two lunch specials today, Carson." Carson was the name of the watery-eyed old shopkeeper. After several days of Camille visiting the shop and livery, Carson still eyed her with distrust, but he took her Node Points readily enough. Carson did not like it when she called him by his first name, so Camille did it often.

"Carson, what is the special today?" she asked while the man turned to load up two lunch sacks.

"Meatloaf. Same's every Tuesday."

"Can you put extra cookies in the bag?" Camille was eyeing a display of what looked like oatmeal raisin.

"Extra cookies gonna cost extra," he said while using a scoop to shovel several into the lunch bags.

"Oh Carson, you're such a tease." Camille gave a fake giggle, then in a more serious tone she said, "I'm transferring Points over," and she flashed her wrist RAP toward him so that he could see how many points she was transferring. "I do love our chats, Carson. The time goes by so fast, it's almost like I was never here." Camille picked up her bags and winked salaciously at the old man. Carson harrumphed into his mustache.

Camille started back up the trail to the old hospital that she and Remy were using as a headquarters. The hospital was once the only netted area for hundreds of miles, but it had become obsolete after the new Omega Net was installed. It was a forgotten holding of an Omega bank until Camille had bought it with a small fraction of her considerable fortune.

Oaza General Hospital was a strange sight. A tall, clinical building surrounded by empty parking garages and empty shops, which were, in turn, surrounded by an empty forest. The parking garages were not quite deserted; the one closest to the hospital was where Camille had been keeping the horses.

If Oaza ever had a painted line marking the start of its mini Net, it had long since faded; so, Camille didn't know where the Oaza Hospital Net started, which made her a little nervous, but not nervous enough to spur her to caution.

Inside, Remy had created a kind of high-tech nest for himself in a nurse's station at the heart of the hospital. Computer entrails spiraled out around him on the floor and ran over every raised surface. A hospital bed, with equipment from Elworthy that had been improved upon, sat ominously in the corner.

Camille placed one of the brown sacks down on the desk next to Remy.

"Meatloaf." Camille sat down a few chairs over and wolfed down her meatloaf. She didn't bother with a plate.

"Are you going to eat?" she asked. Remy shook his head, never taking his eyes from his work. "Why not? Everybody likes meatloaf."

"I'm worried."

"I've never known you not to be, and you haven't starved to death, yet."

"I don't trust him," Remy said darkly. "He's a known liar and a double agent. We don't even know who he's a double agent with. All we know is that he has played us in the past and is likely to play us in the future."

"I told you that we need Cody."

"Yeah, but you never told me why."

"Well, he's late getting up here anyway. You'll have to go in without him here."

"Man, I told you. I can't go into the Node without Cody here," Camille insisted. "You're not going to get it. Just go back to your tech toys."

Obediently, Remy turned to his monitor and resumed typing.

Camille lifted Remy's ignored lunch up from the desk next to him and began to eat it too, although she ate much slower this time.

"Have you ever considered running?" Remy asked her casually.

"From what?" Camille asked.

"For your health," Remy answered.

Camille snorted. Her wrist made a buzzing sound, "Cody," she said, partly because she had been waiting for his call for over a week and partly because he was the only one who ever called her. It was not Cody, however; it was a somberly-mustachioed Carson. Camille turned on the projection.

"Got someone down here at the general store looking for you," the old man said. It was clear he was not proficient with holo-communication. He was standing too close to his own projector, so half of his face appeared in the projection.

"Carson, buddy, thank you for the meatloaf, and the cookies, and the info. What does he look like? Is he an uptight guy in a suit?"

"Nope. A young lady. She's in a pink get-up," Carson said as the malfunctioning hologram zoomed in closer to focus on just one of his eyes.

"Whoa. Okay, I'll be down to the store to meet her shortly," Camille said. Once the hologram was off, which took some difficulty on Carson's part, Camille turned to Remy, "Do we know any young people in pink."

"They could be assassins," Remy commented.

"She doesn't sound like an assassin."

"As reported by an old man who can't work a *holophone.*"

"I'm going down there," Camille said.

"I hope you come back up," Remy said with a mix of sarcasm and actual worry.

Camille trudged back down the steep hill to the general store. As it was her second trip of the day, her legs were sore, and she got a cramp, most likely due to a belly full of meatloaf and cookies.

When Camille walked into the general store, she recognized the young woman immediately. It wasn't that she had ever seen the woman personally, but she recognized her facial expressions and movement. When the olive-skinned young woman turned to her, it Camille saw nothing but echoes of her father.

"Cody didn't tell me he had a daughter." Camille reached her hand out after Nora had introduced herself. She noticed a briefcase on the floor that leaned on Nora's leg.

"My father was a very private man," Nora said stiffly.

"Oh." Camille blinked back sudden, heavy tears, realizing Nora had referred to Cody in the past tense. "Wait. *Was?*" she said, as Nora looked like she was ready to crumple. Her own tears welled up in her eyes and she said, "I am so fucking sorry."

"So am I," Nora said, and grasped the outstretched hand that Camille had forgotten about.

"Yeah, okay. You follow me up the hill to Camp Happy Times," Camille said, swallowing the lump in her throat and turning on her heels. As she headed out the door, she gave a backward wave and shouted, "Goodbye Carson, and thanks."

"Ayup," Carson said.

46
MOSES

The Founder's meeting place had been created by Edith since she was the first Founder, and the first person, to go into the Node. She had modeled it after a rustic lodge her parents once owned, but she made the Node version much grander. She called the place Idlewild.

Idlewild was one of the oldest places in the Node. It was the second place ever created, the first being a recreation of Edith's own home. As a result of being created by an unskilled mind new to the Node, Idlewild had some unique properties. The building itself was a massive cabin made from thick logs, as broad as the biggest redwood. It was perched on a wooded cliff overlooking an impossibly blue and incredibly still lake. Not even raindrops would ripple the surface of the water. Rolling, green mountains ringed the lake, but they were always in the distance; unreachable by foot, or boat, or any other means. The forest around Idlewild was dense and full of small delights. On hikes, beautiful waterfalls or panoramic views would suddenly appear and then vanish just as unexpectedly.

Stars and planets filled the sky at night. The planets were often so close one could see their surfaces, and count their moons or their rings. Sometimes there were meteor showers that streaked across the sky and popped like a galactic fireworks display.

Moses had called the meeting, so he was the first to arrive at Idlewild. He watched moons circle planets out of the lodge's great hall window, which stretched from the floor to ceiling and overlooked the lake, the mountain range and the sky above. Idlewild had a great stone fireplace that eternally burned a crackling fire. Moses settled down in front of the fire, sinking into a well-worn chair.

"Hot cider," he said, and a glass mug appeared on the end table next to him.

"Knowing you, I'm surprised that you didn't insist on pressing the apples yourself." Startled, Moses turned and saw Edith approaching him. She was a tall and well-built woman, with swirls of gray in her upswept black hair. She wore flowing robes that trailed behind her.

"I didn't know you were here," Moses said as rose to greet her.

"I'm always here now." She dismissed his greeting. "I've never made a place that I love more than this," Edith said as she settled into a high-backed chair next to Moses and they sat in silence for some time, the pop of the firewood breaking at regular intervals.

"I gave myself an agent," Moses said. "I forged her out of a hacker who landed in my field. I can't communicate with her yet, but we have an understanding."

"I suppose that was inevitable. Anita will be furious. I doubt anyone else will care." Edith stood so that she could lean on the mantel and look into Moses's eyes. "What is your agent doing out there in the real world?"

"Do you know why we hate complainers?" Moses answered her question with one of his own. "We don't like the people in pain who are loud about it. We don't like them, or the depressed, or the suicidal. It's because we're all in pain and they remind us that there is another option. We don't have to suffer in silence. We don't have to suffer at all if we don't want to. We can be loud about our pain. And, if we choose, we can end it. Those complainers aren't following the rules. We don't want to hear about their agony because it echoes our own."

"What are you getting at?" Edith said, intrigued.

"For a long time, every Node hacker who landed in my fields, in increasing numbers over the years, by the way, was a complainer who was there to tell me about the wrongs that they were suffering. I hated every one of them. I also took no joy in reporting them and getting them killed; they were just trying to fix what we'd broken. But then, they started coming in as explorers and redeemers. They stopped complaining because they were so far away from any semblance of a civilized life that they can't even tell how horrifying it has become. People have been slowly getting hotter, a generational version of the frog boiling in the pot."

"Your agent is going to end the Point System," Edith smiled cryptically.

"It's my System to end. I made it. The rest of the Node is yours, and nothing will happen to the Node, I've thought it all out," Moses explained.

"And what of all the complainers, the sufferers? What will happen to them when they have an easy way out?"

"I've figured that out too," Moses said.

"Does this solution dismantle even more elements of our system?" Edith asked, "such as communication outside of the Node?"

"I've thought it through," Moses said.

"Well, think about this," Edith said, her voice rising and her underlying anger betraying her genteel, Southern roots. "We're trying to cook a grand recipe here, and there's a lot that goes into this stew. You keep taking out ingredients and all we'll have left is heat and bone."

Edith's doorbell rang in a cacophony of church bells. "The other gods are here," Edith said. "Let's see what your vengeance hath wrought."

A few minutes later, Edith led Anita and Gary into the drawing room. Anita was looking dour as ever, with her hair in a severe bun and her lips in a perpetual purse. Gary, who had resembled a stoned Santa Claus when alive, had carried his hippie trappings after death. Today, he wore long dreadlocks, an array of scarves, and he exuded a strong, sandalwood odor.

"Is anyone else coming?" Moses asked as he again rose from his chair to greet his confederates.

"I doubt it," Anita said. "Terry turned off about five years ago, and only his family can turn him back on. They don't consider this enough of an emergency to load his program. Deidra is a flower or something, and she truly does not care. And you know Craig; no one has heard from him in over a decade."

"Four is a majority anyway, should we need to vote," Moses said.

"If we all agree," Edith added.

"Agree on what?" Gary asked, jovially plopping himself down and looking out of place in Edith's refined chair.

"I don't think there's much to agree on. It seems he's gone and done whatever it is without us," Edith said, standing at her beverage cart. "Would anyone like a drink?"

"I suppose this has something to do with my missing computer," Anita said to Moses. To Edith, she said, "Martini, dry."

"You had your agent killed. Your computer could have fallen into anyone's hands," Moses said.

"Which you would know if you had something to do with its

disappearance." Anita took her martini from Edith and lightly sipped it, "Besides, I didn't have my own agent killed. Gary's agent took care of it. You know the protocol."

Gary put two fingers to his forehead and gave a half-hearted salute. "Can you get on with it. I have somewhere much better to be."

"I'm ending the Node Point System. It's too late to stop it; everything is already in place," Moses said.

"Whoa." Gary sat up in his chair.

"So," Edith said carefully, "since you said 'ending,' I can assume that the destruction of the Point System is still in progress. Why tell us now? Why not tell us after your plan is complete? Or better yet, don't tell us at all and wait until new arrivals start talking about zero balances, or whatever you're scheming."

"She has a point," Gary said. "I can call my agent and have it squashed in twenty minutes."

"I think it's because he doesn't really want to end the system. This is a cry for help," Edith said. "Moses wants us to know how serious he is about making revisions to the System." Edith turned to Moses and said, "We understand dear; none of us likes what the Points have become. Just call off this half-baked attempt and we'll work together on a real solution."

Moses stared into the fire. Either he was ignoring Edith, or he hadn't heard her at all.

"He hasn't called us here to talk it out," Anita said angrily. She stalked over to one of the lodge's picture windows. The drapes had drawn themselves in order to keep out the chill of dusk. "Look. He's trapped us here so that we can't stop it." Anita pulled back the curtains revealing a huge chain linked across the exterior of the window pane.

47
REMY

Remy cleared an area of his workspace big enough for Nora to set down her briefcase. Remy and Camille watched in silence while Nora popped the case's buckles and revealed the old laptop's screen, embedded in the lid and keyboard fused to the base.

"I'm guessing there's some kind of software I'm supposed to hack," Remy said.

"In the short term," Camille said, "but eventually I'm going to need you to broadcast the signal over a huge network. You're going to need to copy and distribute its function."

"What's its function?" Remy asked, booting up the computer.

"It sees into the Node and allows for two-way communication," Camille said.

Remy laughed, "Come on, really, what does it do? Reverb detection?" An awkward silence fell over the abandoned hospital lobby.

"That's what it does," Camille said.

"It's a trick. You can't see into the Node. It wouldn't look like anything; just pages of code."

"It's real," Nora spoke up. "My father is –" she choked back some tears, "or was – Cody Priolo, and this was his machine. I've spoken with him through it since he moved on to the Node."

Remy seemed to notice Nora for the first time, then his eyes darted over her sad face and pink tracksuit. He wrestled with his thoughts on Cody, not sure if he should discuss his suspicious feelings toward Cody with his newly-orphaned daughter. Finally, Camille's frustration boiled over.

"We don't have time for this. You have to figure it out, and I have to get jacked into the Node," Camille said.

"Cody is a liar and a known spy. We could boot this up and find him video chatting from the coffee shop up the street," Remy pointed out.

"That's stupid. First off there are no coffee shops around here, I would know I've been dying for a scone. Secondly, you've trusted me enough to set up this lab in the middle of absolutely nowhere. For fuck's sake, just trust me a little more for a little longer," Camille pleaded.

"I don't trust you. You have terrible judgment. But, I'm going to do what you want. I'm going to see this through," Remy said.

"Why?" Nora asked him, fully knowing she was in no position to be asking questions.

"Because the system has to be fixed and if this isn't the way, at least it's a start."

"Remy, I know that this is may be impossible, but I need you to somehow, simultaneously jack me into the Node while you hack this computer. We're running out of time for what I've set up inside the Node."

"I'll start this, jack you in and then finish up in a jiffy," Remy said sarcastically.

"Nora," Camille turned to her, "I'm going to transfer some funds to you. I need you to buy up a ton of advertising space all over Zeta. Find the screens where Toy played her live hack and buy up those same screens."

"How long should the ad spots be?"

"Two minutes, I think two minutes will be enough."

"You're going to try to broadcast from the Node," Remy said. Cody's computer had booted up. The screen displayed a vivid picture of a moor and a single leafless tree.

"No. *You're* going to broadcast from the Node," Camille said. "I thought you were supposed to be quick on the uptake." She looked at the computer screen. "Hey, I know that place. That's Moses's tree, where I landed last time I went into the Node."

Remy leaned into the laptop and began to type furiously.

"I think I saw that tree in the background when my dad contacted me," Nora observed.

"Shhh. Shut up!" Remy commanded sharply.

"What?"

"Listen," Remy said quietly. A low hum was emitting from Cody's computer.

"Ooh, noise." Camille rolled her eyes. "Tell me when you've really got something."

"You don't understand," Remy said excitedly. "This isn't just noise. This isn't a picture. It's a live stream."

"How do you know?"

"The frequency –" Remy was interrupted by a woman's voice emitting from the computer.

"Hello. Hello. This is Anita." Her voice was crisp, but it crackled through the corrupted computer.

"Anita who?" Camille whispered.

Remy shot her a harsh stare and mouthed "Shut up."

Camille, Remy, and Nora held their breath waiting for the woman to speak some more.

"For the love of –" the voice said before the computer noise crackled and fell totally silent. The screen blipped, and the image fuzzed out completely.

"What is that?" Camille asked. "Remy do something, we're losing it."

"Someone is trying to hijack the signal." Remy pushed a few computer keys. The image of the tree on the moor blipped back online, followed by the low hum.

"Good job." Camille clapped Remy on the back.

"I didn't do anything."

Cody's face popped up on the screen, disturbing the view of the moor and its solitary, dignified tree.

"Greetings," Cody said. "Hi honey." He waved to Nora.

"Hi Daddy," Nora said, sniffing back tears.

"Shouldn't you be in here, Camille?" Cody asked. "It's time to get the show on the road."

"Settle down in there," Remy said, tapping the screen. "We're working on it."

"Where's Moses?" Camille asked.

"He's running some errands, I think. He's not very forthcoming," Cody said.

"Last time we spoke, I tossed you out of a truck because you refused to help take down the Node System. What happened?" Remy asked.

"Well, part of me thinks the System works, and the Founders made correct calculations. But, I let my daughter decide. She is, after all, in the land of the living," Cody said. Then, in a louder voice, he shouted, "You made a good choice, dear."

"All right, all right." Remy rolled his eyes. "I'm going to have to turn this unit off to pick it apart and find what kind of backdoor program it's using to read the Node's code. And I'm going to have to jack Camille in while we're blacked out, for the sake of whatever countdown you've got going on here." He turned to Camille, "that means you're going to have to go into this blind."

"Yeah, well if I don't go in, the whole world stays blind," Camille said. "Just fix this shit."

Camille and Nora sat in the hospital's cafeteria for the few hours it took for Remy to make his final preparations. The vending machines were smashed and emptied, and the line kitchen was inoperable. Camille lamented that her last meal may be Carson's meatloaf.

"A cafeteria is why I'm helping you," Nora said, out of the blue.

"How's that?"

"I met a man in my university cafeteria. He helped me learn what I could never understand before, about the Point System."

Camille contemplated this wide-eyed young woman. She looked so much like her father, with her tan skin and short black hair; but she was not like her father at all. Nora was wistful and quietly caring, but immature for her age and Camille regretted that this girl was involved at all.

"Well, whoever gave you this great understanding didn't do you any favors," Camille told her. "We're in danger here."

"My father didn't do me any favors," Nora said. "I've been in danger my whole life because of who he is and I never knew."

•   •   •   •   •

Hours later, Camille was comfortably installed in the hospital bed. Memories of the last time she laid in a bed like this flashed through her mind as she recalled how Dr. Winter hovered at her bedside while Remy made final adjustments to the equipment.

Camille pulled a metal vial out of her pocket and handed it to Remy, as soon as she could catch his eye.

"What's in here?" Remy gingerly took the tube from her.

"Blank nanites. I think you're smart enough to figure out what they're for."

"You want me to finish hacking the signal and then boost you with the virus once your inside," Remy said grimly. "That's as likely to kill you as not."

"Well, you were supposed to have already figured out Cody's computer. It got here too late. Everything got all fucked up when Cody died."

"He's still screwing us over from the grave."

"Cody is using Moses's stolen signal and it won't work. I have to be able to communicate on the go in there. So, does everybody else, but you can start with me."

"You should have told me the whole plan right from the beginning," Remy admonished her.

"You wouldn't have done it then."

"You're right," Remy said, then he called, "I need someone to be a nurse in here," and Nora bustled into the operating room in response.

"Hold this." He handed some tubing to Nora, and she held it while he screwed a hypodermic needle cap on the end. He turned to Camille, "I have to jack you directly into the Node. This isn't going to be all fuzzy and nice like Elworthy. I can do it slowly to ease you in, or I can just do it quickly."

"Just get it the fuck over."

In one quick motion, Remy jabbed the needle and nanotube into Camille's temple. She gasped, out of pain and the need to pull air into her lungs because she had the distinct feeling of pressure and drowning, and she gasped out of surprise because she hadn't meant for Remy to follow her instructions that very moment.

48
CODY

Moses gave his hacked tablet to Cody, all the while stressing the importance of the device. "This is the only one like it, and it can't be replicated. You'll be able to use this to communicate with me, your daughter, and whoever has Anita's briefcase. But just because you *can* doesn't mean you *should* use it all the time. Let's keep things businesslike until our deeds are done," Moses said, clearly not understanding who he was talking to.

Moses also left Cody in charge of his moor and, by extension, the hacker entry point. Moses gave Cody instructions to create any convenience or comfort he wanted, as long as it was in view of the entry point so Camille's arrival could be immediately noted.

Recognizing he had no need for food or comfort, Cody decided to stand and stare at the Node entry point in silent vigil. His vigil was soon invaded by a strange, almost tingly feeling he had not felt since early childhood. It was boredom, and it would not be denied.

Cody decided to try his hand at Node manipulation. After hours of thought and consideration, Cody made himself a plant. It was supposed to be an orchid in a clear, glass vase, but instead, it was a flowering cactus in a red, clay pot.

By the time Camille appeared, with a sudden, startling crack beside the shed on the moor, Cody had made half a dozen identical cacti, but still no lovely orchid in a glass vase. Being a man who was used to always carrying something in his hands, he absentmindedly carried the cactus with him as he crossed a hundred yards to meet Camille.

"Alas, poor Yorick! I knew him. A fellow of infinite jest," Camille shouted to Cody.

"That doesn't sound right," Cody said when he reached her.

Camille eyeballed the cactus. "Is that for me?" she asked.

"If you would like." Cody tried to hand her the plant, but then set it on the ground when she didn't take it.

Without the plant in his hand, Cody, somehow looked even more jangly and awkward, his three-piece suit hanging from his lanky frame.

"You can wear whatever you want to here, you know," Camille said to Cody, when he reached her. "I wore a sombrero hat in the Node once."

"Technically, I'm still on business."

"I just don't get you. Fucking relax already. You know what," Camille rapid fired at Cody, "I don't have time for you. Did Moses leave you anything for me?"

"He did not." Cody was unperturbed. "I'm supposed to contact him if anyone else comes into the Node besides you."

"How are you going to contact him?" Camille asked excitedly.

Cody ignored her. "Because this is an entry point for hackers. It might be the only entry point for hackers. That was not specified."

"Please tell me how you're contacting Moses."

"It's only for an emergency situation wherein a hacker, aside from yourself, enters the Node at this entry point," Cody said in a way that left no room for argument.

Camille clasped her hands tightly in front of her chest as if she was squeezing all of her hard feelings into a ball. "I didn't think it was possible, but I like you even less dead than I did alive."

"I am just following direction," Cody explained. "You seem stressed," he added.

Camille headed over the moor to the location of the nearest transportation gate. She spent the first leg of the journey muttering venomous curses on Cody's name and legacy.

She created a wrist RAP for herself once she calmed down. She was hoping that Remy's code would be delivered to the RAP when, and if, he was finished hacking Cody's laptop. Camille then set about creating her costume. She couldn't stop walking, so she created on the go, hoping for the best.

She made long, black pants with flowing fabric and wide legs. Her shirt was also black, but tight, with a plunging neckline stuffed with blood red lace. The high collar of her shirt was wide, and it reached up to the back of her neck.

When her outfit was complete, Camille checked her wrist RAP to see if Remy had uploaded his hacked communication program. The familiar sensation of obsessively checking her wrist RAP brought on an uncomfortable nostalgia.

The transport gate was as she remembered it: atop a platform at the edge of

Moses's moor. She heard someone calling her name as she approached the platform. She turned and saw Nora running toward her.

"Goddamn it," Camille gasped.

"It turns out that Remy couldn't upload the code from the nanites into you while you were already in here," Nora explained when she caught up to Camille. "So he uploaded it into me and sent me in."

"But there is only one set of equipment," Camille said.

Nora looked down.

"Which one of us is dead?" Camille asked with unexpected calm. "There's only equipment to put one person into the Node." When Nora did not answer, Camille said, "It had better be me," as she walked up the transport platform and entered the coordinates for Nightshade.

"Are you coming?" Camille waved Nora toward the transport.

Nora stepped through the transport arch, unsure of what was happening. To her, it looked like she was going to just walk through to the other side of the platform, but she found herself on another platform instead.

The world that Nora stepped into, with Camille right behind her, was bathed in a deep purple twilight. The sky was a rusty dusk with no sun, or moon, just a generous smattering of sparkling stars.

The Nightshade transport platform was at the end of a seemingly deserted avenue. There were hulking, but distinct, iron gates every few hundred yards; they denoted the entrance to the avenue's gothic manors. The sidewalks were overhung with poplar trees, and the median was a strip of impossible, heavy willows. Even the grass blades themselves were mildly iridescent and spooky.

"This place is," Nora paused to find the right word, "interesting."

"I knew that you would like it. I've never been, just seen it on the holo-visions they have here."

A wolf howled in the distance.

"The music and bars are a few streets to the left," Camille went on. "If the maps are still right. Things change around here like that." Camille snapped her fingers close to Nora's face, and Nora recoiled.

49
TOY

"A few months ago, you heard me declare society sick, and I proclaimed myself its healer," Toy said to her reflection in the cracked, filmy bathroom mirror. She spoke in low tones so she would not be heard by anyone standing just outside the door. "It has taken us some time, but I'm here today to declare victory over the evil and manipulative Node Point System." She continued to speak into the mirror.

Just then, a woman walked into the bathroom. Toy must have been speaking a little louder than she meant to, because the woman gave her a strange look. The woman was wearing all black and had eyeliner winged up to her temples, so if anyone should be giving strange looks, Toy thought it should be the other way around. Nevertheless, Toy retreated from the bathroom and sat back down at the bar.

Toy had grown quite used to sitting around bars, but the clanging navel-gazing of the vampire music was harsh to her honky-tonk-tuned ears. The bar had an off-putting iron smell. Toy was still in her boots and chaps, thankfully she had left her hat at home, but she still stood out in the dive's sea of black, purple, and occasional blood red. Toy was by far the most conspicuous person in the room until Camille entered.

The problem wasn't what Camille was wearing; she blended in perfectly. Camille's companion, however, was wearing a bright pink jumpsuit. Toy looked around nervously, checking to see if anyone noticed the odd pair. None of the patrons seemed to care.

"Who is your friend?" Toy asked when they reached her.

"This is Nora, she's carrying the program that transmits signals outside of the Node," Camille said.

"Then why not send just her in? Why are you both here?"

"It was supposed to be just me. Things got fucked up." Camille rubbed her hands together. "All right then. Let's go."

"Where are we going?" Toy asked.

"Haven't you ever watched The Vampires on the holo-vision?"

"I have no idea what you're talking about." Toy was baffled.

"Come on then, I'll tell you on our way." Camille led Nora and Toy out of the bar and into the street. "It's going to be hard for some people to believe that you're talking to them from inside of the Node. They're going to think it's computer generated. So, I want to increase our changes by broadcasting from someplace amazing. We're going to the Cathedral of Light in Nightshade. I saw it on the Vampire show, the first time I was in the Node. The Cathedral of Light is going to be our proof that we're broadcasting from inside the Node."

The three women wound through the Nightshade's damp, labyrinthine streets and alleys. Every turn was a new surprise, there were gothic mansions, castles juxtaposed with modern city streets full of nightclubs and tightly-packed townhouses. Toy thought they may be lost, but they rounded a corner and saw a shining, golden temple perched atop a gradually sloping hill. It had to be the Cathedral of Light.

"The Cathedral is where vampires go when they don't want to be vampires anymore," Camille said. "You'd know this if you watched the show."

"I don't watch holo-vision," Toy said haughtily.

"Anyway," Camille continued, ignoring Toy's attitude, "if you've been a good vampire, the light in the Cathedral turns you into an angel. If you've been bad, it pulverizes you into dust."

"That doesn't seem right," Nora said.

"Well, it doesn't pulverize you into dust for real. This is the Node, so I'm guessing it just transports you to a field, or some shit, it's all part of the story that you play here. But, it's the perfect example of the amazing stuff people have built in here."

Soon, they were standing in front of the Cathedral, looking at its massive, golden doors.

"I think we should start broadcasting, and you can tell them that you're talking to them from inside the Node. Tell them that the Points aren't real and then we'll open the doors so that they can see inside the Cathedral," Camille directed.

"Then you're going to step in and get turned into an angel," Nora suggested.

"Fuck no," Camille said. "I'd get vaporized."

"What do I do?" Nora asked.

"You're going to have to use the Node to make yourself some kind of camera. Moses said that the code Remy pumped into you will work through any device that you create," Camille said, then turned to Toy. "You need to practice your speech while I show Nora how to use the Node."

Toy began to pace and mutter at the top of the Cathedral's staircase. Camille led Nora to a wide landing.

"Button please," Camille said and a large, red, button – the kind that you might see as an emergency stop on some machine controls – appeared in her hand.

"When Moses taught me, he told me to say what I wanted, press this button, and then the Node would make it appear. You don't really need the button, but it helps you get used to manipulating the Node at first."

"Video camera," Nora said and reached for the button, but Camille moved it away.

"First, you tell me which one of us is dead," Camille demanded. "Is it you?"

"You weren't awake to make a choice," Nora said sadly. "I was. How did you know?"

"I still feel alive, I think. Plus, Remy would never agree to kill me."

"I just … I saw my dad here, and I wanted to be with him," Nora cried.

Toy turned an alarmed look toward Camille and Nora. Camille gestured that everything was okay, so Toy resumed pacing and muttering. Sparse snow began to fall from the sky. It was always the first week of winter in Nightshade. The Shades, as they called themselves, liked the chill and the dark.

"You're making it so that we're starting out all wrong here. We're trying to convince people to live for more than Node Points. We want them to see that they will have the love and encouragement of the people who have already come to the Node before them. You saw your dad here, and you fucking killed yourself. That is the absolute opposite of what we want, and you're one of the people who is supposed to be founding this revolution," Camille said breathlessly.

"Well, I didn't mean to found a revolution," Nora said. "So let's just agree to do the best we can here."

"Are you ladies ready?" Toy called down to them.

50
MOSES

Frost grew into spindly tendrils of ice, spreading across the lake. Moses watched it happen, through the massive chains and out the windows of Idlewild. A few flakes of snow floated through the air, flashing and dazzling before they dissipated. Those few flakes were soon joined by thousands more, blanketing the sky, icing the trees, and obscuring his view.

"You made it winter, Edith," Moses said to her.

Edith roused from next to the fireplace, her full height was quite intimidating. The fire crackled as she stood and even the stone figures on the mantel seemed to take on an ominous cast.

"I thought it was fitting, as winter is the death of the year."

The screen of a small tablet that had been sitting next to Moses blinked on. He saw a beautiful, blonde woman standing in front of a massive church.

"It's begun," he said.

"Well, put it up on the big screen," Gary said. A red and white striped bag of popcorn appeared in his hand. "Let's get this over with."

51

Holo-projectors and billboard screens all across the United Nets played a very special message. The mysterious, but wealthy, transmitters of the message made sure the signal went out simultaneously on several of the most popular channels.

In the cloudy haze of late spring, residents of Zeta city thought they were seeing a rebroadcast of Toy's message; they thought perhaps there had been some more news about the hack she had attempted almost a year ago, but closer inspection showed she was in a different place. And even closer inspection revealed her to be in another world. Finally, Toy started to speak.

"Node Points are not real," she said after a brief introduction. "The entire Node System is an ancient set of lies designed to keep us doing what people who are long gone want us to do. You can communicate with people once they've passed into the Node; that's how I'm talking to you right now. It's also where I'm talking to you from. Once you are here, you can do whatever you want, and you can have whatever you want. You are not limited by Points earned throughout life. Your only limitation is your imagination and will to use it.

"This church behind me is the Cathedral of Light. It is a collective creation of the citizens of in a part of the Node called Nightshade. We have chosen to show you this place because of its brilliance. It is an example of the limitlessness of life within the Node."

A thick woman with a large mop of black hair slipped behind Toy. She was only on screen for a second. The camera panned to show the inside of the Cathedral Light. There was an entire world on the other side of the church's ornate doors. A perfect, green meadow stretched to a mountainous horizon, pierced by a blue brook and a sturdy wooden bridge. All of it was bathed in bright, warm sunlight, and all in contrast to the dark, wintery, Nightshade twilight on just the other side of the heavy door. The camera panned back and forth, letting the viewers take in the views of both worlds.

"Fuck it. I'm going in," Camille said, off camera.

She got a running start and dove through the Cathedral doors, her thick legs pumping and her short, dark hair bouncing. As she entered, her black and red dress unfolded into an explosion of flowing white robes and massive, golden wings sprung from her back. She ran faster and faster through the meadow, soon gaining supernatural speed, her toes barely touching the grass, and then, not touching the ground at all. She lifted higher and higher, until, wings flapping, she flew off, full speed toward the mountains.

All across Zeta and the rest of the United Nets, screens blinked back to regular programming and Node Point accounts started counting down to zero.

ABOUT THE AUTHOR

Alison Lyke is a fantasy and science fiction author and professor with a master's degree in creative writing. Her debut novel, a modern mythology titled *Honey*, was published in 2013. She lives in Rochester, New York with her partner Jon-Paul and two sons, Jonah and Isaac. When not reading or writing, Alison enjoys spending time in nature, practicing meditation and yoga, and playing video games.

Thank you so much for reading one of our **Sci-Fi** novels.
If you enjoyed our book, please check out our recommended title for your
next great read!

Culture-Z by Karl Andrew Marszalowicz

In the year 2190, mankind has made great strides forward in the worlds of
technology, science, and greed. However, when all three get together one
last time, this oblivious generation may not exist much longer.

CPSIA information can be obtained
at www.ICGtesting.com
Printed in the USA
BVHW031148280319
543971BV00001B/7/P